"No reason to worry." His devilish grin made her insides clench in a way she thought impossible after being sated twice in one evening. "At least not tonight."

"Why? What's different about tonight?" Her breath caught as a familiar hunger returned to his eyes.

He cupped her cheek in the palm of his hand and kissed her once more. Fire rose between them again as if it had never subsided. His voice was low and sensual as he whispered into her ear, "Everything."

PRAISE FOR YELENA CASALE AND TINA MOSS

"A TOUCH OF DARKNESS rockets you along a pulse-pounding story and sucks you into the characters. You'll want to cheer for Cassie's feisty spirit and loyalty and you'll come to love Gabe and all his wonderful flaws."

- Award Winning Fantasy Author, Heather McCorkle

"An enthralling, fast-paced tale filled with sexual and social tension…Wise-cracking smart, eerily spooky, trendy and unputdownable! Just like an addictive chocolate candy bar, you can't stop at one bite!"

- Amazon Reviewer, Michele L.

"A great read, utterly engaging with a main character I totally supported, trusted and loved as well as a supporting cast of good and bad guys."

- Author and Artist, Nikola Vukoja

"A keeper with a great and unexpected ending you don't see coming. Enjoyable reading and good start for the series."

- Top 500 Amazon Reviewer, Douglas C. Meeks, Book Reviews

"This new paranormal urban fantasy series is a mesmerizing and intriguing read. A fascinating world of angels, fallen angels and demons with some unique elements and surprising twists."

- Amazon Reviewer, Evampire

A TOUCH OF
DARKNESS

YELENA CASALE 🔑 TINA MOSS

CITY OWL
PRESS

A TOUCH OF DARKENSS
Key Series: Book One

CITY OWL PRESS
www.cityowlpress.com

ISBN: 978-0-9862516-0-3

Cover Design by Tina Moss. All stock photos licensed appropriately.

For information on subsidiary rights, please contact the publisher at info@cityowlpress.com.

First Print 2015 Edition: March 2015
Second Print 2015 Edition: May 2015

Printed in the United States of America

For my husband, Joe.

A lifetime of love and laughter would

still not be enough time.

- Tina

To my best friend and soul mate,

my husband Tommy.

- Yelena

ONE

The primal scream died in his throat, a foreign sound he couldn't set free. The surrounding quiet enfolded him, thick as oil. Air hissed through his gritted teeth as he struggled for control.

He knelt at the edge of a dark lake, watching his muscles contract beneath smooth skin. With a shaking hand, he reached back to touch the empty space by his shoulder blades. He grunted at the contact, an alien noise in the absolute silence of the night.

City lights shimmered in the distance, the sole signs of life. No creature stirred in this desolate place. It was as if humans and animals alike felt the dangerous current in the air and chose to stay away. Only the full moon reflected in the water, an indifferent observer to his torment.

As his thoughts unraveled, he caught his image through the water's ripples and stilled. The face staring back at him, usually so stoic, now contorted in agony. His eyes held wildness, framed by a mess of disheveled black hair and topped by a forehead damp with perspiration. Nothing remained of the control, of the precious order that had been the pinnacle of his existence.

The light autumn breeze cooled his naked body but offered little relief. His blood burned from the inside out. The scorching fire threatened to consume him. Every inch of his skin, from the tips of his nails to the ends of his hair, buzzed with soft electric blue energy.

He reached back once more and ran his fingers along the ridge of a burn scar, first on the right side and then on the left. A jumble of images flashed through his mind in chaos. Pain. Pain was everything to him now, his lone reality. He had nothing more to hold him to the ground.

The scream returned, ripping past his lips and into the night. He had arrived.

#

"What you want to know, niña? You have questions about your love life? Your career?" The woman's thick Spanish accent caressed each word. Her dark eyes bore into Cassie as her hands shuffled a colorful pack of Tarot cards. Swift fingers travelled over the tops, never losing their place, like a Las Vegas dealer.

Cassie glanced over her shoulder at the tall woman behind her. Her best friend, Zoey, had been the one to find this psychic and insist on the visit.

"You sure about this?" Cassie mumbled under her breath.

Zoey nodded, twisting a strand of her golden curls

around a slender finger.

Lord, save me. Cassie faced the psychic, plastered on a straight face and adapted a business like tone. "Well, actually I was hoping you could tell me about all the weird stuff. You see... I'm a total freak." She said it without any reserve whatsoever. The paralyzing headaches, the shadows emerging from nothing, the purple energy consuming her life, all of it warranted the *freak* label. Now, this strange vision to top it off. She sighed, eyeing the room. Crystal skulls, long tapered candles, and navy colored drapes with stars filled the space.

I do belong here.

"Weird? Freak?" Luna stopped shuffling her Tarot deck in the middle. She plopped the cards on the table and inclined her head to one side, which made her look like a curious dog.

Cassie would have laughed at the thought if the situation weren't already so strange. Instead, she rested her elbows on the table and let her head fall into her hands.

"Where to begin?" She tapped her fingers, enjoying the swishing noise they made against the velvet. "How about my hands? I get flares of purple energy around them. Want to take a stab at explaining it?"

Luna's grin faltered for a split second, then snapped back into place. She put her hands palm up on the rich cloth. "Lemme see your hands, niña." She leaned forward. "Don't be afraid."

Cassie complied without protest, allowing her hands to fall into the older woman's warm moist palms. Luna closed her eyes and mumbled something in Spanish. Cassie took the opportunity to give Zoey a well-deserved eye roll. Her friend slapped the chair's back and pouted her bottom lip, a small line furrowing her brow. Cassie resisted the urge to stick out her tongue.

As the minutes ticked by with Luna studying her hands and mumbling as if in a trance, Cassie observed the psychic in more detail. The modest wrinkles in her forehead and dyed auburn hair could have placed her anywhere between forty and fifty. Her sharp nose and beady eyes against a round face gave her a wild, off putting look. Couple it with her black gypsy style skirt, flowery peasant top and red headscarf and she had the whole psychic image packaged just right.

"Hmm...Sí," Luna muttered, more to herself than her audience. Her eyes snapped open. "Yes. You have a strong aura, purple ringed. A color of wisdom and strength."

"I do?" The corner of Cassie's mouth quirked up.

"Oh, yes," Luna said. "You're a brave soul. But you haven't had an easy life."

Her smile died. *No, watching your parents die wouldn't be defined as easy.* She sucked in her cheeks. The memory of the awful day threatened to break through the surface, but she pushed it down hard. Choking back the bitterness, she erected a mental wall to block her emotions. She shook her head at the psychic and tried to keep the scowl off her face.

"You have health issues." The psychic tilted her head forward as if challenging Cassie to fill in the blanks.

"I guess you can say that." Cassie slanted her eyes toward Zoey, who flashed a triumphant told-you-so grin. She sunk into the chair, resolved the psychic was nothing more than a charlatan, but not wanting to disappoint her friend. "I have these bad headaches..."

"How long you had them?"

"Long as I can remember. They've been getting worse and more frequent though. The doctors could never find anything wrong." She tapped her fingers on the table again and huffed.

Luna nodded as if in understanding. "Well, let's see your cards." Picking the deck of Tarot cards from the table, she flipped them into her hands with ease. After a quick shuffle, she laid them face up, explaining each card.

"See, here, the High Priestess. There's a secret knowledge about to be revealed. You've some of the supernatural around you. Soon you'll find out. Soon you'll know. You must trust yourself." She patted the next card twice. "And here's the Lovers card. Someone is coming. The stranger will become part of you. You'll be unable to resist." Glancing in Cassie's direction, she wriggled her nose before shaking a long pointer finger. "The stranger brings challenges. Many changes are coming. Be careful, niña."

Cassie stared, unable to resist inching closer despite her doubts. She looked at each card. A nagging thought tugged at her rationale. *Should I tell her about the vision?* It had happened just once, but the dream had been so vivid, so real. A man shaking as he kneeled naked by the lake in Central Park. Two massive scars ran down the length of his back. His beautiful face twisted in anguish under the moonlight. Then, the scream erupted, forcing her to rise while echoing through her waking hours.

The words remained on the tip of her tongue, never moving past her teeth. For as the psychic continued laying out cards, Cassie glanced down at her hands. They rested on top of the table innocently except for the light purplish glow beginning to encircle them. *Oh God, now?*

The purple energy kept growing in strength. Cassie tried to relax and will it away but the force shone brighter. She shoved her hands under the table in an effort to hide them, but the light slipped out the sides and ignited the rounded table edges in color.

Luna slapped the deck on the table. Her face ran pale, illuminated by the unnatural purple glow lighting up the room.

"Qué esto?" Luna's strangled whisper echoed in the small space. "What...what's that?"

"It's the energy I was telling you about." Cassie grimaced.

"I never see anything like this." The psychic's accent grew thicker as thin beads of perspiration formed on her brow. "I mean I see auras...sometime, but not like this!"

"So you can't help me? You can't explain it?" Cassie said, though she already knew the answer.

"I...I don't know...I...maybe the cards." The psychic fumbled and grabbed the cards from the table. She tried to shuffle, but lost her place and the cards fell from her grip, spilling onto the floor.

Cassie sagged in the chair, not knowing whether to laugh or cry. Just as she was about to storm out in frustration, the pain assailed her. Flashing across her brain like a lightning strike, it set her entire nervous system aflame. Her heart thudded, then skipped a beat. She knew what was coming next but could do nothing about it. The agonizing headache rocked her to the core and pushed the air from her lungs. Her body tumbled to the floor, as if something had pushed her out of the chair. She couldn't move, couldn't think. Paralysis took over. The waves of panic became stronger, deeper. A few more minutes of this and her head would either split open or she'd suffocate.

She scarcely registered Zoey kneeling by her side. Her friend's arms tightened around her shoulders, trying to hold her up. From the corner of her vision, she could see the psychic standing close by, terror clear in her eyes.

Feeling close to passing out, Cassie tried to get her breath under control. The encroaching oblivion threatened to swallow her up as a shadow appeared before her. Fear became more palpable. She opened her mouth to scream, but nothing came out. She tried to throw her arms up without success, trying to protect herself from...what? A shadow? Insanity? She wanted to get up and fight despite the pain. Her body had other plans as she curled into a fetal position. A weight pressed upon her and she found herself fading away. She let go. Blessed darkness descended and for a time she found calm inside the void.

A hair-curling scream, forced her to awaken while it boomed through her consciousness. She jolted upright, eyes snapping to life, head still spinning. As her mind focused on the present, Zoey's face came into view. Worry lines shaped her eyes. A woman shouted from behind in a Spanish frenzy.

"El Diablo!" The psychic's voice rang in a high-pitched tin, grating Cassie's ears. "The devil has touched her. Get out! Get out! You don't bring this here."

Zoey yelled a few nasty expletives back and helped Cassie to her feet.

"Are you okay?" Gentle hands guided her to the door.

"Come on, let's get you out of here, sweetie."

"What happened?" Cassie whispered, finding her voice hoarse.

"I'm not sure. When you were down, there was a weird fog around you and then..." Zoey sucked on her bottom lip. "I don't know, Cas. Something came out. I don't know what it was. It looked like a shadow. And it went under the door."

"She's full of demons!" Luna kept screaming from the far side of the room.

Zoey spun around and gave the psychic a sharp glare. Luna wisely shut up, but continued to point at the exit.

As they strode through the main door, Cassie took Zoey's arm for support. They crossed into the waiting area, to find an elderly woman sitting calm on a red velvet couch. Her long gray hair touched a black shawl draped over her shoulders. Her head was downcast, eyes focused on the plush carpet. As they passed, the woman's head shot up and two bottomless black eyes beamed from large sockets.

"Thank you," the woman said. Then, she started to laugh, a hideous cackle.

Pain spiraled through Cassie's head. She leaned on Zoey, struggling to stay on her feet. "Get me out of here, Zo." They rushed from the psychic's den and into the cool night. The woman's laugh trailed behind as if chasing them.

"I'm sorry," Zoey said when they got into her car. "I didn't know this psychic would freak out."

They sat in the car in silence, not turning on the ignition despite the chilliness. The cold and quiet helped ease Cassie's mind, until the headache faded. They'd been friends for five years, long enough for Zoey to have witnessed the purple energy and the paralyzing headaches. But, it had never been so extreme before, and never both at the same time.

"What was it?" Zoey asked finally, flicking a hand to the window. "That was the weirdest shit I've ever seen."

Cassie shook her head, not knowing what to say. After some deep breaths, she said, "I don't know, Zo, I really don't." She drew an X on the fogged up windshield, then banged her fist on the dashboard. "Aura my ass, this has to be something else. It's getting worse and I need to find help. Real help." When the silence lingered too long, she scrunched her brows and added in a lighter tone, "Did the psychic call me the Devil?"

Zoey snickered. "Technically, it was 'El Diablo'."

"Wow, how's that for a stereotype?" Cassie scratched her head.

"Seriously, walking cliché." The tension broke as Zoey started the car, then turned on the heat. Leaning back against the headrest, she added, "We need a drink or two...or ten."

"Yeah, for sure. But, I've got work tomorrow and I need sleep before dealing with Mr. Turpis." Cassie laughed, forcing the burden on her heart to lift a bit. "Besides, I'm a lightweight."

"The best kind, a cheap date, right?" Zoey raised her finger in the air. "No. Don't answer."

"Wasn't gonna." Cassie smiled, but the happiness disintegrated. *Am I ever going to be okay?* She didn't have the heart to voice the concern to her friend, so she kept the smile plastered on her face. The wind blew cold through the open side window. *What the hell else could happen?*

TWO

Cassie was determined to spend the next day basking in the bliss of positive energy where nothing could touch her. Sure. And pigs would start flying any moment now. A gloomy chuckle as she hurried along the narrow semi-industrial road toward her job. Yesterday's little episode and the intense headache had wiped her out and she barely dragged herself out of bed.

"Late, as usual. Damn! Damn! Damn!"

No wonder the little hostess job at the diner was about the only job she could keep, despite a college degree burning holes in her finances. The thought made her laugh out loud. She picked up the pace, forcing her exhausted body to get into a rhythm and her mind to keep up. A slice of sun cut through the overcast sky as if lending brief assistance.

The dark blue sign of Chez Hudson came into view a few minutes later, its large glass windows following her with accusation as she crossed the road. She stuck her tongue out at them--and at the annoying man of a boss inside, who was probably yelling at some poor soul in the kitchen, before he would switch gears and scream at her for being late. Cassie sighed, her heart beating a double staccato, as she ducked down and walked in almost a crouch under the windows to get to the back of the low square building. Maybe if Mr. Turpis didn't see her entering late, it'd be easier to make up an excuse.

She almost made it to the back entrance when her hand scraped on a nail sticking out of the wall. Blood welled up, but it wasn't the pain that made Cassie swear. A dark purple cloud swirled above the small wound. The skin around it tightened and grew hot. As she watched in horror, the wound stitched itself together.

"Holy shit!" Her voice sounded taut and desperate to her own ears. "I can't deal with this today. I seriously can't."

Before she could utter another curse, the metal door swung open and Zoey's concerned face appeared out of the gloom of the kitchen.

"It's about time you showed up," the other woman exclaimed in a loud whisper. Cassie would have laughed at the absurdity of that but humor was fast escaping her this morning. "I was about to call you," Zoey continued. "Are you okay? I mean, after yesterday and all…" She trailed off.

Cassie forced a smile for her friend's benefit and gave her a quick hug.

"I'm fine, Zo," she said, brushing past to enter the building. A lonely chef with a baby face was cooking at the large stove. He exchanged a quick nod with Cassie before turning back to his pans.

"Mr. Turpis is in rare form today." Zoey said, catching up and placing a hand on her shoulder.

"Crap. I can't lose this job."

"You're not losing anything" She gave Cassie's shoulder a gentle squeeze. "Not today, and not on my watch."

"Zoey. What are you doing back there?" Mr. Turpis bellowed from the hall. "Hiding in the kitchen is not what I'm paying you to do!"

"Just a minute," sang back Zoey in her sweetest voice. "Cassie's jacket button broke and I'm just helping her fix it up."

"Cassie?" Their pudgy boss appeared in the kitchen, his round sweaty face warped in a sneer. "Where've you been?"

All hope of keeping her job faded into oblivion. Cassie stared open-mouthed at her boss. His baldhead gleamed in the kitchen's fluorescent lights. Stubby hands balled into fists and rested on his flabby waist.

After a moment of silence, Mr. Turpis repeated louder, "I asked, where've you been?"

"I didn't want to upset you," Cassie said. She lowered her eyes to the floor trying to look repentant. "I thought it would be better to rush to the back and fix my outfit first, since the way we present ourselves to the customers is so important here." The lie came without restraint, but a pain pressed down on her heart with each word. She hated lying and was not any good at it. Her mother had once caught her in a lie when she tried to blame missing cookies on a neighbor's dog. She was only six at the time. Two days later, on her seventh birthday, both of her parents died in a car accident. Cassie had a hard time lying about anything after that day.

"Well, I suppose it is better," Mr. Turpis said as he stuffed his hands into the pockets of his pleated slacks. "Just hurry it up. The busboy is out today, and I'll need you to help set up and clear tables." He shook a finger in Cassie's general direction and stomped out of the kitchen. The cabbage soup and fried pork scent followed him out.

Cassie's breath whooshed out. Working in a diner as she headed into her late twenties wasn't exactly her dream career path, but she needed this job to pay the bills. "I thought he was gonna fire me." She gave Zoey a half-hearted smile, the best she could manage as she fought for composure. "Thanks for the save."

"Don't mention it." Zoey waved her hand in a dismissing gesture. "It's not a big deal." With a shrug, she continued, "Not so shocked you're late this morning anyway. In fact, I'm wondering why you're here at all. You should be resting." She fidgeted with her sleeve. "Are you really okay?"

Cassie hesitated. The image of the weird shadow after her...*incident*...still remained fresh in her mind. Not to mention, the old woman's cryptic words, the psychic's freak out, the vision of that naked man, the unrelenting purple aura...aw hell. *What do I tell her?*

"Cassie, sweetie, it'll be okay. We'll figure it out." Zoey nodded weakly.

The show of support made her decision easy. *Not a damn thing. She's been scared enough.* Attempting another smile, she said, "I promise, I'm fine. Don't worry."

"Uh-huh. I'll let it go for now." A smile shot across her friend's face. "Only because I have a great idea!" Zoey burst into the main room and glanced at the tables. No one around. Grinning like a kid, she leaned against the hostess' stand and motioned for Cassie to take up residence.

"I'm afraid," Cassie said laughing. "An empty diner gives you way too much time."

She stood behind the stand and set the menus in order. Shifting the wrapped utensils in the wicker basket below occupied her for another few seconds.

"Ready now?" Zoey tapped her foot to a silent, yet upbeat tune. When Cassie didn't answer, she continued, "Good. Now, I'm thinking dancing, or better yet, a date."

Cassie slammed the menus against the wooden stand. "Zo."

"No. Don't start, Cas. You're not getting out of this. You never date anyone. You never hit the clubs with me." She pouted her lips and rubbed the tip of the counter. "Is it fair I should be partying without my best friend? And you are too young to be a hermit!"

"I'm not a hermit, Zo. I'm just not in a very social mood. Plus do I have to remind you of the last time you dragged me out to a party?" Cassie's nose twitched as she recalled the unhappy event.

"What? A cute guy was trying to get you to go home with him? Oh, horror." Zoey grabbed her cheeks with both hands and formed an O with her mouth.

"He called me for the next two weeks. Every day. Even though I told him three times, I was busy. I didn't pick up the rest of the time. You'd think he'd get a hint."

"You could've given him a chance. Is it so bad guys find you attractive? Oh, come on, just come party with me. Have a good time for a change."

"Partying leads to men. And I just don't have the best of luck with them." She grimaced recalling her own and only sweetheart, a college love…and a cheating bastard.

"Sweetie, you won't have better luck if you don't put yourself out there." Zoey leaned in closer. "Next time, you're coming. Promise?"

Cassie started to respond, but the bell over the front door halted the conversation. Over the next hour the diner picked up six tables. Cassie did her best to place them all in the same area. Not only did their busboy call in sick, but the diner's other waitress, quit last night. Mr. Turpis was kind enough to wait until midmorning to inform Cassie and Zoey. *Greedy pig.* As Cassie let her thoughts wander over a fitting revenge plot, the purple energy flared up again.

"Oh my God! This can't be happening. Not now!" She shoved her hands in her jacket pocket, gunning for the bathroom. Locking the door behind her, she ran the cold water and soaked her hands under the icy current. "Go away, damn it! Go away!"

Ten minutes later, the energy still hadn't disappeared and Mr. Turpis pounded on the door. "Cassie. Get out here now or you're fired!"

"Just a minute!" Panic tightened inside her chest. "Breathe. Just breathe."

As the freezing water washed over her hands, she let the numbness calm her. With aching slowness, the energy pulled back into her palms and dissipated. The tingling sensation remained behind. She shut off the water and ran her hands under the dryer to warm them. "Shit that hurts."

"Cassie. This is the last warning."

"Coming!" She pulled her hands away from the

soothing air and went out to face the boss.

"What were you doing? Don't you see the circus out here?"

"Sorry, Mr. Turpis." She tried to hide a grin as she thought of the perfect excuse. "Woman troubles."

He groaned. "Just get back to work."

The brute clunked back to his office. She headed back to her post to find Zoey looking wiped.

"Hey, would you mind grabbing the water pitcher from our resident gossips?" Zoey said, motioning to the old ladies' table in the corner. Her hand went to her chest as she tried to catch her breath. "They've already gone and the table needs to be wiped down. But, I've got to run to the ladies' room."

"No problem." Cassie gave a quick glance down the aisle to make sure the resident gossips, Mrs. Finney and Mrs. Dunblar, were really gone. She hadn't seen them leave and didn't want to be roped into long and boring small talk. When she was sure the booth was empty, she headed down to retrieve the water pitcher. It was the sole item Zoey couldn't manage after clearing away all of the other plates and cups.

Fate sometimes has a strange way of intervening, Cassie thought as the shock hit her. If Debbie hadn't quit the previous evening, if the busboy hadn't called in sick, if Zoey hadn't gone to the bathroom, if their gossiping customers had tried another diner for once, if the water pitcher never made it to the table, then Cassie would have never been at the booth at the exact moment when he appeared. She wouldn't have turned with the water pitcher in hand and stared out the diner's large front window. She wouldn't have seen his piercing eyes and the man staring back at her would have stayed in her dream.

The sound of the water pitcher shattering on the floor echoed off the diner's brick walls.

#

Gabe watched the dark haired woman through narrowed eyes. His gaze never left her as he moved to the front door and stepped inside. The vibrations from the broken water pitcher rang in his ears mixing with the doorbell overhead and a man's high-pitched shriek.

"What was that?" A red-faced man appeared from behind a door marked *Office*. He scanned the diner and zeroed in on the broken pitcher. The man's gaze moved to the dark haired woman and he shook a stubby finger in her direction. A violent chord rumbled through his voice. "It's coming out of your paycheck." Lucky for the man he ducked back into his office or Gabe might have hauled him off his feet and chucked him into the nearest wall--head first.

Whoa. Where the hell did that come from? The innate protectiveness over the woman didn't bode well for his solitary nature, but it did point him in the right direction. A quick, and irritating, reminder of why he was here. He clamped down on his emotions, a cold mask of pure control settling over his features.

The woman turned away from him to pick up the pieces of the pitcher and wipe the spilled water with a towel. He motioned toward her, hand outstretched to help her to her feet when she finished, but caught himself and snatched his hand back. *Easy. Settle. You don't know anything yet.* Crossing his arms over his chest, he leaned against the wooden stand in front and waited for her.

Rising to her feet once more, she walked toward him with eyes lowered. He could tell he made her uneasy, the feeling apparent through her spicy scent.

"Welcome to Chez Hudson," she mumbled, eyes still on the ground. "Table for one?"

"For the present," he said in a rich baritone, the sound unfamiliar to his ears. Even his voice was different in this place.

Her gaze drew up his body, taking him in. His adrenaline spiked. When their eyes met, she gasped. A light pink stained her cheeks. The air between them charged with energy, a lightening he could almost feel on his skin. Silent moments passed between them, before she tore away and studied the floor again.

"Your waitress will be right with you," she said, voice small and timid uttering the rehearsed phrase.

"You're not my waitress?" He raised an eyebrow, suspecting she wanted to avoid his presence.

"No, Sir. I'm the hostess." Spinning on her heel, she gave a discreet nod to the waitress in the corner. The tall blonde practically skipped to the hostess' stand as Gabe took his seat at a window booth. "Here's a menu. I hope you enjoy your meal."

"Thanks." He wanted to smile to put her more at ease, but the simple human gesture eluded him. His mood was just too damn dark to indulge in such annoying and unnecessary things. *Yeah, well, you better get with the program if you ever want to get out of this hellhole,* he thought as he watched her walk back to her stand.

The blonde squeezed the dark haired woman's arm and whispered the second she was within striking distance. Gabe's ears perked up while he glanced over the menu and eavesdropped on the conversation.

"Cas, did you talk with that fine male specimen?" The blonde said as she peeked over the stand in his direction.

"Lower your voice, Zoey," Cassie said, pulling her friend further behind the stand. Under her breath, she mumbled, "First party talk, now her man alert's gone off. Great!"

This time, Gabe couldn't help but smile.

"Oh, come on, Cassie, even you can appreciate that..."

The one called Zoey sauntered over, hips swaying with each step. She was gorgeous but his instinct told him she wasn't it. No, it had to be the other one, the dark haired woman, Cassie. He was almost certain.

Zoey went over the breakfast specials with a sultry flare. Gabe raised an eyebrow. His human form seemed to be as impressive to women as his original one. Without glancing at the menu, he picked the Big Breakfast Special, then turned his attention back to watching Cassie. *Focus. Don't waste time, just get it done.* He stared at her hard. His eyes narrowed. Little currents of energy buzzed at his fingertips. He had to touch her to be sure.

Gabe rose, waiting for her to finish with the customer, then strode toward her with confident steps. She didn't see him coming and shuddered the moment he laid his hand on her shoulder. A strong electric current ran through him, making his heart thump and little beads of sweat slide down his back. He had his confirmation.

Cassie stared at him like a frightened deer, her hazel

eyes wide. Her breath hitched. The sound ignited his blood like an erotic caress.

"Where's the men's room, please?" Gabe asked after his senses relaxed. Something inside him made him wonder at the lost look in her eyes. *So fragile.* He trampled the thought and firmed his resolve. He didn't give a damn.

"In the back, to the right," Cassie pointed the direction, and he slowly walked away.

In the bathroom he made sure he was alone before slamming his fist into the wall, leaving a small dent behind. How could this happen? He was a warrior, meant to always be one. If he only followed the rules, he wouldn't be here, trying to figure out what human he had to baby-sit and why.

He stared at his reflection in the mirror. But he *was* here. And he had a mission. He needed to pull himself together and approach it like he would approach any other operation. Do it fast. Do it efficiently. And get the hell out.

By the time Gabe got back to his seat, Zoey reappeared and covered every part of the table with his meal. The spread smelled and looked like heaven. Scrambled eggs, bacon, toast, pancakes, a tall glass of orange juice and a cup of steaming black coffee beckoned him with magical aroma`. A little bottle filled with amber-colored syrup and a small plate with butter completed the picture. Gabe felt the rumbling in his stomach grow forceful.

As Gabe tried all the foods laid out in front of him, chewing, savoring it all, his brain worked overtime. *How do I get close to this woman without scaring her off?* His assignment depended on gaining her trust. How to do this was left up to him. A direct confrontation seemed out of order.

He needed time. Time he now had in abundance, whether he wanted to or not. Yet patience was never his virtue and he was not about to begin practicing it now. His fingers twirled the fork in his hand, then tapped on the table. He slanted his eyes toward Cassie, watching her fiddle with a basket of utensils. *She looks like she's ready to jump out of her skin.*

Relishing the taste of black coffee on his tongue, Gabe became absorbed by his internal musings. It took him a moment longer than usual to notice Zoey back at the table.

"Looks like you're enjoying the breakfast," she said, a sly smile tugging at the corners of her lips. "Can I get you anything else, anything at all?"

"No thanks," Gabe said.

As Zoey left the bill on the table and walked away, Gabe made his decision. He'd come in a few more times. Get to know her better. Maybe ask her out the way humans did. Meanwhile, he'd trail her, figure out what it was about her life that got her in trouble. *It'll buy me time. The more information on this mission, the better.* The plan was simple and reasonable. He brushed a stray hair from his eyes. *What happened to make this Cassie so jumpy, anyway?* He pushed the thought aside with annoyance. Genuine concern had no place in his situation. He needed info, yes. But he would not let emotion enter into the equation. This was a job, pure and simple. Nothing and no one would interfere.

THREE

Cassie turned the key and heard the diner's front lock click into place. The day's tensions melted away as the thought of going home for some much-needed rest took center stage.

"Are you sure you don't want to come? Last chance," Zoey pleaded at her elbow.

"I'm positive. All I want to do is see the back of my eyelids." It wasn't a lie by a long shot. "Go, have a great time." She yawned for good show.

Zoey gave her a quick hug and a smooch on the cheek. Then, she disappeared, or so Cassie thought.

"See you tomorrow. Love you." Cassie heard Zoey's goodbye from somewhere around the corner.

"Love you too," Cassie said softly and sighed. The exhaustion threatened to overwhelm her. The long workday let itself show in her aching muscles and throbbing feet. But, fresh air called to her despite the sleepiness and she decided to walk along the river back to her apartment.

The West Side Highway stretched along the riverfront, unusually empty. A few late-night runners jogged along the Hudson pedestrian walkway. The waxing moon hung yellow and dim above the murky New York water, while a few dark clouds floated across the horizon. The air started to smell of rain. Clean and crisp. Cassie breathed it in. *I hope it rains all night.* A vision of raindrops falling upon her face came to mind. The image shone so vivid and pure she shuddered. It evoked an almost sensual response. *Maybe Zoey is right and I do have to get laid soon.*

Cassie walked down the path, enjoying the moonlight glow on the water. The sky crackled, the promise of a thunderstorm coming in its call. Her senses tingled. Something elemental and powerful came over her during a storm. She could never understand it, but the energy ignited around her in those times, even summoning the purple glow from within. She never felt it more than when she was at her childhood home, upstate. There, in the shade of the old trees, the isolation she so often felt in the giant metropolis of New York disappeared.

"It's about time I go visit," she said aloud. Yet, home also held painful memories. Those same memories she tried to avoid as much as possible.

Lost in her thoughts, Cassie stopped in midstride when the feeling of being watched haunted her steps. *Oh, you've got to be kidding me.* Her internal voice sounded annoyed even in her own mind. *It's way too late for anymore freakiness.* She tried to brush away the feeling as if it were a fly in front of her face. "Well, I guess it really is the day I snap."

When Cassie whirled around to try to spot her peeping

tom, it was with a frown on her face. Yet, irritation gave way to shock as she located the stranger from the diner, the man from her dream, watching her from far across the highway.

#

Gabe walked on the far side of the West Side Highway studying the girl. As if alerted to his presence, she swung around scowling in all directions. He stood too far back for her to see even if she looked his way, but his vision was sharp enough to see the frown on her face.

What the hell? He wondered, then sucked his teeth. *Poor choice of words.*

Cassie's face changed, as she seemed to have spotted him. "It's not possible. She can't detect me from there." The narrowing of her eyes in his direction spoke otherwise. "No way. It's too far for a human." He tried to deny the obvious even as his shoulders tensed. *I don't misjudge stuff like this.* Yet there she stood, staring at him, and with his keen eyes he could see her go pale.

His eyebrows shot up. "Damn. Plan B it is. Introductions now." As he started crossing the highway, he had to think fast. Their meeting needed to put her at ease, not spook the hell out of her. Mistakes didn't sit well with him. He'd always been right before, certain of his decisions, and that fact wasn't going to change for some simple human.

Gabe noticed the uncertainty flicker in her eyes. It was clear she contemplated whether to stay and hear him out or run for it. He had to admire that she even considered staying. It made her more appealing, knowing she had the strength in her. She impressed him further when he saw her legs lock straight. *Brave. Or maybe foolish.*

Gabe stood within ten feet of her when she crossed her arms as if to protect herself and asked in a strong voice, "Why are you stalking me?"

Well, she cuts straight to the point. The silent declaration had him smiling inside. Aloud, he answered formally, "Please let me apologize for scaring you. I found you very interesting when we met earlier today. I was trying to think of how to approach you. You see I'm not very good at meeting women." He had to restrain his laugh or give away the ruse. In what universe was he not good at meeting women? Or having them do anything he wanted?

"I doubt that," he heard Cassie say but her voice didn't sound as confident anymore. "But even if it's true, I'm sorry. I'm not interested." She sidestepped him, waving her hand in dismissal, and began to walk away.

"No, please, wait." Gabe matched her steps and touched her arm. "I'm not from around here. This city...well, it's not something I'm used to. I'm from a...more open place. You know big blue skies." He let her arm go as something sparked in Cassie's eyes. *Got it.* He let a small smile play on his lips. "I was just hoping maybe you could show me around. I've only been here for a day or so and it's a bit overwhelming." Another internal laugh bubbled up. He was starting to feel like a fool, like one of those base humans walking around, ignorant of anything but themselves.

He sensed Cassie's suspicion in her scent, a hint of dark berries beneath the spice. "My name's Gabe," he said, extending his hand, hoping the simple gesture would put her at ease. She remained unmoving.

"Gabe what?" she asked instead. Her posture stiffened.

Oh, shit. He attempted to cover, "Just Gabe."

"'Just Gabe'," she mimicked him. "What like 'Madonna' or 'Cher'?"

"Pardon me?" he said trying to hide his doubt. *Another mistake.* He'd watched these pedestrian creatures for years. He shouldn't be confused about these things. "Yes, I suppose so. For now at least. Until we get to know each other better."

Cassie's face changed again, a mask of mistrust and weariness settled over it. "You've got to be kidding me. You want me to go out with you but you can't even give me your last name? Do you know how creepy that makes you?" The situation spiraled out of his control. "Look, I'm not interested and now that we've established that, move on or I'll be forced to stop someone and ask them to help me because a strange man's following me." She said the entire sentence in one breath, her chest rising and falling faster under her blue jacket.

Before Gabe could speak again, Cassie spun around and walked away once more. Her strides lengthened as she seemed to try to catch up to some joggers. Gabe moved to follow, but before he had the opportunity, she stopped dead. The jogging couple moved off into the distance leaving Cassie and Gabe alone on the pathway once again. Yet, Cassie remained stock-still. Gabe wondered if she was considering giving him a chance after all when he saw her shudder once, twice, a third time. Her whole body shook. A musky smell of standing water permeated his nostrils.

This can't be happening. As soon as the thought flashed

through his mind, Cassie went rigid and fell on the asphalt, only her palms stopping her face from smashing into the concrete. Energy singed the air around them. He knew very well what would follow. The sidewalk stood empty now but it might not be for long.

He reached Cassie in two steps and grabbed for her, but the electric waves around her body ignited, too intense for him to break through. "Where do you live?" he shouted, as though he was trying to get her to hear through static. Gabe knew it was what she heard inside her head. She didn't respond, her body going more rigid. He had to get her away from here. Every minute counted.

"Please tell me where you live. I can help you. Don't be afraid, I know what you're dealing with." But it was a lie he covered under a calm tone. *I shouldn't be telling her that. She should be scared.* As he searched for an answer, his gaze fell onto a small leather purse. He snatched it from where it'd fallen and sifted through it. He came up with a wallet. Inside, her driver's license revealed what he needed.

"Cassie Durrett. 18 Washington Street." He had her address. A fact she would be none too pleased to find out once she was back to normal, he was sure. Tough. He had no other choice. A brief side thought gripped him. *No pictures of a man or children. Good, less complicated.*

Cutting through the energy at last, Gabe picked up Cassie's limp body, put her purse over one of his wrists, and started to haul ass. The path walk remained empty and the traffic was light as he crossed the highway toward Washington Street. One block more and he stood in front of the door to her apartment building, an old bricked structure surrounded by warehouses. Balancing Cassie in his arms, he reached into her bag again and dug out a set of keys. The very first try resulted in the right key. "Lucky."

A few flights of stairs later, Gabe entered her apartment using another key and looked around. "They call this adequate living space?" he muttered to himself. A Siamese cat meowed at him from the couch, and then scampered into the bedroom as he approached. Gabe placed his fragile package down on the cushions and looked her over. He didn't observe any visible injuries except for the scrapes on her palms, but he did note the compactness of her body, the smallness of her feet, and the beautiful contours underneath her clothing. *She's not bad looking.* Heat spiked through his blood. *If she wasn't my mission, I might be interested in finding out more about this one, intimately.* Yet as it was, he had a goal to keep in mind and he wasn't about to let himself get distracted.

#

Cassie moaned as the remnants of the attack wore off. She opened her eyes to stare into her dream man's gaze. *Oh, just great. I need to dream about him again?* Her body already tingled with pleasure at the familiar vision. A trench coat molded to his tall frame. Across his chest droplets of water clung to a black shirt, then dripped down to run over his dark jeans and heavy boots. *Gabe.* The name came to her. *How do I know his name's Gabe?* Reality flooded back with a vengeance, the whole encounter snapping into focus as if the picture emerged from a snowy TV. What she didn't recall was what happened after and why this man was now here, in her apartment.

Her gaze darted around the room, looking for

something to use as a weapon. Bookcases lined the far wall with plenty of thick books inside, but she'd never make it past him to reach the shelves. A tiny statue of a marble angel stood on top of the old TV just a foot out of her reach. Next to the TV sat an opaque yellow vase with a couple of long-stemmed white calla lilies. Neither the statue nor the vase, she decided, would be adequate for the job. When she couldn't find a satisfactory weapon, she tried to yell.

Before she could utter a sound, Gabe moved so fast she saw him in nothing more than a blur. His hand covered her mouth and he breathed into her ear. "You fainted. I had to get you home, off the street. Please don't scream. I mean you no harm. I promise." As if to punctuate his last words, he took his hand away.

Cassie suppressed the rising terror as she considered the situation and chose anger instead. She narrowed her eyes and curled her hands into fists.

"How did you find out where I live if I was unconscious?" she said, her body tensing in the fight or flight response.

"Your wallet. I went through it."

"Oh..." Her hands remained fisted.

"You're a strong woman, but you shouldn't direct your anger at me." He went to touch her shoulder, but she flinched away. "Look," he said. "There's something we need to talk about. But first tell me, how long have you had these headaches, this pain?"

"How do you know about them?" Her voice raised an octave higher.

"I just know. I also know what they mean. Do you?"

He seemed eager to hear the answer.

"I've had these episodes forever," Cassie said, unsure why she answered him. "They've been getting worse lately." Her head titled to the side. "Are you a doctor or something?"

"And have you ever felt any other feelings or sensations during or after the headaches?" Gabe went on, ignoring her last question.

"Yes...Maybe...But how on earth would you know?"

"Tell me more," Gabe insisted, his voice flowing smooth like water.

She pressed her lips together and shook her head. "Enough. I'm not telling you anymore until you tell me what the hell is going on, who you are and what you want from me."

Cassie heard him whisper under his breath, "Easy..." It seemed more instructions to himself than to her. She ignored it and waited for his answer.

"Cassie, I know what I'm going to say will sound crazy, but you've got to listen to me. Haven't you ever wondered at all the weird things happening to you over the years, at the feeling you get with the headaches, the energy?" She was about to interrupt but he raised his hand to silence her and continued, "This is not going to be easy for you to understand but...there's more to you than you think."

And I thought I was crazy. Cassie started to tremble. "What's that supposed to mean?"

"Well...you're not exactly...technically...you're not..." He struggled with whatever he was trying to get out.

"Just say it."

Gabe locked his gaze with hers. She didn't look away.

She couldn't.

"You're not completely human."

Silence hung thick in the air between them. Then with one swift motion, she sprang off the couch and into the kitchen. Without pausing, she jerked one of the drawers open and grabbed a steak knife.

As he followed her toward the kitchen, she turned to face him with the knife extended. The light in his eyes faded, but a glimmer of humor appeared in them. She was not, however, in a humorous mood. "Listen Gabe, or whoever the hell you are, you're crazy and I want you to get out of my house now! They have places for people like you."

Cassie inched toward her bag, which Gabe had dumped onto a little stool between the kitchen and the couch. She held the knife pointed at him with one hand while she rifled through her bag with the other. She never took her gaze off the man. Her hand came out holding an old model flip cell phone. With a flick of her thumb, she opened it and pressed three numbers.

"If you don't get out now, I'll call 911."

Gabe's brows lowered as he gave her an intense stare. After a few seconds, he raised his hands as if in defeat and said, "All right, I'm leaving now. But I want you to think about what I said. I would know. I'm not quite human either. As a matter of fact, not at all." Gabe walked to the door and opened it as if to leave. At the last moment, he turned to her and added in a gentle voice, "You may not be safe anymore, Cassie. I'll come back when you're ready."

"Mister, you should seek serious help for your problems," Cassie said. "If I ever see you again, I'm going to call the cops and get a restraining order. Do you understand me? Now, get out."

Without another word, Gabe left. Cassie slammed the door shut and slid all the bolts in place. A tremor ran through her. *Maybe I should change the locks tomorrow.* The idea of going through all the work made her miserable. Yet, she couldn't help but wonder about the man who came into her life in such a bizarre way. "Every day just gets weirder and weirder." She slid against the closed door to the floor and put her head in her hands. A dim purple glow radiated from her palms. "You've GOT to be kidding me!"

FOUR

"**A**h. Here comes another one," said the old man, cocking his brow. "Look at him strut as if he *is* somebody. Humph. We'll soon lay that arrogance to rest." He grabbed the nearest book and turned his back on the would-be visitor.

Gabe stepped into the room and pretended not to have heard the old man's remarks. He bit the inside of his cheek, trying to suppress his displeasure at the mess. In every space he found objects strewn about – books, magazines, newspapers, tapes, and even napkins with scribbled writing. Anything ever printed, written, or put into media in some form, probably existed somewhere in this hobble. Past issues of *Gossip Queen* magazine were stacked in a pile nearest the old man. *What am I doing here?*

"Revered One," Gabe said with an attempt at civility. "I seek your counsel." He waited for the old man's attention. When silence ensued, Gabe repeated louder, "Sir, I would seek an audience with you." Still no movement, no answer from the old man. *This is a waste of time.* As Gabe turned to leave, a gruff choking noise crossed the room.

"You would give up so easily?" the old man said, more statement than question. His fingers tapped along the armchair. "If you cannot manage twenty seconds of inconvenience, what hope have you with a lifetime of it?"

Gabe narrowed his eyes. No one had ever spoken to him in such a manner. It was as if ice water had been doused on his fiery pride. Contempt rose up like battery acid while he studied this old one. Silvery hair with streaks of brown stood up in every direction. A large bushy moustache of the same grayish-brown color lay at the end of an elongated round nose and covered a wide oval mouth. His eyes were dark, drooped, and set too far back in his face. It made the old man appear tired yet alert, an unsettling combination. Gabe decided a change of tactics might be in order.

"Inconvenience I can manage," Gabe began, pausing deliberately. "Wasting time, I cannot."

"I wasn't aware the two were separable." The old man grinned like a loon as Gabe seethed under his feigned cool demeanor. Gabe knew the more ancient of his kind rarely received visitors and enjoyed riling the younger fallen, but he found it difficult to ignore the slights. After a pause the old man added, "But come young one, tell me your troubles."

Gabe nearly exploded at the term "young one" but restrained as it would serve his purpose better to let the insult drop. "I seek answers from one who has inhabited the Earth these many centuries."

"Back to formalities. Do you think it matters to me whether you are formal or casual, humble or rebellious?"

The old man's zany laughter filled the room. "Young ones. What a hoot!"

The old man bolted across the room quicker than Gabe would have thought possible. With one rapid motion, a ferocious hug captured Gabe, pushing the air from his lungs. He sputtered and coughed as the old man stepped back.

"My apologies. I forget how fragile you are when you first arrive." The old man patted Gabe on the back and led him to a leather chair. "Have a seat. Tell me your woes, but first a name please?"

Gabe sat down and tried to hide the discomfort the old man's embrace had caused him. *Do all the ancient ones gain such incredible strength here?* In a flat tone he answered, "Gabe."

Another medley of laughter filled the room.

"Gabe he says." The old man clutched his stomach. "Gabe. Not very original, my young friend."

"It serves my purpose and fits with me well." The insults to Gabe's person began to tax his nerves. He shifted in the seat. With a hint of irritation creeping in his words, he said, "And what name do you go by now?"

"Why Albert, of course," the old man said with blatant astonishment. "A bit outdated for this time, I know, but I have found none better as of yet."

"Well it explains the appearance." Gabe swept a hand in Albert's general direction. He sat across from Gabe in the same worn out chair he'd occupied before the abrupt embrace. Tan slacks encompassed his short legs. His sweater was navy blue, a wool material. His face resembled the famed scientist. Yet, minor differences assured mortals would not concern themselves with the similarities. This old one enjoyed mimicking famous humans.

"Of course," Albert said beaming. "But, you did not come to admire my looks, now did you?" His eyes narrowed and his head slanted to the side.

Gabe couldn't hold back a smirk. "No. I didn't." He folded his arms across his chest and said no more. *I know your weakness now, old one.* He continued to smile at Albert as the silence wore on.

Albert squirmed in his chair, before jumping up. "I see you know more about me than I first anticipated, young one." He shuffled across the room, opened the double oak doors, and yelled, "Maribel."

Maribel appeared within the span of a minute. "What do you need, sir?" Her large dove eyes glared.

"My guest and I may be talking well into the night. Please bring us some tea," Albert said. Maribel strolled toward the kitchen. "Oh and some of those cookies. The peanut butter ones." He yelled at her back.

"Lousy, lazy, infuriating," Maribel cursed under her breath.

"Lovely woman," Albert said, oblivious to his servant's seething. He closed the doors and turned back to Gabe. "Now, where were we?"

Several hours, dozens of oatmeal cookies, and cups of tea later, Gabe had still not revealed the purpose of his visit, but he learned a great deal about his new plight. Albert was one of the oldest fallen he knew.

"The life of our kind, Gabe, is service to the Light," Albert said. "But, I was far too curious about Earth and its inhabitants to be content. I chose to remain here and give up the path of redemption for all time." He sighed. "I've been here for almost two thousand years, and still it is not enough to know the ways of this world."

"You may never be satisfied," Gabe said with genuine concern. "Don't you wish for peace of mind?"

"I miss the Light and its wondrous power." He paused. "But I do not regret my decision."

Gabe stayed silent. He could not imagine wishing to stay here for so long. Worldly temptations and the allure of free will did nothing for him. He was a warrior of peace, a servant of the Light. As if the old fallen had read his mind, Albert said, "And what of you, young one? What will you do?"

"I will seek redemption. My pride brought this upon me." Gabe's heart swelled with the pain of the admission. "I have accepted guardianship."

"I see. And would your charge be the real reason you've sought me out?"

"Yes," Gabe said. *If I lose the upper hand now, I may never get the information I need.* The old man waited. *It seems I have little choice.* Gabe inhaled, seeking the right words. "I do not understand her."

Albert's laughter burst forth. "You sought me for advice about women?" He choked out each word between chuckles.

"It is far more serious," Gabe said, awaiting Albert's silence. When the mood of the room changed once more he continued, "She has abilities. Yet, they have not matured. She can't control anything. It doesn't make sense."

"How old is she?" Albert's tone sobered with the

gravity of Gabe's words.

"I don't know. Late twenties, perhaps. Far past the age."

"Do you know her birthday?"

"We haven't exactly been social." Gabe's discomfort over the situation vexed him. He should have found out more information before seeking the old one's counsel. He rubbed the back of his neck. Disadvantageous positions didn't sit well with him. Neither did asking for help. But here he was. "What are you thinking?"

"I don't know for certain, but if she is what I think she is, we're all in danger." Albert rose and scrutinized his bookcase.

"What do you think she is?"

"Ah-ha! I've got it." From amongst the shelves, Albert extracted a black leather bound book. Its pages yellowed from the beatings of time. In gold letters on the front, the title blazed one word – Keys. He opened to a page at the very back of the book and read the following passage allowed:

> *Darkness and Light together mixed in blood*
> *Shall produce the Key to Earth's kingdom.*
> *Born on the day of order and balance*
> *Arising on the seventh cycle of birth*
> *To bond in power with the worthy.*

"The day of order and balance," Gabe said. "What does it mean?"

"If the girl, your charge, is the Key of this passage then she holds the future of Earth in her grasp." Albert slammed the book shut and placed it on the pile next to him. It shook as it made contact with the stack of texts on the wobbly side table.

"Impossible. Keys gain their power at seven years old. Not twenty-something." Gabe ran a shaking hand through his hair. "I don't see how this is possible."

"Gabe, we all knew this day would come." Albert reached across the narrow coffee table between them and patted him on the shoulder. "The Sacred Key will be born on the day of balance. I believe humans call it Leap day. Humans believe they've created it to keep the seasons aligned. Little do they know the true power it possesses."

"Then, her powers wouldn't mature until her seventh birth cycle."

"Yes, by human estimations it would be, let's see now..." Albert counted each finger twice then eight more. It seemed the great mathematical abilities of the man he resembled didn't transfer to him. "Her twenty-eighth birthday."

"That time could well be drawing near." Gabe scrubbed a hand down his face, making no attempt to hide his concerns. "The increasing attacks by dark forces, the surges of her powers, even my presence."

"Yes and you should know," Albert paused as if unsure of how to proceed, "Some will want to eliminate this Key. And not just those of the Darkness. If she is the one, and chooses one side over the other, think of what will happen to the other. Many will see her as too dangerous a threat to let live."

Gabe clasped his hands together in front of him and leaned his forehead on them. "This can't be." His heart sank at the weight of his predicament.

Albert remained silent.

The information was a lot for anyone to absorb, even a fallen angel. Gabe couldn't get his thoughts in order.

When the silence wore on, Albert added, "I am afraid it is so, my young friend. I do not envy your position. But, you have freely chosen this road. Take comfort in the choice."

"I care nothing about free choices or will, about humans or this world." Gabe's anger coursed through his blood. The rage fired his soul. "I would have remained in the Light forever. I was a fool."

"Perhaps. Or perhaps, you are needed here." Albert tapped the Keys book. "Perhaps you have far more to learn and care more than you yet realize. Have you considered that?"

The light shone from the old one's eyes in shades of amber and gold. Gabe's doubts subsided bit by bit. "Perhaps," he admitted with some reluctance. "Regardless, I have sworn to guardianship. I can't abandon her, no matter the cost."

"True. If you ever hope to see the Light again, you must maintain your pledge." Albert rose as he spoke. "I hope it is not your undoing." He offered Gabe his arm. "Nor the undoing of us all."

Gabe pushed away all thoughts of pride and accepted Albert's arm. He rose unsteadily to his feet. Their conversation had taken all of his strength.

Albert held him up under his arms and walked with him toward the door. "Remember, my young friend, your choice of guardianship has allowed you to maintain the

Light's powers, but you are still susceptible to the needs of your human body." He cocked his chin at Gabe. "And right now that body needs rest. You may stay in one of the spare bedrooms."

"Thank you," Gabe said without a trace of his earlier attitude. "I am grateful."

Albert stopped. "No protest. I'm shocked. Pleased, of course, but shocked."

"After what you've told me today, I'll be thankful for all of the help I can get." Gabe struggled to keep his head up and out of the fog threatening to enfold him as they continued out the door and toward a guest bedroom.

"Well now, there may be some hope for you yet, young one." Albert placed Gabe on a full bed covered in an elegant gold satin blanket.

"Excuse me," Gabe called as Albert was leaving. "You may call me Gabe, not young one." Some of the defiance of the morning sparked at the insulting title.

"Then again, maybe not." Albert slammed the door as he left.

Gabe chuckled as he lie back on the bed and fell into a restless sleep.

FIVE

"Up, now! Up!" An irritating baritone echoed about the room.

The bed shook with unnatural tremors as Gabe struggled to resist the interruption to his sleep. Flipping to his stomach, he placed the pillow over his head and ignored the sunlight pouring from the window. Even the sun felt different in this world.

The same grating voice called out again. "Come now. Up! We have so much to do. Arise, young one."

"Young one?" Gabe mumbled into the bed sheets. He turned, shaking away his mind's cobwebs. Squashing the pillow in his fist, he tossed it in the general direction of the door. "Who are you calling young one?"

Albert grinned, dodging the throw with a step to the side. "I see you're feeling better this morning." He picked up the pillow, smoothed the ruffles from the protective covering, and placed it on the foot of the bed. "Your strength will improve further with some food. Now, be quick."

Gabe didn't have time to muster a reply. After shaking the bed one final time, Albert disappeared back the way he'd come and shut the door behind him. The grandfather clock in the southwest corner chimed a soothing melody. Its polished brass hands read 10:00am. Gabe had slept longer than he intended. Considering the rest felt anything but restful, the late hour didn't surprise him.

Grumbling about the nature of older fallen, Gabe rose to his feet and skulked across to the bathroom. The cold marble tiles sent pins and needles into his bare feet. He adjusted the shower handles. Steam rose from the glass and encased the room in warmth in a matter of minutes. He let the water run over him, loosening his knotted muscles and washing away his new and unsettling emotions.

"Damn this place." He smacked the faucet bringing the stream to a halt. Bracing his hands against the shower wall, he fought to regain composure. As an angel of the Light, he never had to contend with baser emotions. Yet, he always wondered why Earth's inhabitants behaved so irrationally.

"Now, I know." His words tasted course like sand across his tongue.

The steam soon dissipated and more pressing urges garnered his attention. Hunger seized him with a growl so loud it could most likely be heard in neighboring rooms. He balked at the absurdity, then dried off and dressed. If he'd learned anything about Earth, it was you didn't ignore an empty stomach.

\#

After breakfast, Albert insisted taking Gabe on a tour of his new home – both the apartment and the city. "Can't have you living like a beggar," Albert had said as he waved his hand around yet another guest room. "You'll stay with me as long as you need."

Gabe had wanted to turn down the invitation, but since his options were limited, he accepted the hospitality as graciously as he could. Once the tour of the apartment hit the forty-minute mark, he wished he hadn't agreed. Albert had shown him every square inch of every room, along with a persistent recitation of the history of the building itself. Now, outside on the street, Gabe took a breath of city air. He leaned against a tree just in front of the building and stared at the sky above. A perfect vision of blue cast from one end to the other as far as his eyes could see. Not a single cloud blocked the sun from shining overhead.

"No daydreaming. Too much to do. Too much to see." Albert bounded down the front stairs like an excited puppy, the ends of his olive tweed jacket flapping behind. "This way."

Gabe followed a few paces back, not sharing the older fallen's enthusiasm. At the end of the next block, they came to a set of stairs leading into a concrete void below. The sign read "C" in a blue circle followed by "72nd Street Station." Gabe angled his head, wondering silently just what he'd gotten himself into.

"Down we go, like Alice into the rabbit hole." Albert's exuberance manifested in the form of rhyme.

Snorting, Gabe said, "Okay. I'll bite. Who's Alice?"

"What? Oh no, never mind." The old fallen waved his hand as if shooing the question away.

The pair lumbered down the steps and into the station. Albert demonstrated the proper method of swiping the fare card and entering through the turnstile. The infuriating machine read, "Please swipe again" four times before allowing Gabe entry. By the time the train arrived, fifteen minutes later, he had to ease his hold on the train's metal handgrip to keep from breaking it.

"Settle down, young one, before you cause an unnecessary scene."

The reprimand, along with Albert's use of the damn nickname, did little to dissuade Gabe's anger, but he managed not to cause the subway car any damage. Well, at least for the next few stops. When the train reached the stop at Forty-Second Street, it jerked forward into the station. At the same instant, Gabe's hand left the guardrail. The movement caused him to slam his shoulder into the back wall of the train.

Surprised by losing his balance, but otherwise unharmed, he examined the space where he'd landed. *Hell.* A huge dent remained behind. He leaned back, covering the damage with his body.

"Stop messing around," Albert cried from the station platform. "Lots to see."

Gabe resisted the urge to pull the emergency door from its frame and chuck it at the old coot. Barely. Grinding his teeth, he took one last look at the dent, shrugged, and then walked from the train without comment.

The forty-second street station had a long connecting walkway packed with people. Albert said it led to an area called Times Square. Pushing through the mob, they exited onto the street above, which proved equally as crowded.

Gabe couldn't believe the sight. Humans of every age and size, every shape and color, rushed through the streets with single-minded speed and purpose. The shared goal to get to their destinations as fast as possible created a synergy amongst the people.

Gabe had heard about the pace of city life from other angels who had travelled to Earth from time to time. He'd known the stories, but avoided the world he considered inferior. Being here, amongst these creatures, felt surreal and set his heart racing. He expected to feel disgust or pity. He expected to hate it now as much as he had when he'd been part of the Light. Yet, he didn't. *Amazing.* Blood rushed through his veins, a fiery adrenaline shot. The sensation excited and unnerved him all at once.

Albert cleared his throat, breaking the strange mood that had descended upon Gabe. After additional coughs, he said somberly, "This city is a microcosm of the world, my young friend. It is a living, breathing concrete reflection of every person on the planet." Pointing to a street corner, he continued, "Just look there. You see those people standing in line at the hot dog cart?"

"Yes," Gabe said, his hunger gnawing to the forefront as the scent of meat and grease pervaded the air.

"What do you see when you look at them?"

"Humans." Fighting to keep the bitterness from his tone, he said, "Emotional, unpredictable, ordinary humans."

"Ah, that's the angel talking." Albert chuckled. "The angel from the position of superiority we're bred and fed." He leaned in. "Know what I see?"

Gabe took a step back not wanting to buy into

whatever the old fallen was selling. "You still going to tell me if I say no?"

Continuing as if uninterrupted, Albert said, "I see life." He pointed at individual humans as he spoke. "The man there. The one with the dark hair. He's a college student from Beijing studying at NYU. He likes this all-American blonde from his class. He never talks to her, too afraid she'll be turned off by his accent or mock his English." He sighed. "Behind him, the woman in her twilight years has twelve grandchildren, twelve. She thinks about each one of them every day. She prays at night she doesn't forget their names, their faces, that she'll keep her memories and senses until her final breath."

Gabe folded his arms across his chest and sucked his teeth. The knowledge of these humans' lives... His chest tightened. "Why are you telling me this?"

"This is Earth, Gabe. This is the freedom and the passion you could never have as part of the Light. These people worry because they have something to worry about. They love. They care. They feel in a way no angel ever could." Albert inhaled. His nostrils flared. "I love this place. Light and Darkness mix on Earth, but this world belongs to neither of them. It never should." He moved closer and gripped the younger fallen's arm. "Stay here awhile and you'll understand my words."

"I have no intention of understanding." His temper resurfaced as Albert's motives became clear. Gabe jerked back his arm. "You won't tempt me with this life. Human emotions are undisciplined. This world is erratic. Choosing to stay here, instead of earning your redemption, was a choice of anarchy over peace. A fool's choice. I will not be such a fool."

Albert shook his head and sadness filled his gaze. "It's through chaos we learn who we truly are." He turned and fled down the street. People parted for him as if he possessed some type of invisible force around his body.

Standing alone, while in the middle of so many people, had Gabe chewed over his emotions. *This is Earth. This is its power; its temptation.* He tried to convince himself and silence the inner turmoil. As an angel, his pride grew from his confidence and certainty in his decisions. Doubt was not part of his genetic makeup. At least it's what he'd always believed. Since falling to Earth, every thought he had, each decision he made, he called into question. *Is it this place? Or is it truth?* He glanced further down the street to find Albert standing at the end of it watching him.

"I can't care," Gabe said aloud to no one in particular. "I have to steel myself against emotions, against these people, against this Key." He pictured Cassie, strong and determined, kicking him out of her apartment and denying the truth about her true nature. "Especially against her."

A woman's shrill scream rang out a pace from where he stood. He turned toward the sound without thought. The woman hung onto a traffic pole as if too frightened to support her weight. Just beyond her, a yellow taxicab barreled down the road faster than any other car. It approached the intersection where a small boy with curly hair and wide eyes stood immobile in the middle of the crosswalk. In a breath, the boy would die under the cab's unmerciful force.

All of Gabe's doubts and indecisions melted away. No question remained, only action. Later he would claim to

Albert it had been instinct driving him, not concern. But, it would be a lie. He wanted to save the boy. He desired it down to his bones. It went beyond rational thought. He felt it and the emotion could not be denied.

Gabe grabbed the boy just before the taxi could make impact. He rolled on the pavement with the tiny human cradled in his arms. When he rose to his feet, he made sure the boy could stand and the mother wouldn't pass out from shock, before he wished them both well and moved on. People applauded and slapped him on the back as he found Albert once more amongst the crowd. Someone even called him a hero.

"So," Albert said with a smile as wide as his face. "Are you hungry, hero?"

Gabe didn't respond. He paced the streets with the older fallen at his side. The noises of cars honking, people talking, pigeons chirping, lights buzzing and infinite sounds bombarded his senses. He concentrated on each of them in turn to avoid his own thoughts. If he listened enough, maybe he could block out all of his internal struggles. Maybe he could pretend he was an outsider, an observer and not part of the fabric of Earth. He could try.

"Come on, young one," Albert said with a knowing look. "I promise things will look brighter after a pizza."

"Pizza?" Gabe asked, too tired to argue.

"Now you see, no one, and I mean no one whether angel, fallen, human or other should ever be denied the experience of classic New York pizza."

"Why not?" Gabe sighed and a stray thought ran across his mind. As they entered the pizza parlor, he turned to Albert and gave the idea voice. "You know, maybe you should tell me more about this Alice and the rabbit hole."

Albert's boisterous laugh brought about a few stares from patrons. He whispered to Gabe. "I think you might be right, my young friend. I think you might be right."

SIX

Parallel lines of light and shadow streamed across Gabe's face. Weeks had passed in a blur as he spent the time learning from Albert and contemplating his decisions. On this morning, he stared about the room. Everything came rushing back. All that had occurred since the moment he'd fallen from the Light hit him with crushing force.

"What have I done?" he asked to the empty room. "What do I do now?" He resisted the urge to place his arm over his head and wallow in self-pity. Not his style. Instead, he pushed himself to a sitting position, put his hands behind his head, and leaned against the oak headboard in thought.

As Gabe pondered his situation, three knocks sounded on the bedroom door. "Mr. Gabe, sir," followed the sweet voice of Albert's maid, Maribel. "Are you awake?"

"Yes," Gabe said after a brief hesitation. "Can I help you?"

Maribel entered the room with a breakfast tray in hand.

She wore a black shirt, black slacks, and white apron about her plump waist. If the slacks had been a long skirt, she could have passed for a domestic servant of an earlier age. *Albert's soft spot for history.* Gabe's smirked. *Then again, I suppose in essence he is living history.*

"Mr. Albert said to attend to you this morning," Maribel said. "And for as long as you may need."

"Really?" He cocked a brow. "And where is Mr. Albert?"

"He's gone away on some business. He left you this note and told me to give it to you with breakfast." She placed the tray on the edge of the bed, picked up the letter and handed it to Gabe.

"Thank you." He took the letter and placed it face down on the bed. The meal's sweet aroma reached his nose. It smelled far too tempting to bother about the letter just now. A large stack of pancakes doused in syrup, bread with butter and jam, bacon, sausage and scrambled eggs beckoned to him. His stomach rumbled. His hunger as fierce as it had been the first day in the diner. The memory brought with it a pang of annoyance, but he pushed it aside. There would be time to worry about rectifying the situation with Cassie later.

Maribel stood silent, staring at him. She coughed, then asked, "Aren't you going to read the letter, Mr. Gabe?"

Gabe looked up from the breakfast. *Another one too curious for her own good.* He picked up the letter again, opened it and read it aloud for Maribel:

"Dear Gabe,

I apologize for not being there to greet you this morning. The revelations of the past few weeks leave me with many questions. I have gone away on trip, one of discovery. Please feel free to continue to utilize the house and any of my possessions at your discretion. I have left explicit instructions with Maribel to give you free rein. See my trust is not misplaced. I expect all will be in order upon my return. Until we meet again, my young friend, good luck!

Albert

PS Enjoy the oatmeal cookies"

He folded the letter and placed it back in the envelope. Without pause, he began to dig into the ample breakfast. Maribel exited the room. As Gabe's hunger subsided, the earlier emotions churned in his stomach. He pushed the now empty tray aside and lay back on the bed once more. Staring up at the bare ceiling, he contemplated his next move.

#

Cassie shuddered and resisted the urge to scream. *Another dream.* The remnants of it swam in her head. Since the day before they met in the diner to the incident in her apartment a few weeks ago, Cassie had been having nightly dreams, and sometimes daytime visions, about Gabe. Some shook her to the core. Creatures, far beyond what her imagination could conjure, tormented her while Gabe watched. Other dreams starring Gabe were all too sensual, all too enjoyable and reminded her of just how long it'd been since... *Oh jeez.*

Yet, tonight's dream was perhaps the most disturbing of all. It gave a full account, with all the tiny details, of the night she threw him out of the apartment. Time and distance from the event gave her more clarity. One thing she could not deny, no matter her feelings, was Gabe had saved her from...something. Whether or not he was crazy was another story. She owed him and the debt poked at her conscience.

"What do you think, Maia?" Cassie rose from the small couch and stretched her tired limbs. She'd fallen asleep just after dinner while watching the six o'clock news. It was nearly nine now. "Is he nuts?"

Maia, her Siamese cat, mimicked her master's movements by arching her back and stretching her long legs. Her nails dug into the wool fur on her tiny bed. "Meow."

"Yeah. I'm not too sure either." Cassie picked her up and placed the sleepy cat on her lap. She'd found Maia as a tiny kitten over ten years ago and they had formed an instant bond. *Two orphans.* It'd been Cassie's first thought upon plucking the homeless kitty from a filthy garbage can. She sighed at the memory, scratching behind Maia's ears as she let her mind wander over the incident with Gabe. "What if he's not crazy?"

The troubling thought didn't have time to linger as a loud chirping distracted her. Chirp. Chirp. Louder. More persistent. Chirp. Chirp. It seemed to be coming from her leather bag. Cassie had thrown the bag across the room earlier in a fit of temper. "I'm coming," she called towards the continual chirps.

"Hello," she said into her cell phone.

"Well, hello there, hermit," said a peppy Zoey from the other end.

"Hi Zoey." Cassie tried to get in coughs for good measure between words. "What's up?"

"Don't even bother, Cas. I know you too well. You're not getting out of it tonight. So save your coughs for someone who believes them."

Cassie rolled her eyes and sighed.

"Save the sighs too. And the eye rolling. I can practically hear them through the phone."

"How could you possibly know?" She couldn't help laughing at her friend's perception. "I guess you *do* know me too well. It's not fair."

"True. But, I'm also a genius, silly. I thought you knew by now." Zoey's happy energy rang through the receiver.

"Uh-huh. Well, then tell me this, oh genius one, what will be my method for getting out of this evening?" Even as Cassie asked, she strolled over to her bedroom closet and began to rummage through it for an outfit. She knew she'd been defeated but didn't give up just yet.

"Hmm. Let me consult my trusty and very scientific..." Zoey paused for emphasis, "Magic eight ball." Her hums vibrated over the line. "Sorry. It seems fate is against you. It has decreed you must keep up your promise of going to the club with your friend tonight."

"So I thought." Cassie considered volunteering for a night shift at the diner.

"Cassie." Zoey's tone turned serious. "I will be over there in twenty minutes. I expect you to be ready, or at least in the process of getting ready. You've been stuck in your apartment for too long. You *are* coming out tonight, even if I have to drag you myself."

"Yes, mother."

"That's right!" Zoey cried, perking up. "See you in a bit."

"See you, Zo." Cassie clicked the phone closed letting one more sigh escape. She had no desire to go anywhere let alone to a crowded club to mingle with a bunch of drunk and sweaty strangers. *Then again, all of this questioning hasn't done me any good either. A distraction could help.* She paced around the room before returning to her closet, all the while wondering if she was going crazy. She hadn't told anyone about the incident with Gabe and all of the strange dream visions, not even Zoey. She didn't know how to explain it, and she'd already worried her friend enough by telling her about the headaches. She owed it to Zoey to put on a happy face tonight.

"At least she'll stop nagging me for a little while." Cassie chuckled as she pulled on a black mini skirt, red halter-top, and black leather knee high boots with serious heels. A silver choker with a ruby in the middle and small silver hoop earrings completed the outfit. Smiling to Maia, she said, "If I'm going to go, might as well look good." She brushed out her thick hair and let it hang straight, where it trailed midway down her back. Her hair was one feature she actually liked, though she often wondered whether the black color came from her biological mother or father. She huffed at her reflection. "Don't go there. Happy face, remember?"

As Cassie finished applying a smoky eye shadow,

mascara and dark burgundy lipstick, the doorbell rang. *Jeez, Zoey isn't messing around.* She grabbed her bag and black leather jacket as she called a loud, "Coming."

From the other side of the door a voice answered, "You'd better be." Cassie laughed as she opened the door to face an awestruck Zoey.

"You're ready." Zoey gave Cassie the once over and nodded her head in approval. "And you look great."

"Ah, thank you," Cassie said, pulling the door shut behind her. She gave Zoey a quick hug and then stepped back to admire her friend. Zoey wore skintight black jeans that screamed designer, a low cut metallic blue shirt with a long silver necklace, and stilettos whose height demanded attention. "You look incredible."

"Naturally." Zoey wiggled her brows. "Thank you." She took Cassie by the arm and dragged her into the night. "I'm so excited you're coming tonight. I feel like a teen." Zoey hailed a cab with expert finesse.

"I'm sure we'll have a good time," Cassie said with as much enthusiasm as she could muster. She added under her breath, "Just like a root canal."

When they pulled up to the building a few minutes later, her last drops of hope for escape faded. Brick, painted a midnight black, encased the club's exterior walls. It possessed no windows and the glowing red sign above the entrance read "Private." *Why do I do this to myself?* Cassie swallowed hard.

As they got out of the cab and walked to the front door, a narrow alleyway to the side of the building caught Cassie's attention. She paused and peered in. It was impossible to see down, but she'd bet anything there was an emergency exit for the club somewhere within the darkness. *Escape plan – check. Now, I just need an excuse.* But before she could think of one, her friend's voice interrupted her scheming.

"Come on, Cas, it'll be fine." Zoey led the way into the club, past the cliché burly bouncer who nodded to Zoey like he knew her. Considering how much she went out, he probably did.

Blaring music hit them full force. The house beats intermingled with rock metal, the noise so loud identifying the song playing became impossible. Cassie could feel the pounding of bass drums deep in her chest. The lights dimmed to create a dark enigmatic mood. The crimson neon signs pointing out the bar area and the restrooms were the sole bright spots in the club.

"What's the name of this place again?" Cassie said struggling to be heard over the racket.

"What?" Zoey cupped a hand around her ear. Cassie repeated the question. "Oh. It's 'Crimson'. Great, isn't it?"

"Yeah." Cassie plastered on that happy face and tried to sound enthused. "Great."

Zoey yelled what sounded like, "Be right back," and disappeared through the mass of moving bodies. Cassie scanned the area and spotted an empty corner toward the back of the club. She made a beeline for the spot. Just as she was about to have a little peace, a guy grabbed her wrist and spun her around.

"Hey. Come dance with me, baby." The man's breath reeked of alcohol. His disheveled sweaty hair spilled forth from a ponytail. A pair of tattered jeans, dirty construction boots, and "More beer here" t-shirt pegged him as trouble.

"No, thanks." Cassie tugged her hand away from his grip. She took a pointed step back to put more space between her and the stranger. His muddy blue eyes glared at her with menace.

"That's how it gonna be, huh?" The man slurred his words and made a grab for her again. She sidestepped him and watched as he stumbled forward. When he regained his balance, he turned and hissed. "Bitch!"

"Get lost, asshole!" Cassie braced one foot forward and felt the floor beneath her feet. It'd been a rough couple of weeks, and if she got the chance to take out her frustration on this moron, she'd welcome the challenge.

The man laughed at her. "Watcha gonna do bitch?" He lunged again, trying to circle her waist.

She out maneuvered him. With her leg extended to one side, she used his body weight and forward motion to propel him to the ground. The jerkoff fell head over heels for her – literally. He laid flat on his back in a heap as his eyes stared at the ceiling.

A martial artist for many years but a pacifist by nature, she tried to keep the grin off her face. She failed. "Perfect."

SEVEN

"Excuse me, miss. You okay?" A booming voice said from behind her. Cassie spun around, the grin still on her face. Taking down the jerk had her adrenaline pumping. She tried not to bounce around as she eyed the voice's source. A hefty bouncer, with Zoey at his side, stood like a mountain. He observed the man in the corner with the poise of a true professional.

"I'm fine. Thank you."

The bouncer towered over Cassie, a good head and a half taller. His biceps bulged larger than her thighs. A black t-shirt and jeans matched his ebony skin. His deep-set eyes projected an all business gaze. Anyone would be a fool to mess with this man.

"Okay, buddy, let's take a walk." The stranger might have been sleazy, but he evidently wasn't a fool. He staggered to his feet with a groan. Shooting Cassie a drunken glare, he followed the bouncer out without argument. The crowd parted way for the pair, and then swallowed them up again in a mass of bodies as they passed.

Zoey embraced her around the neck in a tight hug. "You sure you're all right? I'm so sorry. I thought you'd be safe by yourself for two minutes." She stepped back and swatted the air, exasperation making the simple motion more dramatic. Another hug around Cassie's neck cutoff the airflow. "I'm so so sorry. You okay? Really?"

"I'll be better after you let go." When Cassie could take a deep breath again, she said, "No worries, Zo. You know I can handle myself. Besides it wasn't your fault. Let's just forget it and try to enjoy ourselves."

"Okay. As long as you're sure." Zoey's peppy spirit switched right back on. She took Cassie by the hand and led her to the main dance floor. People swayed to the beat all around them. "No more craziness. Let's have some fun."

Cassie made it through five songs of house and techno mixes, before she signaled to Zoey she was heading back to the bar. Zoey made a move to come with her, but Cassie waved her off.

"I'll be okay. I'm just going to get a drink and rest. Keep dancing," she yelled at Zoey's ear to make sure she heard her.

She needed some alone time - or as alone as you could be in a club. Thankfully, an empty metal bar stool assured her reprieve from the crowd and the blisters forming on her feet.

"Diet coke, please."

The pretty blonde bartender worked fast, sliding drinks across the counter with ease. Cassie grabbed her drink from the pile and turned to watch the people dancing. The music had died down a bit but the crowd was just getting started. The mass of wriggling, straining bodies on the floor made for an almost hypnotic show. Zoey danced with a cute guy who had more than dancing on his mind. His hips gyrated in an obvious demonstration of his thoughts.

What a meat market. Cassie blew out a breath, then let her gaze wander from the display and travel around the room. *I'm getting too old for this.*

Out of the crowd, she spotted a familiar face. It was the same one she'd seen so many times in her dreams. Gabe's heated stare captured hers from the other side of the room, giving her heart a little jolt. *Shit! Hell! Damn!* Curses flooded her mind without direction. He walked toward her with confidence, his step never faltering. Before she could think straight, he stood in front of her.

"Hello Cassie."

The suggestiveness in his simple greeting melted her. A weak "Hi" was all she could manage as his eyes pierced her in a way that suggested he saw into her soul. *Aren't I supposed to dislike him or something? Is he following me again?* It skipped across her mind, a fleeting pebble of a thought before she lost all reason and resolve. The golden color in his gaze entranced her.

"We need to talk," he said, eyes narrowed.

Before Cassie could do little more than open and shut her mouth, Zoey appeared on the scene. Her sly smile warred with her mother hen hovering. She winked at Cassie, and then turned to Gabe. "Hello there. You look familiar." She beamed a row of white teeth. "I never forget a face. Now let's see...the diner right?"

"Yes. You're Zoey, the waitress. I remember too." Gabe returned the grin. "I'm Gabe. Nice to see you again."

"Nice to see you too. Cassie failed to mention you two knew each other." She huffed and peered at her friend. A shrug was Cassie's lone reply.

"We know each other somewhat," Gabe said. With a wolfish grin, he added, "But I'm hoping to change that."

"Well then, you going to stand here chatting it up all night, or are you going to take my friend and hit the dance floor?" She nodded in Cassie's direction.

"I don't dance." The muscles in his arms flexed as he slipped his hands into the pocket of his overcoat. "Besides, your friend and I need to talk."

"Oh really?" Zoey said, raising one eyebrow skyward. She giggled. "Well, you see, bars are for talking, clubs are for dancing."

"And what about bars inside of clubs?" Gabe pointed at the neon bar sign.

Zoey crossed her arms looking a bit deflated. "Guess there's no steadfast rule about it."

"Then, do I have permission to talk with your friend?" The sudden sweet change in his voice made it impossible for any woman to resist.

"Sure." Zoey titled her chin toward her chest and lowered her lashes, clearly affected by Gabe's tone.

"Ah Zoey." Cassie said, tapping her friend on the shoulder. "I think Gabe and I are going to get some fresh air. Will you be all right?"

"Of course, silly. I'll see you later." She examined Gabe, her gaze running the length of his body. A brief nod to Cassie followed. "Or if I don't see you later, just give me a call," she said with a wink. Zoey kissed her on the cheek, then turned to Gabe and pointed her long finger at him. "You take care of her."

"Yes, ma'am." Gabe gave a polite nod. "Wouldn't do otherwise."

Before Cassie could protest she hadn't meant anything more than a simple walk outside, Zoey leaned in and whispered into her ear, "Please be careful." Then, her friend disappeared into the swarm of people on the dance floor.

"She's got the wrong idea."

"Oh and what idea is that?" Gabe's smirk implied the type of idea Cassie wanted to avoid.

"Never mind. What do you want? How did you find me?" Zoey's earlier distraction pulled Cassie back to some of her senses. *This isn't some dream. This is real. And he's not to be trusted.* The conviction would be a lot more effective if her body would just cooperate and not get all worked up. She pushed the memories of her dreams away, gripping the cup of soda like a life preserver.

"Easy. I just want to talk to you." Gabe put his hands up in surrender. "Please."

The *please* caught her off guard and she nodded despite her better judgment. Gabe walked toward the emergency exit around the corner from the bar and she followed two steps behind. He cracked the door open, glancing up at the alarm. When it failed to go off, he pushed it wider and scanned outside. He stepped into the cool night, and then held the door open for Cassie. The alleyway looked empty in the moon's glow.

The wind blew past with a chill and goose bumps

emerged on Cassie's legs and arms. Without a word, Gabe took off his long black coat and offered it to her. *Didn't I hold him off with a knife the last time we met?* Cassie hesitated as her internal warning bells triggered. *Didn't he also save you from...?* She didn't know how to finish her last thought, so she put her arms into his jacket and hugged it around her, nodding a silent "thank you". The smell of cinnamon and something stronger, almost like Jack Daniels, reached her nose. She edged the collar of the jacket further savoring the aroma. *Be careful.* Her need for self-preservation struggled against, or perhaps with, her curiosity, depending on how you looked at it. Regardless, she had to know more despite her reservations.

"All right, Gabe," Cassie said with a little too much force. "We're alone. Talk."

"Just a minute." He motioned for silence. "I don't think we're alone after all." Squinting into the darkness, he searched the alley. He pointed to a shadowy figure about forty feet away, by the dumpster near one wall.

"I can't tell. It could be a person. But, I only see..." Cassie choked on the last words as blinding pain invaded her head. She went down hard on both knees, her hands clutching her temples. A scream struggled to escape her throat.

"Cassie," Gabe shouted. "Not now. You have to fight this. It's too dangerous here." He wound his arms around her, willing her to stay with him. Every fiber of his being worked to keep her in the here and now; his energy flared a brilliant blue. She could sense his resolve even through the pain.

Without warning, Gabe flew backward into the brick

wall and the pain in Cassie's head reached its threshold. A buzz and smoke surrounded her. Darkness consumed the space and air where she knelt creating a cyclone without wind. Somehow she'd managed to stay awake through it. Not at all the norm. Every other time these attacks hit, she'd passed out. Yet, now, her mind remained alert.

As the pain eased off, so did the dark whirlwind. But, before it disappeared completely, a shadow emerged from its base. Cassie opened her eyes wide and stared as the shadow moved across the alley floor and toward the dumpster. The figure she'd been unable to see before now appeared very clear. The stranger who'd grabbed her in the club leaned against the metal trash bin, staring at the shadow. Hisses erupted from the spot where the stranger stood and a voice, which could only be defined as demonic, half hiss, half growl, spoke. Cassie couldn't make out the words, but the next thing she saw she was certain would haunt her dreams for all time. The shadow on the floor shot straight up into the man's mouth, nose and eye sockets as if it were a tangible thing.

Cassie's scream finally ripped through the air. In the same moment, Gabe grabbed her from behind and pulled her down the alley. In her fear, she fought him, struggling in his grip and making the job far more difficult. "Cassie, stop," he shouted close to her ear. "We have to get out of here. Now!"

Terror paralyzed her. For so many weeks, she'd been living in doubt of what Gabe had told her, of what the psychic revealed, and of the existence of anything paranormal. The sight of the shadow shooting into the man had her stomach churning. It seemed far too possible Gabe hadn't been lying and all she'd ever known only scratched the surface of reality. She couldn't make herself move.

The stranger turned to observe their behavior. His eyes, which Cassie had remembered as blue, flared black. The pupils and irises mixed, while the white outer layers punctuated the terrifying combination. In a steely tone it said, "No use, Guardian. I know her now." A bitter laugh rang in the night. With inhuman speed, it lunged toward them.

Gabe reacted as fast. He pushed Cassie aside and out of harm's way as he turned to face the oncoming stranger. The pair clashed in a sickening thud. Blood splattered on the alley's aged pavement as the two exchanged blows. Gabe gained the upper hand. He got up into a crouch and his leg shot out to take the other man down. Before the stranger had a chance to get back up, Gabe's elbow collided with the stranger's nose. Cassie gagged at the sound of crunching bone and cartilage. Another blow had Gabe's fist coming down hard and fracturing the man's collarbone. His movements flowed from one to the next, precise and unhesitant. *He's done this before.* The thought held her in stunned amazement.

The stranger swung at Gabe from the ground. In an instant, however, he stopped and lay motionless. Surprise marked Gabe's features as he bent down to inspect the cause of the sudden change. Cassie could see the lifeless black eyes staring at Gabe. A disconcerting feeling formed in her mind's eyes, but she couldn't give it shape. Observing the situation as close as she dared, she reached a tentative hand forward but snatched it back.

"Can't be that easy," Gabe said as he leaned in for a

closer look.

"No!" she cried. "Look out!"

Her words resonated down the alleyway. Gabe couldn't react fast enough to her warning. The black eyes sprang to life and a knife pierced Gabe's side, the blade buried up to the handle in his body. Before crumbling to the ground, he managed to slam the stranger's head into the pavement. The crunch of bone on concrete filled the air. Pain clouded Gabe's eyes and showed on his face in sharp lines. Cassie ran toward him and kneeled at his side. Warmth radiated from his body in an electric blue current when she touched his shoulder. It lasted but a moment before his body went limp and unconsciousness swallowed him up.

EIGHT

"**W**ake up! Wake up!" Cassie screamed. "Oh God, no. Please. Come on." She slapped Gabe's face once, twice trying desperately to bring him back. *I don't believe this is happening.* She snuck a look at the knife jammed in his side. The hilt taunted her, emblazoned in copper with a menacing green python. "What the hell do I do?" The panic threatened to choke her.

Moving with caution, she touched her hand to the weapon. Her thoughts jumbled as she tried to talk through the horror. "Think. First aid. CPR. Do you pull out a knife or leave it?" Her hands shook. "When do you apply pressure? Oh, God!" As she wrapped her fingers around the weapon, a hoarse voice startled her.

"I'll...take...care of it," Gabe said. His face was a reflection of his body, raked with pain. His words came accented on short rough gasps. "Let...go."

A whoosh pierced the air. Cassie hadn't even been aware she'd been holding her breath. Gabe's voice set her back to reality.

"Oh my God! You're alive. Thank heaven," she said in one breath. "But you were unconscious. And is he...?" She glanced around Gabe at the stranger's motionless body. Blood covered the pavement like a macabre rain puddle. A moan from Gabe dragged her eyes away from the spectacle and back to his injury. The wound continued to trickle blood past the knife, down his body and onward to stain the ground. "Where's my phone? I have to call an ambulance."

"No!" Gabe cried, grabbing a firm hold of her wrist. His lips pressed together, jaw locking. She winced, but he took a short breath and said evenly, "You can't do that. I said 'I'll take care of it' and I will. Just give me a minute."

"You're hurting me." He let go. Cassie rubbed her wrist. "Okay. You're hurt, so I'll let that go, but what the hell's going on?"

"Damn it." The knife erupted from Gabe's body in one rapid motion. He stared at it, then tossed it across the alley. His eyes ignited in raw agony. His breathing ragged. "I asked for a minute."

"Why did you do that?" She watched in horror as the blood poured from his side unchecked. "We have to get you to a hospital now."

"You can't, Cassie. I'll be fine. Just..." He turned to one side and covered the wound from her sight. "Please. I think you know I can't go to a hospital."

The pleading look in his eyes tugged at Cassie's heart. She didn't know why and she didn't trust him, but she knew he wasn't lying. He couldn't go to a hospital. "All right." It was a bleak acceptance. "What do we do?"

A weak smile crossed his lips. "Thank you." It was probably one of the few times he'd ever used the words or so she guessed. "Let's get to...the end of the alley...cab...your apartment." He choked on his words as the intensity of his injury flared up. She looked at him with renewed concern. "I'll heal. No hospital."

"What about him?" She asked, more grounded with a plan in place. "What do we do with the body?"

"Leave it." Gabe rose to his knees. Beads of sweat formed on his brow, but he pushed on. "Cops won't be able to decipher anything more than a bar fight gone bad. They'll run into a dead end."

Cassie nodded, not being able to come up with any rational arguments – plenty of irrational ones, none rational. Her mind raced with the thoughts of how they were going to accomplish the next part. *Oh shit. Lots of blood. How do I get him out of here?* She puzzled through the problem while rubbing her crossed arms. The coarse fabric of Gabe's coat met her cold hands. He'd given it to her when they stepped outside. Now, it was a lifesaver. She took it off, draped it around him, and pulled it taut to cover the gash. She rose over him.

"Give me your hand." She stretched out an upward palm. When he made no motion to take a hold of it, she sighed. "Sure. Let's make it more difficult." She raised her eyes skyward for an instant, bent down again, and dragged his arm across her shoulders.

Gabe peered at her with passing suspicion, but allowed himself the support. "On three?" He laughed.

"Just try to stand up." Cassie's spine stiffened, not in a joking mood. With a little effort, and a little luck, she managed to walk down the alleyway to the street supporting at least half of Gabe's weight. He leaned against the side of a building as she hailed a cab.

A yellow-checkered taxi pulled up within minutes. The driver, an Indian man wearing a clean white turban, gave them a funny look as Gabe struggled into the narrow backseat. With bravery she didn't feel, Cassie said, "Eyes forward. The stop is on Washington Street by the West Side Highway, and here's a tip." She handed the driver a folded fifty-dollar bill from her purse. It was all the money she had on her. "Get us there fast."

"Youse got it," said the driver with a heavy New York accent. It didn't match his appearance, but it made Cassie smile. *Appearances are deceiving.* The irony struck her and she chuckled lightly. *Don't I know it all too well.* She looked at Gabe's sprawled form. She tried not to go over the night's events in her head but it was a struggle. There would be time enough for that later. Right now, she needed to concentrate on getting the man at her side taken care of.

Within mere minutes, her apartment building came into view. Cassie nodded her thanks at the driver, then took Gabe by the arm and half dragged, half forced him out of the cab toward her building. Gabe's strength was waning fast. The ample stairs made the task even more difficult.

"Just a few more steps," she cried, tugging at his waist. "We're almost there."

The space between the cab and her front door seemed insurmountable, but she managed to get him inside without falling over. At her apartment, the key clicked and the door opened. Maia came to greet her master and meowed her surprise at seeing someone else. Cassie maneuvered Gabe through the door, around her curious cat, and to the couch. He sunk down with a thud.

At once, he tried to lie back, but Cassie knelt next to him and held him by the shoulders. "Not yet. I have to check this first," she said, pointing to his injury. "So, we need to get your shirt off." Any other time Cassie might have enjoyed the prospect, but in the moment, all she could think about was treating his wound. Not a nurse, in any sense of the word, she tried to keep her nerves under control.

Gabe didn't reply. His head swayed in a semi nodding motion. Slowly, he raised his arms upward. Cassie yanked off his shirt, then guided him to lie on his uninjured side. He followed her lead as he slipped into unconsciousness. The sight of his torso covered in blood almost made Cassie shake him awake. She restrained herself and ran to the kitchen to grab a dishtowel. Soaking it in warm water, she returned to Gabe's side and dabbed the blood away. It *doesn't look so bad.* She shook out the towel. *Just need to put some pressure on it.* She ran to the bathroom and located thick athletic tape, gauze and cotton. With her limited first aid knowledge, she managed to cover his wound and bind it.

"What a night." Cassie said, inspecting her work. Maia strolled up and rubbed against Cassie's leg. "Come on. We'll let him rest." She picked up the cat and returned to the kitchen. Setting Maia down on the counter, she tapped her fingers in an offbeat rhythm. "Better give Zoey a call too."

Her mind flitted from one mundane chore to the other as she fumbled around the kitchen. She had to concentrate hard to keep to her task of calling Zoey. It took twice as long as normal to locate her discarded purse, spill the contents of it on the counter, and extract her phone from the mess. Her fingers trembled as she tried to steady them on the keys. With a clearing of her throat, she placed the call. Zoey answered on the fourth ring and Cassie could hear the noise of the club in the background.

"Hey Zoey," Cassie said, her pitch a bit higher than usual. "I, um, wanted to let you know I got home okay."

Without a word of greeting, Zoey began babbling. "What's wrong? What happened? Did he hurt you? I can't believe it. The first guy you take home."

"Zo. Zoey," muttered Cassie trying to get a word in between her friend's ranting. "I'm fine. Gabe didn't do anything wrong." With a pause, she thought, *Well, not to me anyway*. She shook her head. "I just wanted to call and let you know I was okay. I didn't want you to worry."

"Cassie. If you were okay, then you wouldn't be calling me, would you? I can hear your voice shaking."

"Of course, I would! I also want to see how you are." Her stance shifted to defense mode. "It's not every day I leave my friend in a club alone to go home with a relative stranger."

"So, then you did go home with him? Now, we're getting somewhere." Zoey's tone changed from worried to suggestive in a snap.

"Maybe...No...Yes... But, it's not what you think. He's asleep on the couch."

"You tired him out that quickly? Jeez, Cas."

"Okay. I did what I was supposed to. I called you. You now have ten seconds before I hang up this phone." Cassie's patience had reached the end of its rope.

"Wait. I want details. Oh come on, you have to tell me now." Zoey begged to no avail.

"7...6...5..." She emphasized each number with a bizarre delight.

"Don't you dare! Cassie!"

"2...1...Time's up. Goodnight Zoey." Not waiting for a response, she clicked the phone shut. Maia meowed her approval and stretched on the counter. "Serves her right." She nodded at her cat.

Cassie's eyes surveyed the room. Her heart began to pound harder and faster as she glanced at the sleeping form on the couch. *I won't think. Not about anything. Not now. Not yet.* She turned away and opened a cabinet door instead. Extracting a glass and turning on the faucet, she filled up her cup with water and chugged it down. The cool liquid eased her parched throat.

After an awkward pause and with a false sense of urgency, she started cleaning the kitchen. She wiped down all the cabinets and appliances, scrubbed the sink, cleaned Maia's food and water bowls, and swept the tiled floor. Spotting her mess of a purse and the lack of money in her wallet, she pulled out her meager *rainy day* fund from her ceramic cookie jar. Two hundred dollars. It wouldn't go far in this city, but she'd been able to save a little out of each paycheck. Not thinking about it, she stuffed it all in her wallet. Some small internal voice told her she'd need it.

Afterward, with nothing left to do but think, she tried again to block out all thoughts from her mind. But the image of the dead body in the alley kept flashing in front of her eyes and the crunch of breaking bones still filled her ears.

"Maybe we should check on him," she said to Maia and lifted the sleepy cat in her arms. "Make sure we did it all right."

Cassie lowered Maia to the floor by the couch, then knelt beside Gabe. Working with care so she would not wake him, she undid the wrappings around his wound. She stared at his injured side trying to figure out the problem. Her breath caught when she realized the issue--he was already healing. The cut was not as large or deep as when it first happened no more than an hour ago. "How? Should've needed days. Maybe stitches even." Her fingers grazed the delicate skin over the cut with feather light strokes. Without thought, she let them wander up his back. Two long burn marks caught her eye. They ran parallel from the tops of his shoulder blades down to the hem of his pants. "Wonder how he got those." A blush crept up her cheeks making her face hot. *And how low they go.*

Gabe spun around. Awake. She jerked her hand away.

He grumbled at the pain caused by his sharp movement, then looked Cassie dead in the eye. "Go away, woman," he said with a dismissive gesture.

"Excuse me," Cassie spat as the shock wore off. "I am trying to make sure you're all right. And I get this?" She copied his hand motion.

Gabe grinned. "You were doing far more than seeing if I was all right, weren't you? Tell me about your other intentions, Cassie." Stunned silence from her, then he laughed.

Cassie knew her face flushed beat red. To save her pride, she shrieked, "You've got to be kidding. You are so dirty and smell so rotten even if I wanted to, I wouldn't bother." She crossed her arms over her chest.

"Hmm..." Gabe seemed to ponder it as he looked himself over. "You're right."

As if in perfect health, he sprang to his feet and strode toward her bathroom, his step firm. There was no sign of his earlier weakness from the injury. On the way, he shook off his boots and socks, then began to unbutton his pants. Cassie had a delayed reaction watching his movements, before she followed behind him. With an exasperation she couldn't hide, she slapped him on the back and shouted, "What the hell do you think you're doing?"

He looked over his shoulder at her with an amused gleam in his eyes. "What does it look like? I'm taking your advice. You said I was unappealing. So, I'm fixing that with a bath."

"In my house? Are you completely insane?"

"Don't you think a bath is something you can offer a person who just saved your life?"

Cassie stood still, wavering. *He did protect me.* She rubbed the back of her neck without responding. *But I did bring him here, and I took care of him. I did what he asked. What more does he want?* She tapped her foot on the carpet. "Take a bath, but don't expect anything else. I want you gone by morning."

He grumbled, but didn't say anything. Turning back toward the bathroom, he removed the rest of his clothes. Without a word of thanks, he pointed to the dirty pile, and muttered something suspiciously like, "Wash". The bathroom door shut behind him.

Cassie stared in a daze at the closed door, before the sound of running water knocked away her astonishment. "Ewwwww," she said. "Unbelievable! Infuriating...Man!"

She sat down cross-legged outside the door. *Do not bang on the door and scream at him. Do not bang on the door and scream at him.* As she snorted air in and out her nose, her eyes drifted toward the clothing pile. She spotted the bloodstain left on his pants from the injury. As a pang of guilt hit her, her anger subsided.

With a deep sigh, she went to the kitchen for the third time and got a black trash bag from underneath the sink. She picked up all of his clothes, including his boots, from the floor and stashed them in the bag.

"Be back in a little while," she said to Maia. Grabbing her purse from the counter, she headed down to the basement with the trash bag slung over her shoulder. It took her only a handful of minutes to stomp down the stairs. Bathed with white fluorescent lights, the basement's cement floor and ceiling shone in a ghostly glow. As she looked around, she felt all too grateful no one else had the crazy idea to do laundry at this hour. After removing coins from her purse, she threw all of the clothes into the washing machine, poured in an ample supply of detergent, deposited the coins, and set it for Heavy Wash. The boots she swiped with a rag and set them by the machine. With nothing else to do, she plopped down in a plastic folding chair and finally gave into thinking about the night's events.

"Ok, Cassie, let's recap tonight, shall we?" she said aloud because she needed to chase the unnerving silence away, even if only with her own voice. "So, you went out with Zoey to some club, got hit on by Mr. Sleazy Guy who later was possessed by a..." She didn't know how to finish that sentence so she skipped it. "By something. Mr. Crazy Man aka Gabe who you kicked out of your apartment a few weeks ago because he said you weren't human, shows up at the club." Her hands shot up to rub her temples. "You go outside with Mr. Crazy Man despite your usual good judgment and get attacked by Mr. Sleazy Guy, now possessed by something. And then, you take Mr. Crazy Man back to your apartment after he was knifed in the side by Mr. Sleazy Guy." She took a deep breath. "And oh yeah, Mr. Sleazy Guy was killed, and Mr. Crazy Man is upstairs in YOUR bathroom. And he's healing like..." Once again, she had to skip over that one. "What is wrong with this picture?" Hah. Where to start.

The old washing machine rumbled its agreement. Cassie couldn't piece together one rational thought or explanation after her recap, so she slunk back in the chair and listened to the mechanic clink-clink. She closed her eyes and prayed for a few minutes of peace. Just as her body was starting to cooperate and relax, a high-pitched DING signaled the clothes reached the end of the cycle. Begrudgingly, she unfolded herself from the chair. Reaching into the machine, she pulled out the wet clothes, flung them in the dryer, slipped more coins into the contraption, and set it for High Heat. With an evil laugh, she said, "And if something should accidentally happen to shrink, so be it."

About thirty minutes later, the dryer signaled end of the cycle with another shrill DING. Cassie tucked the clothes under her arm, grabbed the boots by the laces, and headed back upstairs. As she opened the door to her apartment, a funny feeling knotted in the pit of her stomach. She called out. "Gabe?" No response. "Gabe?"

Dropping his clothes on the kitchen counter, she

tiptoed through the apartment. Since her place wasn't very big, she eliminated all of the obvious spots – kitchen, living room, and bedroom. "He can't still be in the bathroom, can he?" Maia gave a noncommittal meow, but sauntered over to the closed bathroom door. "Seriously?"

"Gabe, you still in there?" Cassie called as she rapped on the bathroom door. "It's been over an hour." She knocked louder. Not a sound. Turning the knob, she tested the lock. It clicked free. The door creaked in protest. "Gabe?" Still not a peep. With a sigh, she opened the door and examined the bathroom. She let out a small yelp when she spotted Gabe sound asleep in the tub.

Cassie turned to leave when an errant thought struck her. *What if he isn't sleeping? What if his injury's gotten worse? What if he is...?* She swallowed hard. "Just check that he's breathing, so you don't freak out. Then, leave." Mustering up her courage, she walked toward the tub, trying to avert her gaze from the obvious lack of bubbles in the bath. She bent down and listened for sounds of his breath. Her own breath caught as she struggled to hear. *Nothing.* Her heart started racing. *He can't be dead. There can't be a dead person in my tub.*

Without further consideration, she shook him and yelled in alarm, "Gabe! Gabe!"

Gabe's eyes snapped open. In a speed faster than a wink, he pulled Cassie into the tub. He held her about the waist with her arms pinned to her sides. She wriggled against him, soaking wet and as mad as a hornet.

"Let go. What's your problem? Let go now!"

"Calm down. Stop flailing. I didn't know it was you." He said. "Relax. Relax."

The gentleness in his voice brought her temper down a fraction. She stopped moving, deciding instead to squeeze her eyes shut and wait for him to let go. *Do not freak out. Do not freak out.* She repeated it to herself like a mantra. *Ok. So you're in a bath with a naked man.* She clicked her tongue against the roof of her mouth. *Why's that bad again?* Her body started to betray her as she remembered her many dreams over the past weeks about this very same man in similar circumstances.

"See, I knew you had bad intentions," he said, his voice pure masculine teasing. "And now, I'm all clean." He let go of her waist to run a hand down his clean, and very naked, body.

The tinge of sarcasm in his tone brought her right back to the present. Angry, embarrassed and wet, she sloshed out of the tub with as much grace as she could muster. She stalked across the bathroom resisting the urge to turn and stick out her tongue. Dripping as she went, she stomped across the apartment and slammed her bedroom door.

#

"Women!" muttered Gabe as he watched her go. Yet, something inside him stirred at her exit. He hadn't wanted her to leave. With a shake of his head, he stood up, dried himself off and wrapped the towel around his waist. He looked over his injured side and nodded at finding it healing well. He followed her trail of wet droplets across the apartment, but paused at the kitchen when he spotted the pile of his clean clothes on the counter. "Aw, hell."

A surge of guilt swept him. *Who cares if she's mad? She's being irrational. SHE woke ME,* he thought, trying to push away the feelings of regret. "I have nothing to be sorry for." He ran a hand through his wet hair, and then stood a heartbeat with his hands on his hips, undecided.

"Damn," he whispered. Resolved, he dressed and walked toward her bedroom. He raised a hand to knock against her door, but paused. At a loss for words, he stared at the door for several minutes. Exhaustion hit him. "It'll have to wait until morning." He swayed on his feet. "Besides, what's there to say?" he asked to the air. "Nothing...and yet...everything."

NINE

The sun blazed down forcing Cassie to shield her eyes. The light had an odd disorientating effect and she struggled to make sense of her surroundings. Squinting against the rays, she caught the glare of light upon the pavement. A flash of recognition seeped into her thoughts. *I know this place.* She reflected, listening for any sounds, any noise at all. *But, how?* The rumble of an approaching car shook her to the core.

"It can't be," she gasped, shaking away the mental cobwebs. "No. I can't be dreaming again. I can't."

Cassie squeezed her eyes shut and begged to wake up. As the noises grew closer, she opened her eyes to stare at the highway in front of her. She stood upon the shoulder of Route 6. The vertical drop of Bear Mountain loomed behind her. The day was February 29th, twenty years in the past. Atypical warm weather encompassed the area despite the early hours of this winter morning.

The scene before her had played out so many times over the years in her dreams, Cassie fought not to turn her back on it altogether. She knew the results. A family from a small town in upstate New York drove to the big city to see a play on Broadway. The little girl bounced up and down in the back seat, too excited to stay still. She always wanted to see the lights and sounds of the stage. It was supposed to be her birthday present. But, she didn't get her gift that day. They would never make it past the mountain, past the bend in the road.

"Why?" she said to no one.

A strange sensation crept over her as the boxy blue Oldsmobile Cutlass Supreme squawked around the curve and spun on the pavement. Its tires screeched in protest. The commotion reached deafening levels, but Cassie's attention locked on a shadowy figure looming over the wild, out of control car. The presence of the stranger ignited her apprehension and added to her confusion.

"Wait! Wait!" she screamed. "I'm not supposed to be here. The car. In the car."

For the first time, Cassie realized where she was in relation to the accident. Every dream she had of this event placed her as the child inside the car. This time she stood on the side of the road as an adult looking upon the scene. She could see the dark presence standing in front of the vehicle. The car crashed with an echoing boom followed by ripping, tearing and crunching against the rocky mountainside. She watched in horror as the dark figure lifted the little girl from the car at the instant of the crash. It placed her on the ground. The girl's eyes shut and her hands gripped the sides of her head.

Cassie avoided the sickening remains of the car, instead walking across the road toward the girl. As she moved closer, she noticed the shadowy figure looked humanoid in its shape. Well, it had the outline of a human at least, but its face was turned away from Cassie and toward the girl. At this angle, there was no way to tell who or what it was.

A commanding voice erupted from the stranger, "Hello child." It began speaking to the girl. "I've been waiting for you. It's time to awaken and make the blood bond with me."

The girl on the ground didn't look up or move her hands away from her head. The creature inched toward the child. "Come now. Awaken. The time is here. Your seventh year has come. Join me."

A chill gripped Cassie's heart. Trying to keep her voice even, she said, "Get away from her. She isn't yours."

The creature turned to face Cassie. His cold black eyes bore into hers. "You're right, my child. You weren't mine then. But, you will be now. We are blood."

A horrible thought began to form in Cassie's mind. The creature in front of her was oddly recognizable though some form of...*other*. The black bottomless eyes mimicked those of the possessed man in the club alleyway. Yet, it was far more than eyes that frightened her. His black hair, his fair skin, the shape of his mouth, all of it spoke of a family resemblance.

"It can't be. It's not possible," Cassie said just above a whisper.

"Of course it is, child. I always knew you would be a Key. It's why your mother hid you from me." His nostrils flared. The black eyes widened. "Oh, but to be The Key, the Sacred Key, the one who can bring this world to its knees. I should have guessed. You come from *my* blood after all."

"No." Cassie said. "I'm Cassiel Ann Durrett." She bit out. "I'm from a small town. I live in the city. I work as a hostess." Listing the simple pieces of her life on her fingers did nothing to stop her rising fear. "Zoey's my best friend. I'm normal. Normal." Her body trembled. The facts did little to assuage her. "I was born from normal, regular people. They may have given me up, but they were human." Her voice shook. "The people who raised me, my parents, were human. I'm human. This is nothing but a dream. This isn't real!" Cassie screamed her protests, barely recognizing her own voice. She glanced to her right as the girl on the ground began beating the sides of her head.

"Oh, it may be a dream." The stranger spat. "But, this is very, very real. And you will be one of us, soon, so soon now, my daughter." He smiled, his teeth gleaming white in the light.

The girl's eyes popped open as her hands pounded the pavement. She looked upon the stranger in absolute terror before he disappeared into the morning without a trace. A raw cry pierced the skies.

Cassie awoke screaming and clawing at the air. Someone's strong arms wrapped around her, while soothing words repeated in her ears. She came out of it slow, her head swimming. Gabe's face snapped into focus.

"Where is he?" she asked aloud and scanned the room for the stranger.

"Who? No one's here, Cassie. It's just you and me," Gabe said, sweeping a hand across the room as proof. "See?"

"Gabe?" The name fell oddly from her lips. She

straightened up and shot him a dark look. "What's going on? What happened last night? Who are these...creatures?"

"Whoa, one step at a time." Gabe put one foot on the floor, off the bed, and placed his hands palm out in the air. "Let's just take this easy, okay?"

"You take it easy! I just saw my parents' deaths again in my sleep." She choked out the words, fighting back tears. "But something wasn't right." She paused a heartbeat, struggling to find her voice. "A weird shadow, like the thing from last night... It was there. And it looked like me. It looked like me! Why did it look like me, Gabe?" She shrieked losing control. "What am I?"

"If you'll calm down for a minute, I'll tell you what you want to know." He sat down on the edge of the bed, but looked over his shoulder toward the door. "Why don't we go inside, get something to drink and talk?"

"Fine." Cassie agreed. She hopped off the bed and went storming out of the room. Once in the kitchen she filled up two glasses with cold water and slammed them both on the counter. "Now, talk."

Gabe followed, glancing between the cups and her face. He put a leg over the kitchen stool and leaned forward. He sipped the water, then asked with absolute calm, "Where do you want to start?"

Cassie sucked in a breath before responding. "Last night. What happened to the man in the alley?"

"He was possessed by a demon," Gabe said without hesitation or emotion.

The cold directness had her pushing away from the counter. She leaned back onto the refrigerator and stared at the water glass as if searching for an answer in its contents.

"A demon." Doubt gnawed at her, but the realization that it might be the truth began to take shape. Last night, she'd seen the shadow enter the stranger with a horror she couldn't deny. Swallowing hard, she searched her feelings. *I've seen it. I've seen it with my own eyes.* She wavered, digesting the information. When she felt brave enough to continue, she said, "Okay, I'll bite. Why did he attack?"

"I told you before, you're not human. Are you willing to accept that now?" He glared at her, eyes narrowed.

"Do I have a choice?"

"You have more of a choice then you realize." The corner of his mouth pulled up. "But first things first. You're a Key. The parents you knew were your adopted parents."

"I already know I was adopted," she hissed.

"Good. Makes it easier." He cracked his knuckles. The sound grated on her nerves, but she said nothing. Rolling his head and stretching his neck, he sat up straighter on the stool and continued, "Your birth parents weren't human. One was a fallen angel, which is also what I am. And the other..."

"A fallen angel?" Cassie interrupted before he could finish. She thought back to her Sunday school classes in the tiny church basement. After her parents' deaths, she'd given up on religion altogether, but the traces of those lessons remained. "Like angels who go against God and are thrown out of Heaven?" Her thoughts started to spin.

"No. I don't know anything about what you call Heaven and Hell, Cassie," he said, a trace of weariness evident as he ran a hand through his hair. "I can only talk about what I know. Angels of the Light live on a different plane of existence, but they are very much a part of the world, as much as humans."

"I have no idea what you're talking about." She rubbed her temples in frustration.

He sighed, his shoulders sagging on the exhale. "If your Heaven is above and Hell below, then Light and Darkness are to the left and right. Another dimension, if your science fiction helps you understand." He sipped the water once more. "And you are a Key. Keys are born when the creatures of the different worlds... mate."

"So, one of my parents was an angel, or fallen angel. And the other was...?" Her eyelids popped wide open. "My mother was the angel. My father was the man from my dream. What is he?"

"Cassie, your mother was cast out from the Light, making her a fallen angel. She chose not to follow the path to redemption, and instead sought out your father." He'd sidestepped the question.

"What is he?" Her top and bottom teeth ground together.

"A demon." He paused as if to gauge her reaction. When she remained silent, he continued, "They're evil greedy bastards, creatures of the Darkness. There's not a shred of light in them." Emotion at last entered his voice, passion bubbling just past the surface of his words. "They remain on Earth by preying on humans and possessing them."

After a few deep breaths, Cassie said solemnly, "I'm a daughter of a fallen angel and a demon." She swallowed that pill with as much courage as she could muster. "Makes me...um...a Key? What does it mean?"

He stood and leaned further across the counter, closing some of the space between them. He spoke softer than before. "It means angels and demons can seek you out to enter this world. They can use your abilities to cross over."

A light went off somewhere in the dark corner of her mind. "My headaches." She answered the unspoken question, which had plagued her for so long.

"Yes, your headaches."

An understood silence ensued. Cassie used the time to decipher her thoughts. She stared at her glass as if she could burn a hole through it, or as if all the answers could reveal themselves in its depth. Her hands clenched around the edge of the counter. Finally, she snuck a peek at Gabe from under her lashes. He sat back on the stool watching her, worry written upon his furrowed brow.

Probably thinks I'm going to lose it. Tension ran through her body's every nerve. *Hell, maybe I am. I deserve to.*

The minutes ticked onward as the silence wore thin. Just as Gabe began to reach toward her, Maia entered. The inquisitive cat sprung onto the counter, stared Cassie in the eyes, and meowed her sympathies.

Cassie stroked the cat's soft fur with automated movements. A familiar purple glow began to illuminate around her hand. She ignored it, unable to deal with any more freakiness just now. After some quiet internal reflection, she kissed Maia's little head and stepped back from the counter hiding her hands behind her back.

Courage, Cassie. Courage. She tried to work up to her next question while willing her mind and body to relax. Squaring her shoulders, she met Gabe's stare.

"Can I stop them?" she whispered.

Gabe understood without explanation. "No, they, the headaches I mean, won't go away." He peered at her as if seeing her soul. "But, you'll be able to control them better once you choose a side. You'll have power over all of your abilities, Cassie." He cocked his head to the side and raised an eyebrow. "All. Your. Abilities." He emphasized each word and inclined his chin toward her hidden hands.

He saw. Damn it. Cassie shrugged. *No use hiding it, I guess.* Bringing her hands in front of her body, she prayed they were normal. She shut her eyes, too afraid to look, and placed them palm up on the counter. A warm heat glided over her fingers. Opening her eyes, she found a blue energy encircling Gabe's hands and mingling with her own purple glow.

"We're not so different, Cassie," he said with a twitch of his lips. "Inhale. Exhale. Then imagine the light returning to your body." The blue began to fade leaving her own energy to swirl around her hands. "Relax."

She did as he suggested. Her breathing slowed. Emptying her mind of all thoughts, she focused on pulling the light back through her open palms. With great effort, the plum color faded to a cool lavender shade, and then dissipated altogether. She stared down at her hands. "I usually can't do it when I'm upset."

"The closer the time to the bonding, the more you'll be able to control your powers." His fingertips grazed her arm. "Once you choose a side, you'll have complete control."

"Choose a side? You said that before." Something in the statement rang close to her dream. She riffled through her brain before it dawned on her. "Does it have to do with a blood bond?"

"How?" Gabe started to ask, then paused. "Your dream?"

"Yes. The creature...demon...from my dream spoke about a blood bond. He said I was from his blood." She swallowed hard. "That...thing, it's my father, right?" The tears welled in her eyes as she began to tremble.

"Cassie." Gabe hesitated. He dropped off the stool and approached her. Placing a hand on her right shoulder, he bent to meet her eyes. "You are *not* a demon."

"But...my...father?" She asked between sobs.

"Was a man from this world, a good person who raised you. He was your father." He placed his other hand on her left shoulder and shook her lightly. "Anything else is just genetics. A fluke of nature. Demon blood doesn't make you evil." He winked. "Besides, you're half angel too."

"Fallen angel," she said with a hint of a grin.

"Semantics. Don't get crazy about the wording."

As Cassie brushed the tears away with the back of her hand, Gabe stepped back, giving her space. She sucked in air, calming her nerves. "Okay," she said. "Now that decision, blood bond, whatever. What is it? What do I do?"

Cassie thought she heard him whisper, "Brave girl," as he swept a lock of hair from her forehead. But, before she could comment, he pulled his hand away. "I promised I'd tell you everything and I will, but I think it'd be better to show you some things first."

"Lead the way." She gestured a hand toward the front door.

"Just like that?"

Cassie managed a snicker as she rummaged through the

apartment. As quick as she could, she located her bag, cell phone and keys. She was about to pull on her boots when Gabe gave her a questioning look.

"Well, I'm glad you're so trusting now," Gabe said. "But, don't you think it would be better to change into something a bit warmer." He pointed to her attire.

With an awkward pause, she glanced down at her clothes. She was still dressed in her yellow pajamas. She burst into laughter at the sheer insanity of it all.

Taking up his former seat on the kitchen stool, Gabe sighed and leaned back against the counter. "Earth," he said dripping with sarcasm. "What a world."

Cassie upon hearing his proclamation sat on the floor cross-legged, grabbed her stomach, and laughed until she cried.

TEN

Cassie remained sitting on the floor studying the diamond pattern in the pale beige linoleum. After an agonizing twenty minutes or so, Gabe clasped her by the shoulders and hoisted her to her feet.

"Enough." He shook her, stopping only when she swatted at his hands. "You want the truth, then on with it. Get dressed. We need to leave." He turned her toward the bedroom, and practically dragged her through the door.

"All right. All right," she said as she pulled her arm free of his grasp. "I can manage myself." He left her alone in the sanctuary of her bedroom, and she unceremoniously shut the door behind him. Her hand gripped the knob making her knuckles go white. *No freaking out. Not now.* She squeezed her eyes shut, willing herself to settle down. That did nothing to calm her nerves, but she forced herself to move about the room.

Within minutes, Cassie managed to throw almost every piece of clothing she owned into three different piles –

sleeping, casual and dressy. The minor exercise helped alleviate some of the tension in her muscles, but her mind still wandered adrift. She surveyed the mess trying to focus on something simple, normal.

"Just get dressed. Pick whatever is at the top of the middle pile and put it on." A worn comfortable pair of old blue jeans and battered olive sweater caught her eye. She shrugged. "It works."

"Cassie. Let's go." Gabe called from outside the door.

"I'm coming. Just hold on." She pulled on the clothes, stashed her hair in a messy ponytail, and shot out of the room. As the door opened, Gabe jumped back faster than a shadow. She blinked trying to gauge whether or not she'd seen him move. When she couldn't decide, she put up a hand and begged, "Just don't say anything else until we get wherever we're going. I've had all I can handle just now."

"Fine with me." He crossed his arms over his chest.

Without another word, Cassie pulled on her boots, grabbed her coat and bag, gave Maia a quick peck, and followed Gabe out the door. Quick and quiet, they made their way to the subway station. Cassie resisted the urge to ask where they were going as they boarded the uptown C train. Instead, pinpricks crept up her spine. A bing-bong chime of closing doors signaled the beginning of something she couldn't quite name.

As the train passed from one stop to the next, her eyes wandered the crowd from person to person. All of the faces looked odd and out of place. As she caught her reflection off the glint of a plastic poster cover, it dawned on her. *She* was the stranger now. The chilly thought penetrated her soul and made her shudder.

"Where are we going?" She blurted just as the automated train announcer rang, "This is an uptown C train. The next stop is 72nd street. Stand clear of the closing doors please."

"Next stop," Gabe said, but offered nothing more.

A baby cried out as the train jerked into the Central Park West station. Before the doors could close, Gabe and Cassie pushed their way off. The empty platform offered a nice reprieve from the crowded train.

Gabe pointed to the exit sign ahead and muttered, "That way."

"Jeez. You think?" Cassie rolled her eyes.

A blazing midday sun assailed them as they left the darkness of the subway's underground. The late autumn weather put a chill in the air but the light streamed down strong from above. Cassie squinted in the direction of Central Park. An inherent love of nature pulled her in its direction, but Gabe had other plans.

"The house where I've been staying is only a few blocks from here," he said, gesturing in the opposite direction. "It's owned by one of my kind, one far older than I."

"Another fallen?" Cassie asked, stealing her gaze away from the park and toward the direction he indicated.

Gabe cast a glance up and down the street before whispering in her ear. "Yes. He knew what you were before I did. There's a book which contains an important inscription."

She stared at him, unable to hide her confusion.

Sighing, he added, "It's a prophecy, Cassie, about you, about the decision you'll have to make."

"Yeah, you mentioned this decision already," she said, ignoring the *prophecy* part. "But, saying it doesn't explain it."

It was his turn to roll his eyes. "I'm aware of that." Turning his back to her, he continued down the street. She struggled to keep up with his pace. Thankfully, she only had two blocks to go before Gabe stopped in front of a beautiful five-story brownstone. "Here."

"Seriously?" Cassie regarded the decadent facade. Black ironwork handrails guided the visitor up the stairs to the double pine doors, highlighted by golden knobs and thick paned glass. She couldn't even begin to imagine the money this kind of place would cost.

"Why wouldn't I be serious?" Gabe's tone hinted at his puzzlement.

Cassie shook her head and scrunched her eyes at him. "Never mind." She waved a hand motioning him forward. "Let's go."

As they passed through the front door, Cassie let her gaze wander over the lobby. Marble tiles in ivory and gold covered the floor. A semi-circular counter constructed of dark grey granite took up one wall. A Lenox vase with a single white orchid sat upon a long metal table in the center of the room.

Gabe inclined his head at a young doorman whose nametag read *Claude*. Wearing a stiff burgundy uniform, Claude resembled one of those English guards outside of Buckingham Palace. He stood tall and straight at well over six feet. His clean-shaven head gleamed in the overhead recessed lights.

"Nice to see you again, Mr. Gabe," Claude said as he buzzed them in and pressed the elevator button.

"Yeah, you too," Gabe answered, almost polite. He nodded a goodbye as he and Cassie stepped into the elevator. The speed of the elevator didn't match with its ancient appearance. Before she could blink, the doors opened onto the top floor apartment.

The front parlor consisted of two pale green armchairs and a round glass table. Behind them lay a pair of massive double mahogany doors leading into the interior of the home. Cassie stood in absolute amazement. She hadn't even reached the inner apartment, and yet, already she was surrounded by more beauty than she could imagine-- exposed solid oak walls, a black marble floor, and three exquisite oil paintings. She turned from left to right examining each canvas in detail. An idea dawned on her as she stared at the works of art.

"These paintings?" she said. "They represent the worlds you were talking about. Don't they?"

Gabe's brows rose. "You're more perceptive than I thought." When she looked down at the floor he added, "I meant it as a compliment." Her lips twitched into a quick smirk and he continued, "Yes, you're right. These represent the three worlds. This one..."

"Wait. Let me see if I can get it." She interrupted, waving her hand in front of him. "This one over the doors, it represents Earth. I can tell from all of the places depicted. Let's see..." she mused. "The Grand Canyon is an easy one. So are Stonehenge and the Great Pyramid. And I recognize Mount Fuji and Mount Everest. Um...What are the rest?"

Gabe seemed a great distance away as he said, "The Wailing Wall of Jerusalem, the River Ganges of India, Lake

Manasarovar of Tibet, Mount Pico da Neblina of the Amazon Rainforest, and the remains of the Oracle at Delphi in Greece."

"Why all these spots? What's so special about them?"

"These are all places of power on Earth. It's where angels...or demons...can connect with others here, without Keys." Gabe paused. "They can't stay for long though. To stay permanently on Earth, you need a Key's power or...you fall."

Gabe's solemn look disturbed her. She tried a distraction to take his mind off the dark thoughts she could read on his face. "So, what about these two?" She pointed to her left and right.

"This one is a representation of the Light," Gabe said, pointing to the right. "Although a poor one."

Cassie scrunched her face in surprise as she examined the incredible painting. Luminescent shades of yellows, oranges, and reds danced in harmony across the canvas. It was as if the artist had captured a thousand sunsets or the explosion of a star. Words eluded her.

"Now this one," Gabe continued waving to the left picture. "This is how I'd imagine the Darkness."

A black abyss covered the painting from one end to the other. The more Cassie observed, the more it pulled her. Not a trace of warmth was present in the color or design. She fell deeper and deeper into its void. She didn't believe in hypnosis or trances, but if she had, she would have been frightened.

Gabe smacked the armchair with an open palm. The thud broke her reverie. "Have a seat."

Cassie clasped one elbow. "I don't get to see inside?"

"Of course. But, you want to know about your decision, right?"

"Yes," she said. "I mean, I think so." She sat down opposite Gabe and placed her hands folded on the table.

"You aren't a normal Key, Cassie. Keys come into their power on their birthday at age seven. You're different, but I'll explain when we look at the prophecy." She motioned to interrupt, but he waved her off. "Just listen. All Keys regardless of when they come into their powers have to make a blood bond with either an angel or a demon, Light or Darkness. Whoever they bond with dictates how they can use their powers."

"So, I bond with an angel and I'm good. I bond with a demon and I'm screwed."

"Crude, but not incorrect," Gabe said. "A blood bond isn't a small matter, Cassie. Because you're making this bond at your age, your powers will be much stronger – amplified by who knows how much." He paused a heartbeat. "If you decide wrong, it could be devastating. Neither side will want you to choose the other."

"I get it. But why me? Why didn't this happen when I was seven? You said this happens to Keys then. Why not me?"

"Your birthday, February 29th. It only happens every four years."

"That's ridiculous." Cassie couldn't help laughing. "It's an arbitrary day, made up by some mathematicians."

"No!" Gabe stood. His voice echoed through the small room. "It is a sacred day of balance. Each side has equal power to inhabit Earth. If one side should claim the power for themselves, it could mean the destruction, if not complete annihilation of the other."

"Whoa." She rose from her seat. "Easy. I didn't mean to offend you."

The anger left Gabe's face as he gripped the armchair. "It's fine. Perhaps you'll understand more when you see the prophecy for yourself. It's no laughing matter."

"I can see that now," she said wide-eyed.

He nodded. "Let's go inside."

Cassie followed behind as Gabe pushed open the double mahogany doors with ease. She almost collided into his back when he stopped. Straining around him, she stretched to see what made him halt. The sight before her stole the breath from her lungs. She tried to scream but found her voice captured in silence. Gabe turned, grabbed her around the waist, pushed her back into the parlor, and closed the doors behind them.

Yet, the image would not leave Cassie. In the next room, a woman hung by electrical wiring from an enormous gold chandelier. Her arms and neck were bound to mimic the form of a puppet. Dark hair fell upon a kind round face. Her skin had turned ashen as if the poor woman had been left there for a while. The wide eyes remained open, shock and horror evident in them. Cassie's imagination ran wild as she pictured the killer manipulating the wires around the woman's wrists and moving his victim like a marionette. This last piece of the scene had her choking down vomit.

Gabe captured her in a fierce embrace. Already stunned, she didn't try to move. A warm energy poured from his body and into her. She tried to turn her head and look into his eyes, but he held them shut muttering a language she couldn't understand. A heartbeat later, she was still and steady on her feet. He let her go very slowly and then led her to sit in a chair.

"What?" she said in an alien voice. The noise sounded so far away, but it was all she could manage.

"Listen to me, Cassie," he said while holding her hand. "I have to go back inside. I won't be gone more than a minute. Stay here."

She simply nodded, then closed her eyes and leaned against the chair's soft padded backing. Her whole body seemed to be swimming in some type of trance and she didn't try, or even want to try, to go against the soothing current.

#

With care, so Cassie would not be subjected to the horrific scene again, Gabe opened one of the double doors and slid into the next room. Once inside, he glared at the remains of the poor maid.

"She didn't deserve this," he whispered trying to keep his emotions in check. Fury flooded him like a tidal wave as he thought of Maribel's simple kindnesses--an image of her bringing him breakfast, a flash of her cleaning the apartment. He fought to bury such memories, but he couldn't shake the rage. He allowed the anger to wash over him. It seeped into his muscles as if a tangible force and pushed him to act.

Gabe scanned the room. In a far corner he spotted a large navy blue blanket folded on a leather chaise lounge. In a short series of blurred movements, he managed to retrieve the blanket, wrap it around Maribel's remains, and hoist her body down from the chandelier. The electrical wires had bound her in a doll-like pose snapped with ease under his hand. He threw them aside disgusted, then carried the body to the sofa. The leather creaked as he placed her upon it. A pair of lifeless brown eyes looked up at him. He closed them gently and wiped some of the blood from her face.

"I'm sorry." The apology choked forth.

With nothing more to be done for the dead woman, Gabe rose and made his way through the apartment. He glanced in each room as he walked the long hallway, but all seemed untouched...until he reached Albert's study. The double oak doors hung open to reveal the wreck inside. Every stack of newspapers, magazines, and books had been strewn about the floor as if a whirlwind had entered the small space. The two large bookshelves, which encompassed the walls from floor to ceiling, were knocked on their sides and the contents thrown about. On closer inspection, Gabe noticed many of the texts had also been shredded. The markings hinted at some type of serrated knife.

"Damn it!" He ran a hand through his hair, then paused. His eyes narrowed on a familiar black leather bound book placed open on the small table. The chairs had been knocked over but the table stood straight displaying the book. Gabe inhaled as he stooped to examine it. It was the same *Keys* book Albert had shown him many weeks ago. The page with the prophecy of the Sacred Key was neatly torn out.

A bang filled the air as Gabe slammed the book into the nearest wall. He almost put his fist through it as well, but just refrained. A jumble of incoherent thoughts filled his mind. He struggled to keep his cool and think of a plan instead. The first step was getting the hell out of the apartment.

Within sheer seconds, Gabe blasted through the outer mahogany doors. "Come with me," he muttered to Cassie and hauled her out of the chair.

"Wait. What about... Where are we...?" Cassie struggled to complete a sentence. Seeing a dead woman's mutilated corpse was far beyond her coping ability.

Gabe stopped in his tracks and turned toward her. "Cassie, I'm sorry. I know you're scared, but I don't have time to explain. We have to get out of here now." He brushed her cheek with the back of his hand. "Please, just trust me."

Cassie swallowed. "What are we going to do?"

"The prophecy is gone. Someone knows about you. I don't know who it is yet, but I'm going to find out." He took both of her hands in his grip. "But, we need help. More than anything now, I need your trust. Your life may depend on it. Do you understand?"

"Yes," she said without wavering. "I don't know why. I know it doesn't make any sense, but I trust you."

Her blatant honesty and trust struck a chord buried deep inside him. "Thank you," he said trying to mask his amazement. "This next part's going to be hard to believe, but I need you to do something."

"What is it?"

"I need you to come with me to Arizona for a few days, maybe a week." Not a trace of jest in his voice.

"Should sound crazy, right? But after all this..." She

shook her head. "When do we leave?"

Gabe couldn't suppress a smile. "Right now."

ELEVEN

When Gabe had said they were going to Arizona "right now," Cassie feared he would blink them there like a genie. She was relieved to find he'd meant heading to the airport.

"The airport, right," Cassie said. "But, I have to run home first."

"Are you insane?" Gabe's jaw clenched. "I've got to get you out of here."

"Listen, I get it." Her stomach rolled as the picture of the dead woman in the next room flashed through her mind again. She blinked over and over to will the image away. When that failed, she pressed on. "I understand. But, I still can't just leave. I have to go home."

"Anything you think you need to do at home, we'll do on the way." His arm shot around her, pulling her toward the exit.

"No!" She dug her heels into the ground, refusing to go without a fight. "I'm not leaving until you agree to let me go home first."

"Cassie, you're being unreasonable."

"I need to check on Maia. I need to call Zoey. I need to get some clothes. I have responsibilities. I can't just takeoff without a word."

Gabe exhaled, rubbed the back of his neck and mumbled something unintelligible. "Fine. You get five minutes. If you take one second over five minutes, I'll throw you over my shoulder and carry you to the airport."

"Uh-huh. Fine."

They stepped into the elevator from Albert's front doors. Gabe's hand wrapped around Cassie's wrist. She cursed him inwardly, but said nothing about it.

As the elevator descended, Cassie blurted out the second biggest question on her mind. "Aren't we going to call the police?"

"We shouldn't be here for it. We'll place an anonymous call from outside."

The elevator dropped to the bottom level and her heart went with it.

"Come on," he said as the doors opened on the first floor. He switched from holding her wrist to her hand and pulled her to the counter.

"Everything okay, Mr. Gabe?" the doorman said.

Gabe stood in front of him and caught the doorman in a cold stare. He muttered a set of foreign words, similar to those he used to calm Cassie down earlier. Claude looked surprised at first, but soon relaxed, remaining eerily still.

Gabe leaned across the counter, ever closer. "Claude, we were not here. In fact, I haven't been here in days, do you understand me?"

The young man nodded. His gaze blanked.

"Good." With that problem solved, they exited to the street.

"What did you do?" Her voice quivered. The afternoon breeze blew cold. "Is he going to be okay?"

"He'll be fine. He's going to snap out of it in a few minutes, but he won't remember us being in the building." Gabe shrugged. "It's less complicated this way."

Cassie choked on the thought of all the terrifying powers Gabe might possess, powers she didn't understand. Her insides did an uneasy flip-flop. She would have to ask him about it soon, very soon, for her own peace of mind. For now she concentrated on just getting out of Dodge.

After the trip to her apartment at record-breaking speed, Cassie convinced Gabe into one more side trip. "I've got to see Zoey and drop off my cat. There's no way I'm leaving Maia here all by herself for who knows how long! And I can't take off without telling my best friend." She leveled him with a no-way-am-I-bending stare. He conceded, but gave her just two minutes to make her goodbyes as he waited at the bottom of the stairs. *Jerk.*

Cassie forced herself to breathe evenly as her anxiety mounted with each step to Zoey's apartment. What could she tell the person who'd been her closest friend--hell, her only friend--for years? Not much, because she refused to put Zoey in danger. Yet, she couldn't leave without some kind of an explanation either.

The cat carrier shook in her hand. Cassie hesitated at the front door and then knocked, listening for sounds on the other side. Nothing. She knocked harder with the same result. Sighing half in relief and half in disappointment, she realized she wouldn't get to see her best friend before this crazy trip.

She fished her keychain from her purse, locating the key to Zoey's apartment. They always kept a spare set for each other's places, although Cassie never would've imagined she'd be using it for such a purpose. Sliding the door open, she placed the carrier down and let Maia out. Heading to the kitchen, she filled up two bowls with water and cat food before finding pen and paper. She wrote in a rush, willing tears not to spill.

"Zoey, I can't explain anything right now but I need you to cover for me at work for a little while and take care of Maia. I can't tell you where I'm going, but I have to take a trip. I'm really sorry. You're my best friend and I hope you'll trust me on this. I'll explain when I get back. Probably in a few days, a week maybe.

Love you! Cassie."

Swallowing hard, she gave Maia a kiss on her tiny head and headed out the door before she changed her mind.

As Cassie gazed into the night outside the plane window hours later, the horror of the past few days, her guilt about leaving Zoey in the dark, and her worry about what was to come hit her in full force. Her head swam in a fog and thoughts jumbled together in chaos. She massaged her temples, wondering if she would ever experience clarity again.

She stole a glance at Gabe. His eyes were closed and he looked made of marble...or dead. His restful state seemed complete. She envied it. Tapping the button with a stick figure over her seat brought a middle-aged flight attendant to her row. She ordered a shot of tequila and paid the $5 fee. Never a big drinker, she shrugged at the plastic cup in her hand. She couldn't think of anything better than to try to stun her buzzing head into some kind of stupor. *Bottoms up!* Three shots later, her plan worked. Drinking the cheap tequila on an empty stomach made her drowsy. With her forehead leaning against the seat in front of her, she fell into an uneven sleep.

The wheels of the plane slammed on the tarmac, making Cassie jerk forward, then back. Her seat belt saved her from injury. *Fasten your seatbelt. No kidding.* She snapped her eyes open, fingered the tangles from her hair, and looked over at Gabe. He'd been unaffected by the rocky landing, but his eyes narrowed as he peered out the plane window.

"What's the matter?" Cassie said. His look made the hair on her neck stand up.

"I don't know yet." Gabe didn't take his gaze from the window. "Just a feeling."

"That never means anything good," Cassie muttered.

Gabe turned to face her. Electricity buzzed in the palm of her hands, an invisible current begging for release. It had become an all too familiar feeling around him. As if in response to her energy, tiny flecks of blue leapt from his body. The sight made her shift back in her seat. Yet, his eyes never failed to entrance her. She could fall into their piercing light.

"Don't worry," he said, the golden color in his irises intensifying. "You'll be fine. My job's to protect you. And I won't fail."

"Yeah, so you keep saying." Cassie looked away.

"Just trust me." He stroked her cheek with a cool finger, turning her head back to face him.

Cassie wanted to melt into his touch, but fought the instinct. *Trust. Always trust.* It was a lot to ask for. Even now, even after everything she'd seen, or maybe more so. *You don't know his intentions.* She wondered if she ever would. Her whole world had been plunged into uncertainty in the past weeks and he seemed to be the lone anchor.

As they stood in line waiting for people to file out of the plane, Gabe leaned over and whispered into Cassie's ear, "We have to rent a car and drive straight to the Grand Canyon." Even though the words were all business, his low whisper was like a caress. Her heart skipped a beat from the feel of his warm breath on her neck. She couldn't help but wonder if Gabe knew what he was doing and what kind of a reaction he was producing in her.

"Just the situation," she mumbled to herself. "Nothing to do with him."

Even as she tried to convince herself this attraction was only due to the extreme circumstances, she knew it was a lie, and that spelled nothing but T-R-O-U-B-L-E.

The next half hour went by in a haze with them picking up their luggage and renting a car. Gabe refused to miss an opportunity to enjoy a new human experience, and so he insisted on a nice sports car, a silver Mustang convertible to be exact. *All men are the same,* Cassie thought, shaking her head. *Even if they are angels...well, fallen angels, whatever.* She'd get it straight...some day.

The drive down helped soothe her nerves as they flew along the open road. As the car accelerated in a rush of power, she couldn't help peeking at him. His muscles flexed under the plain black t-shirt as his hands gripped the steering wheel. She swallowed, then locked her gaze on the window.

When the adrenaline wore off hours later, the silence got to Cassie. She turned to Gabe, willing him to say something. He seemed lost in his own thoughts with his forehead creased into uneven lines. She tried to start a conversation a few times but after getting one-word responses back, she gave up for five minutes. The quiet kept gnawing and gnawing at her.

"You know, it's only polite to share your thoughts with someone you just dragged halfway across the country for some mythical mission," she said exasperated, but looking dead ahead.

In her peripheral vision she saw Gabe slant his eyes toward her.

"I'm thinking about how it will be to communicate with my own again."

"It must be hard," Cassie said, gentler now. "Being cut off from your own kind, I mean."

"Yes...it's hard to be away from the Light."

"Tell me about the Light. What is it?"

Gabe fell silent. The breeze rushed off the windshield as the car whipped around turns. When the road straightened out, he turned to Cassie. With a focused stare into her eyes, he said, "The Light is pure. It's peace. It's...indescribable."

"So then, why do some of your kind end up here?" She could see from Gabe's rapid blinks he hadn't expected the question.

He shook his head and turned back to the road. "We all have different reasons. You humans have different reasons for your actions." The steering wheel shook under his hands. "But, it's almost always a fall. We don't tend to leave by choice. Pride and arrogance can get in the way. You can't be a part of the Light if you let such things take over..." He shifted in the driver's seat. "...for any reason."

The pain in his voice warned Cassie not to ask anything further. Fidgeting with the glove compartment as a distraction, she sighed. Not wanting to push him away, she decided to give him an easy out and change topics.

"So what do we do at the Grand Canyon?" she said with false cheer.

"We speak with my kind, those of the Light." The blood flowed through his knuckles once more as he eased his grip on the steering wheel.

"Angels, you mean? We're going to speak with angels?"

"I am going to speak to them." The car swerved between lanes. "You are going to stay silent and watch."

Cassie ignored his last statement. "Do you think the angels will give us some answers?" The highway curved ahead as she held her breath and waited for his response.

"I can only hope they will." Gabe glided the car around the winding road.

After the brief conversation, they settled back into silence. The scenery drifted by hazy and unidentifiable as Gabe competed with the speed of sound. Cassie checked her seatbelt for good measure. *Demons, angels, weird powers.* Her lips twisted. *It would be my luck to die in a car accident.* The memory of her parents' death and the irony of her present circumstances turned her mood sour. A fuzzy noise filled her ears as the car's purring engine replaced her inner musings and the wordlessness between them. As the minutes ticked by she thought she'd crack up, but said nothing.

They only stopped once to use the bathroom at a service area and grab a bite to eat, cold turkey sandwiches and nacho chips. By the time they got to the canyons, dusk had descended onto the world. They parked at one of the tourist lots and planned to wait until full darkness to start their trip down. Gabe knew the place they'd have to reach and it was out of the way of standard hiking routes.

Stretching as they exited the car, Cassie eyed a picnic table on the far side of the parking lot. She walked toward it with Gabe following behind. They sat down on the low wooden bench. Cassie tilted her head toward the sky, then to the right. She noticed Gabe watching people with an intent expression on his face.

"It's amazing how many emotions you humans feel. How do you deal with it?" He broke the silence.

"I'm not human myself, remember?" Cassie's tone had a bite to it. *Now, he wants to talk.* Sitting in a car for hours with nothing to do and no one to talk to hadn't exactly lifted her spirits.

"No, you're not. But you've been brought up human. Look at all the emotions you have." His voice turned acidy as well as he swept his hand toward her.

Cassie sighed. There was no point in fighting. Even if she could summon the energy through her exhaustion, she didn't have the heart for it. *Too much. It's just too much.* She held up one hand for a truce. "Look, I'm sorry," she said softly. "I'm still dealing with all the revelations about myself. And these creatures supposed to be myths or a bad bedtime story. Cut me some slack."

"Sure." Gabe turned back to watching the crowd.

She slammed her hands on the tabletop. "I'm taking a nap." She put her head down onto her arms on top of the picnic table, closed her eyes and drifted off to sleep.

Black eyes glared at her, bottomless, terrifying, and unfathomable. They wanted her life, or her soul, or maybe both. Nothing, nothing but those eyes surrounded her in an airless void.

Cassie whimpered as someone shook her awake. She raised her head, still half caught in the dream. Blinking, she took in her surroundings and left behind the nightmare.

Gabe bent over her with wide eyes. His face was just inches from hers. Her gaze landed on his full sensuous lips. Acting on pure impulse, Cassie reached up, wound her arms around his neck and pulled him forward. Her tongue danced together with his in an unyielding kiss. He tensed up for a moment, but then his whole body shuddered. His hand came up to grab her hair and angle her head. His tongue demanded entrance. She parted her lips. He was inside, searching and probing with intensity she never knew before. It was like he wanted to find the truth about everything in the world right then.

It wasn't until he pressed his whole body into hers, his arousal firm against her thigh, she at last came fully awake...and became frightened. Her world swirled out of control. She didn't know what the next hour would bring, let alone the next day or week.

Cassie pushed on his chest. He didn't react, his need persistent. She pushed harder, her muscles tensing. He remained an immovable solid bulk. She groaned and pushed with all her might. Gabe pulled away.

"Are you okay?" he said, his voice hoarse from the need she could read in his eyes.

"We can't do this, Gabe. Not now."

He seemed to consider, then rose to his full height. "You're right. We have to focus on what we need to do first," he said. "It takes too much energy. We can't split it."

"Yeah, something like that." She rubbed the bridge of her nose and lowered her eyes. Glancing around, she put her head on the table once more. "Do me a favor and don't wake me until we're ready to go."

#

Nightfall couldn't come fast enough for Gabe. Hours of grating silence with nothing more than her intermittent nagging had worn down his last bit of patience. *And now this?* He brushed the back of his hand across his mouth as if to wipe away the remnants of her kiss. *What the hell does she want from me?*

Shifting off the bench, he paced the parking lot at a feverish rate. The fire she ignited in his blood would not extinguish. "Damn woman," he muttered, kicking a soda can across the pavement. Abruptly, he paused. Soft dings like raindrops on tin echoed in his mind. He struggled to interpret the distant ringing.

"I'm coming," he said to the summons. "Soon."

The noise grew louder, a baser clanging only he could hear. It led him toward Cassie's direction. A profound purple glow began to radiate around her body as she slept. He focused, gritting his teeth and fighting back the growing chimes.

"No," he cried low, not wanting to attract attention. "She's not strong enough yet to bring you through. It's why we're here. We'll use a point of power."

The ringing reached its crescendo. He battled the tide. His hands clasped in tight fists. The electric blue energy buzzed deep inside him, threatening to explode. "We do this my way, or not at all."

The noise ceased without warning. Cassie's energy faded into her body. The remaining silence left him unsettled. He rocked back on his heels and collided with a trashcan. Cursing, he dropped to his knees and let the feeling pass. He hadn't been summoned since before his fall. Compared to the Light, the calling on Earth felt like knives in his brain. The angel reaching for him wanted to use Cassie's powers to come through to Earth and speak with him. He couldn't let that happen. Cassie didn't have the strength for it. Not yet.

He rose on unsteady legs and walked toward her. She still slept on the bench with her head upon her arms and her breathing uneven. The ragged breaths caused his heart to squeeze. "What is this?" he whispered, his hand running through her hair of its own volition. Snatching it back, he forced himself to look away.

"Don't be a fool." The gravity hung on his words. "You can't care for her. You have too much to lose." Looking toward the darkening sky, he searched the distant stars for an answer. They glimmered on the horizon as night set in. When they offered no response, he glanced at her again and exhaled. "Damn."

TWELVE

Darkness encompassed the area by the time Cassie woke up. All the tourists had disappeared, some engaging in night hikes, the rest leaving for their lodgings. Gabe helped her up from the low bench and they walked to the car to gather the supplies for the trip down. The air had cooled since they first arrived. *Thank you for remembering to pack a sweater and windbreaker.* She took both out of her luggage and put them on now. Gabe shrugged into his leather jacket. She eyed his lack of proper clothing for the trek.

"I don't need much to stay warm," he said as if he had read her mind.

They travelled light, each carrying a small backpack with bottles of water, granola bars and flashlights. Gabe told her he could see in the dark with no problems, but she didn't want to chance being left with nothing more to guide them than moonlight.

Gabe led the way down the canyon and off the hiking trails. He claimed he had never been to the Grand Canyon before, but instinct alone told him where to go. *A built in GPS*. Cassie's nose twitched.

The dark night covered them like a blanket. Above, the starry sky started to fill with ominous shapes, sinister looking clouds. The moon wouldn't appear from behind them no matter which way Cassie turned in search of it. "Knew the flashlights were a good idea." She clicked her light on and tried to match Gabe's lead. His pace felt as fast as a marathon runner's. She followed behind. Yet, eventually, as her foot slipped and she stumbled forward catching her knee on a rock, she complained. "Would you slow down?"

Her voice sounded too loud in the nocturnal silence of the canyons. It bounced off the walls with a jarring echo. The tiny hairs on her arms rose and dread filled her. She shook it away. *I'm not scared. I'm not.* The flashlight offered a small comfort. But even with it, the moonless night made it too dark to see much. She had just enough light to see they were standing between two rock columns. She could also hear the swift Colorado River carrying its waters nearby.

Amusement gleamed in Gabe's eyes when he turned around to face her. "Having problems?"

Cassie's already grim mood threatened to turn downright sour. "Yes, I'm having problems." She sprang her foot out of a muddy hole with a curse. "I'm not an angel, smartass! I don't have super powers!"

Gabe had the gall to laugh, a deep sensual sound that sent tingles through Cassie despite her irritation. She chided her treacherous body.

"Well, a fallen angel," Gabe said, still chuckling.

With that he swept Cassie off her feet, literally, and held

her close to his hard chest. He started walking with ease before she could utter a word in protest, and it took her almost a full minute to get over the shock. As soon as she did, she hit him on the shoulder. He didn't react and she had the distinct feeling what she thought was a pretty good punch felt more like a mosquito bite to him.

"Put me down, now!"

"But I'm enjoying this too much," Gabe countered without a pause.

Well, clearly.

He kept walking. She wriggled in his grip and tried not to admit to how much she enjoyed being carried as well. His well-defined arms supported her weight with ease, making her feel safe in his hold. His body radiated heat even through the thick leather jacket. Just as she was about to give up the fight and settle into the warmth, he put her down, setting her on her feet.

"That's better." She huffed and brushed off her pants.

"We're here," he said, traces of laugh lines around his mouth.

Cassie turned to see their whereabouts. They stood on the bottom of the canyon. She shivered, but not from the cold. A buzz of currents danced in the air. It made the hair on the back of her neck stand at attention. Energy never felt so tangible to her before.

Gabe's face smoothed over, a grave line on his lips. He extended his hand to her. She took it now without protest.

A small path wound under their feet. The sound of water grew stronger as they approached their destination. *Is that? It can't be. A waterfall?* A welcome surprise. She wanted to ask Gabe about it, but decided she'd find out soon enough. They emerged between rocks into open space. Glimmering light reflected from the waterfall and shone into a small shadowy lake surrounded by boulders and trees.

Gabe led her to a smooth rock by the water and motioned for her to sit. She complied, shifting on the stone. Her gut instinct told her not to interrupt anything he was about to do.

He walked over to the lake, kneeled at the edge and started bathing his hands and face.

Ritual bathing, she guessed at the actions.

His movements were fluid like the water itself. She couldn't help but admire him from where she sat. The droplets ran through his fingers flowing between the spaces to the pool below. A light blue energy radiated around his body as the washing continued. Thirty-seven heartbeats passed as Cassie counted to keep her mind occupied. Then, he straightened and came toward her.

"This should work," Gabe whispered. "But there's a risk it won't. I haven't communicated with my own since I fell." His eyes gleamed in the waning moonlight, haunted by some unspoken emotion. "Not like this. The process can be draining." He rubbed his hands together, then tapped her on the arm. "I need you to not panic no matter what you see going on. Can you promise me?"

"Well, I'm only human...sort of." Cassie thought it over, then nodded. "I'll do my best. I'm assuming it would be in my interest not to attract much attention to myself?"

"Smart girl." A shadow of a smile ghosted across his face. "Just stay here and if there's something I need you to do, please do it without question."

Cassie had a strong urge to salute and shout, "Yes, sir." She stifled it, obeying the quiet that enfolded her.

Gabe went back to the water's edge and peered up at the night sky. Clouds covered most of the stars and the moon hid too. No sounds of life. No sounds of any kind. *Like the vision.* Her insides reeled and panic seized her. The quiet turned oppressive. *Maybe, I've gone deaf.* She coughed a little just to hear something and prove she still had her sense intact. Gabe glared at her, but she grinned back at him with an innocent wave.

After the hush fell upon the area again, Gabe began to speak. She had to strain to catch his words. They were foreign to her and yet somehow familiar. The words sounded magical, ancient, like the Earth itself. He kept going without a pause, as if he wasn't even drawing in breaths.

Since Cassie had first met Gabe, she'd begun to recognize the signs of energy accompanying the supernatural: quiet, stillness, currents. All of it surrounded her now. The force hummed like electricity in the air. She strained her eyes, imaging she could almost see the sparks. Then, all of a sudden, she did. Actual white sparks flew in the darkness. The mirror of the lake, so smooth and calm before, twisted with ripples covering its surface. The little tree, standing by the stone where she sat, bent as if a strong invisible wind had it in its grasp. A crackle strummed the unseen. The tree exploded like a lightning strike hit it straight on. She screamed and leapt off the stone.

Only then did she realize Gabe wasn't speaking the mystic words anymore. He stood rigid, a few feet away from her, as if in a trance. Waves of powerful energy emanated off him in shades of blue ranging from the light hue of an open sunny sky to the midnight tint of the ocean's depths. Cassie ceased to breathe. She had never witnessed anything so beautiful and terrifying at the same time. If she had any lingering doubts about the supernatural, she let them go.

Still lost in the sight before her, she didn't notice at first the light spreading through the clearing. Now she watched as it became brighter. The flare threatened to blind her. *Great, first I think I'm going deaf, now I'm about to go blind.* As soon as the thought passed, the light dimmed and people appeared in the clearing. Well, not people. More like...beings.

Five of them stood motionless, dressed in crisp white loose pants and shirts. Cassie couldn't begin to guess the material. Four males. One female. All beautiful. *No, not beautiful. Ethereal.* The men had plain short-cropped hair. Nothing special. But the woman's hair, on the other hand, cascaded down her back. Golden waves flowed to her knees.

"Gabe," said the woman.

Gabe narrowed his eyes at the female. "Ariel."

I wonder if she was his lover. I wonder if they can be lovers up there. Cassie shifted her weight between her feet, then sagged to one side. *Oh, what's wrong with me.*

"Why have you called us?" Ariel asked.

Gabe seemed to consider the question, inclining his head. He glanced back at Cassie. His eyes grew brighter as he stared at her, as if too much light resonated from their depths. He turned away, the golden color lingering in Cassie's mind.

"I'm in need of assistance with my mission," he said to Ariel. "I need answers."

"And you think we should be helping you? You, who are a fallen? You, who left the Light?" Ariel said. Gentleness alone in her voice, no contempt or anger, perhaps a twinge of sadness. "You, who deny us?"

"I'm on the path of finding redemption and returning to the Light, Ariel. You know this." Gabe's limbs straightened and he leaned forward, a predatory posture.

One of the men stepped forward from the outer circle. "We can only tell you what's good for the Light. You will have to make your own choices though, Gabe. Earth and free will are bound to your fall."

"I understand, Remiel. I wouldn't ask to communicate with you in this way if I didn't have a choice."

"So be it." Remiel waved his hand, one finger extended with a flourish.

Ariel raised her flawless arms in Gabe's direction. "Tell us what you need to know."

Cassie's ears perked up as she listened. Gabe recounted how he had found out she was a *Key* and, more so, *the Key* from the prophecy.

The angels remained stoic, no emotion showing on their faces. Cassie could have sworn they were zoned out or sleeping with their eyes open. *So much for a human reaction.* She rubbed her arms through the dense fabric of her windbreaker and sweater.

When Gabe finished, Remiel looked at her. "Yes, I can feel the power in this one." The angel's coldness made her flinch.

Cassie knew she stay quiet but something in her wanted

to gain a sense of normalcy in this bizarre scene. The urge to assert her presence rose to the forefront.

"It's Cassie," she said, crossing her arms over her chest.

Gabe inhaled and tensed. His jaw clicked. "Cassie, please be quiet," he said just as softly but in a voice allowing for no arguments.

"A feisty Key," Ariel said.

Cassie's patience broke. *You might be some all-powerful supernatural being,* she thought to herself, wisely now. *But I bet I can still take you.* The rage rose, then fell in a flash. It surprised her to learn it was hard to stay mad at Ariel. *She must be influencing me somehow.*

The tension in the air floated through the trees, the rocks, and those assembled, almost palpable in its force. A hush fell amongst them. Ariel stepped forward claiming the floor once more. With no further preamble she said evenly, "This Key is too dangerous to the Light." She pointed at Cassie without a trace of pity. "She must not be allowed to live."

THIRTEEN

Cassie rocked on her heels. She couldn't have heard right. *An angel can't want me dead.* Her mind rallied against the shock. *This is just a bad dream. It has to be.* The air passed through her lungs in slow breaths as she fought the tide of nausea and struggled for control. *Breathe. Oxygen, air. You remember how to do it.* The pit in her stomach refused to subside.

"What are you talking about Ariel?" Gabe let out a low growl between gritted teeth. The difference between the fallen and the angel became clear. Gabe's far more human reaction showed in stark contrast to the detached attitudes of the angels. They remained calm as they proclaimed the need for her death.

Remiel answered in place of Ariel, his voice soothing. "Gabe, you must see this. She is but one mortal in the grand scheme of things. Her abilities are far too dangerous. No creature should be granted that much control. The events unfolding when she comes into her full power could lead to a global disaster. If demons get to her, if she chooses the wrong side, it may be all over."

Gabe's fury blazed. The electric blue energy vibrated with sharp pulses around his body.

"You want me to redeem myself. You want me to return to the Light. Yet, what you're asking of me is to kill an innocent I have sworn to protect? This must be a joke." Gabe's words remained sharp, on the razor's edge of losing control.

Cassie could take no more. She knew it was foolish but she couldn't allow these creatures to talk over her, deciding her fate like they were determining what to eat for their next meal.

Mustering her courage, she said, "Excuse me."

"Cassie, silence," Gabe said, flashing his eyes wide in warning.

"No, Gabe. I'm sorry but I have to speak up here. You're talking about my life, for God's sake!" Her voice broke and she winced at the show of weakness.

"Let the Key say what she wants," Ariel said, beaming at Cassie the way someone would at an unruly kitten. The mockery gave Cassie the boldness she needed.

"Oh, thank you." Cassie hoped the dripping sarcasm wasn't lost on the angels. "If I'm such a powerful Key, if everyone wants me so much, why doesn't anyone give me credit for choosing to do the right thing? After all, we mortals do have free will."

"You are too unpredictable." The female angel kept her voice calming, as if soothing a child. "You are right. You have the free will to choose the right side. You also have the free will to choose the wrong side. We cannot trust you.

Not in matters of such importance."

"Aren't you supposed to be serving the Light?" She shifted her weight to her heels trying not to crumble under the pressure. The ground felt solid under her feet even as she swayed. "When did killing a person become good for the Light?"

"When it is for the good of all humanity, as well as the cause of the Light," Ariel said deadpan. She turned once more, giving Cassie her back and dismissing her altogether. "Gabe, you know things are not always as simple as mortals would like them to be. Like it or not, we are in the middle of a battle, you know this more than anyone." Ariel's voice rose as she kept talking. It seemed out of place after her dispassionate expression earlier. "We are warriors of the Light."

I'm screwed. Cassie's heart sank. There would be no convincing these angels to see reason. They were soldiers. Warriors in every way, though they didn't look it. Anger boiled inside her as she stared at the benevolent looking creatures, their appearance mismatching their true nature. Yet, she saw them for what they were. Saw the truth. *They'll fight, even blindly, for their cause because they were made to believe in it from the day they were created.* She shook. *There's no other way for them, and no way out for me.*

Gabe seemed to have come to the same conclusion. His face darkened. He was one of them. Cassie wondered how much of what he was in the past still remained in him, and how much of what he became had changed him. She had no answer to either question, so she took a pointed step back.

The silence lingered. Ariel's words hung heavy in the

air. The angels remained a blank circle, their position unyielding. Any emotion glimpsed during the speech was now gone from their faces.

Gabe, at last, as if awakened from his reverie, shuddered and looked at Cassie. His face showed nothing but a grave mask. The tightness in his jaw begged for release. Without a word to her, he turned back to the angels, his energy flaring around him.

"I have to find another way. My redemption depends on it," he said. The hush in the clearing felt palpable.

Ariel and Remiel glanced at each other, then peered at Gabe. The light in their eyes flashed in unison, a blinding white. Ariel came forward, her irises fading to an ivory shade. She took Gabe's hand. Cassie saw him tense up at the contact. His body became stone as if caused by her touch alone.

"Gabe, your redemption lies in doing what you must for the Light and this is what we require. It may not get you back to us right away, but it will be a step in the right direction. You trusted me once," she said, stroking his hand. "Trust me now."

Cassie's heart gave a loud thump. Ariel spoke to Gabe in the most intimate tone. *He can't ignore it.*

An eternity seemed to pass before Gabe shook his head, met Ariel's stare, and repeated, "I will find another way."

Ariel's eyes shifted, something dangerous and dark flashing in their depths. Yet, her voice gave no indication of anything amiss. "You always have to do things your own way. Is it not enough it led to your fall?" She didn't wait for him to respond. "We told you what we had to. You make your own choices here. But remember, if you go against us, we cannot help you anymore. You are moving in the wrong direction, Gabe."

The angels stepped back and bright light flooded the area once more. A few seconds later, Gabe and Cassie stood alone in the clearing and the night enveloped them, darker than before.

#

Cassie closed her eyes. Stinging jolts lapped at her skin. They came from the direction where Gabe stood unmoving in the open space. The energy stung, charged with hot red fury and more, a substance she couldn't name. Gradually, she opened her eyes.

Gabe faced the now empty clearing, his gaze cloaked in amber and far away. She took a hesitant step closer and strained to see his eyes. What she spotted in them had her jerking back. They shone of danger and betrayal, not unexpected feelings, but something more sparked just beyond the obvious. It pulled at Cassie like invisible strings.

"Pain," she whispered. "He's in so much pain."

Cassie covered the remaining distance and took his hand. It blazed with tiny sparks of electricity. The energy flared red instead of his usual blue. The power triggered a tremor to run through her, but she didn't back away. She had to calm him down before this strange red energy erupted and caused damage.

"Gabe," she whispered. He didn't respond. Cassie's heart beat staccato in her chest. "Gabe, talk to me."

He turned his head toward her then, his eyes focusing on her face.

"I'm sorry, Cassie."

Her body stiffened, cold fear creeping up her spine. *Either he's apologizing for my first meeting with angels traumatizing me for life, or...* She swallowed the lump in her throat. *He's sorry he has to do what they told him to and...* Her mind zeroed in with frightening clarity. *Kill me.*

"I'm sorry I don't have any more answers for you than before."

She exhaled, unaware she'd held her breath at all, and offered up a silent prayer of thanks. Her hand clutched her chest. She fiddled with her jacket zipper. "You had no idea they were going to tell you this?"

"No. We're supposed to serve the Light. How's killing an innocent person going to bring me closer to redemption?" Gabe's body trembled. He demanded this answer more of himself than her.

An odd sense of disappointment bubbled up inside her, despite her relief in knowing he wasn't going to kill her. *He isn't concerned about me. He only cares about himself, his redemption.* She told herself it didn't matter. He was cut off from his source, confused by what he had been ordered to do. *I can't worry whether he cares for me or not. It's not important.* She tried to convince herself as she remembered the stoic coldness of the angels. Gabe was anything but dispassionate at the moment. In fact, his emotions, his very human emotions, boiled over.

"Are you scared?" Gabe said. The question was so unexpected Cassie took a small step back. She didn't say anything and Gabe seemed to take it as an affirmative. "I swore I'd protect you and I won't go back on my word." Passion ignited like burning coals. "I will protect you.

There has to be another way." He put his hands on her shoulders and gave her a little shake, as if physical contact would convince her of the truth of his words.

Energy hit harder, almost making Cassie pull away from his grip, but she didn't. Gabe's mouth came on top of hers, hard and fast. *Oh God.* Her heart skipped a beat. *What the hell am I doing? What the hell is he doing?* Her heart soared with the kiss, but unwelcome thoughts found their way through... *What if this is just his way of dealing? What if he thinks I'm...?* She shook the worry from her mind with a silent reprimand. *Oh shut up! Just shut up!* Her body responded in full, charged with adrenaline and pure desire. She moved closer, molding their bodies together. His tongue danced inside her mouth, exploring its depth. Heat spread through Cassie, despite the air around them reaching well below arctic levels.

Gabe twined his fingers through her long hair and leaned over her. His free hand explored her body, touching her cheek, her neck, and her shoulder in turn. He pulled her sweater off one shoulder and shifted his attention to her collarbone.

Cassie clung to him as if her life depended on it and moaned as he licked the sensitive spot at the nape of her neck. The sound only urged him on. His need pressed greedily between her thighs. She wriggled against him and got a guttural growl in response.

He peeled Cassie's thick sweater up and over her head in a rush, then slid her pants off her hips. She expected to shiver once left in her cotton bra and panties, but the liquid heat pumping through her veins intensified. The urgency between them rose like an unstoppable tidal wave.

While Gabe yanked his own shirt off, Cassie fumbled with his pants. She discovered he wore dark boxers underneath. The fabric was stretched to the limit. She moved them down his hips, exposing all of him with one quick motion, afraid she'd lose her nerve. Her experiences with men were not extensive on any level, having only been intimate with the jerk from college. It didn't give her much basis for comparison. Even so, she knew in front of her stood a perfect male specimen, human or angel. Cassie squirmed as anxiety and excitement hit her in equal measure.

She shyly circled him in her hand. His groan had her smiling and her confidence growing. As she worked him faster, the power of the intimate act had her craving more. He seemed to share the sentiment. Grabbing her legs, he supported her back with one hand while laying her on the ground. The jacket and sweater he'd spread out like a blanket tickled her bare back. He stood over her for a brief moment. Hunger showed in his parted lips as he explored the lines and curves of her petite body. Cassie never felt so beautiful and wanted.

In a heartbeat, he was on top of her, kissing her everywhere. He unhooked the bra and pushed it to the side, cupping the full globes of her breasts in both hands. His tongue teased the left peak, pink, erect and ready for him. Cassie shuddered with pleasure, writhing under him. He moved on to the right breast, his tongue lapping at her in slow erotic circles. His hand sought lower pleasures. Her panties slid down to her ankles. In achingly long strokes, his fingers probed the wetness between her thighs. Cassie's insides clenched and released with quick pulses. Her senses working toward overload.

As she climbed higher, to the very edge of control, Gabe pulled up and looked into her eyes. An unspoken question glowed in his gaze. She stared back at him. All anxiety or shyness long past. It seemed he found the answer he sought, because in another second his mouth came down on hers while he plunged deep into her warm core. Cassie's breath hitched as she took him all in. He stilled inside her, yet his tongue never stopped dancing with hers. Then, he started moving and Cassie thought she would be burned from the inside out. She found she was happy to be consumed by the fire. It didn't take long for both of them to reach the height of their ecstasy. As Gabe came to his own finish, Cassie cried out like never before.

FOURTEEN

The sun loomed high overhead the next time Cassie opened her eyes. Her limbs lay still intertwined with Gabe's and the fallen angel lay asleep. She tried to pull away to get up without disturbing him, but his arms squeezed around her more tightly in his sleep. She had no choice but to stay there and think.

"This is my reality," she whispered and stared at the sky overhead. "Sleeping with a fallen angel. Other angels want me dead." She glanced at the clearing where the angels had declared her a threat the night before. "Demonic father. And living between two...or is it three worlds?"

"Yeah, about sums it up." She sighed and threw an arm over her face blocking the morning light while trying to hide herself from her predicament. As if on cue, Gabe stirred beside her.

With a groan, Cassie removed her arm and turned to him. His gaze already ate her up, the pleasant moments of last night shining in his eyes. Yet, as the sun reappeared from behind a cloud, his good mood faded with the rays. He untangled his arms from around her and shot up. Cassie averted her eyes for propriety's sake as Gabe remained stark naked. It may have been silly to do so after what they'd shared but the daylight made her self-consciousness reappear and the situation far too real.

Gabe said not a word of greeting, instead brushing past her to the lake's edge to wash up. She watched him rinse off, disappointed but unsurprised by his reaction.

"Well, this should be perfectly awkward," she muttered. Working out the kinks, she stretched, not in a hurry to face the trip back.

Rising from the makeshift bed, the cold air hit her in force, making her tremble. Pulling on her sweater and pants, she wrapped her arms around her waist. After the initial chill wore off, she picked up her jacket and shook it out before donning it on as well. Warmer and less uncomfortable with her clothes on, she walked to the lake and splashed some water on her face. It dripped down her cheeks in freezing droplets, but felt good nonetheless. The magic of last night had vanished. Reality, as cold as the water, settled in.

"We have to get back on the road as soon as possible," Gabe said. His voice sounded rough in the hush of the clearing.

Cassie nodded.

It seemed like the trek to the car took longer than the hike down the previous evening. She kept slipping on loose rocks. As before, he was oblivious to her plight, walking fast and with purpose. He paid her no attention, not even to offer support over the more treacherous terrain.

"Ass," she cursed him more than once. After the heat and passion of last night, it was hard to believe this was the same man. *Can't forget who he is…what he is.* The quiet declaration fueled her into action. She tightened her jaw, kept her footing firm, and by sheer force of will refused to fall anymore.

By the time they reached the parking lot, lunchtime tourists packed it, scurrying around. They didn't stay long, just enough time to use the bathroom and meet up by the car. Back on the road, Cassie thought she'd be able to relax and nap, but her stomach had other ideas.

"We need to stop and eat something," she said from the passenger seat, slapping her hand on the glove compartment for emphasis. "I'm starving."

He didn't look at her. His gaze was fixed on the road ahead, his profile hard in the sun's rays. "Food isn't important right now."

"Maybe not to you, but it is to me. I'm not adding hunger to my growing list of annoyances." She tapped her finger against the window.

"Then have one of those energy bars you brought," he said flatly, still looking straight ahead.

Cassie considered punching him. *With my luck, he'd be just distracted enough to turn the wheel and land us in a ditch.* The tension level reached its zenith inside the little sports car. She huffed, pulling out a chocolate protein bar from her bag. She nibbled it. He didn't ask for one and she didn't offer. It tasted terrible. The chocolate bits packed with who knows what.

"Enough silence. What's the next step?" Cassie said when she finished choking down the poor excuse for food and gulping down half the water bottle.

"We're going to Las Vegas to gather more information."

"What's in Vegas? Why there?"

"It's a well-known center of fallen and demonic activity." He rolled his shoulders while keeping his grip firm on the wheel. "I also need to find Albert. He might know more by now."

"I've never been to Vegas." Under her breath she added, "What a way to visit Sin City."

"This might prove dangerous, but we have no other choice. And I'd rather have you with me so I can protect you," Gabe said, ignoring her last comment.

Cassie leaned back in the seat and let her thoughts wander. Despite her frustration with Gabe, she couldn't help but imagine their intimate exchange from the night before. It brought a stinging heat to her cheeks and a fire to her blood. The feeling faded, however, as the image changed. She pictured Gabe kissing Ariel, holding her in his arms, making love to her with abandon. She winced. Any thoughts of the cold angel would make her cringe, but thinking about her with Gabe turned her downright vicious.

"One night," she chided herself. "And already you're acting like a love sick kid."

"What was that?"

His question broke her daydream. She considered asking him about his relationship with Ariel, but shook off the thought. She decided she didn't want to know the answer. "Nothing."

They drove almost nonstop, making a couple of pit

stops throughout the day and grabbing some real food. Although, Gabe refused any of the food she offered.

"A waste of time," he'd said.

Cassie grumbled none too happy to be eating in the car again, but figured it was better than choking down another energy bar. Just as she'd finished her meal and began to drift off to sleep, a sharp ringing echoed in her mind. The noise was too high, as if mortal ears shouldn't hear its pitch. She clapped her hands to her head in an attempt to block out the sound.

"What is it?" Gabe said, his hand reaching to her shoulder and shaking it. "What's wrong?"

"Pull over," she cried, unsure of what to do. "Pull over."

As Gabe steered the car onto the shoulder, the internal chimes became louder. She concentrated on blocking the clamor. Pushing against it with her will worked just enough to keep her from passing out. A melodious voice came forth beyond the horrible ringing.

"Is it a demon?" The car idled. Gabe's hands sparked a soft electric blue as he reached for her.

She pushed his hands away, focusing on the voice. "No. It's something else. Wait."

A woman's high soprano whispered in her mind, "Cassiel. My poor Cassiel. Guard yourself. Danger is coming."

Before Cassie could respond, the woman's soft tones faded as if they'd never been. She tried to trace the notes as they disappeared from her mind, but couldn't hold them anymore than air. They floated away.

"What happened? Are you all right?" Gabe leaned

closer, his hands reaching for her once more.

Cassie let him hold her this time. The incident shook her to the core. Never before had she heard a voice so soft and pure. When demons manipulated her powers, they caused her agonizing pain. As if the very essence of her mind would rip apart under their weight. *This. This was so...different.* She couldn't find the words.

Gabe shook her and asked again.

"A voice," she said. "A gentle voice." Sorting through the memory, she turned to face him. "A woman. She told me danger was coming."

Gabe nodded without comment and released her from his embrace. Shifting the car back into drive, he changed into the same stoic creature he'd been before. "Best try to get some rest," he said without feeling. "Don't worry about this voice. It's harmless."

The change in him reignited some of her previous anger. She huffed and shouted a quick, "Fine." Turning away from him, she curled into a ball on the passenger seat. The events of the last few days put her mind on overload. She'd take any chance she could to rest. Pushing all of it from her mind came easier than she anticipated. Her body slumped down further in the seat, exhausted beyond belief.

At some point she fell asleep. Gratefully, the nap stayed dreamless. When she opened her eyes again, she stretched her arms high over her head. Staring out the window, she found the sky painted with deep sunset colors of red, yellow and purples.

"We're not far now." Gabe glanced in her direction.

Cassie looked into the distance and saw city lights peeking out from between the mountaintops. She sat up straighter as a quiver of excitement rippled through her.

"We're going to check into a hotel," Gabe told her. "I want you to stay there and rest while I go talk to some people."

"Like hell I'll stay at the hotel!" Calm flowed out of her like a bullet. Somewhere in the back of her mind, she knew he was right. It'd be better for her to hide. She didn't give a damn. They were in this crazy mess together. "Hell if you're leaving me behind."

Gabe's tone turned to steel. "Cassie, I can't protect you if you don't listen to me. This isn't the time to argue over such things." He shot her a warning look. "Half the population of the city would love to get their hands on you."

Cassie chose not to answer. He didn't say another word, and she was glad to remain quiet this time. Her irritation with him rose unbidden and she wondered at it. Gabe produced so many contradicting emotions in her and made the whole situation even more confusing. So far he'd proven he could be trusted.

Even with my life.

The nagging did not subside with the revelation. If she were honest with herself, she'd admit she didn't trust him entirely. No matter what he'd done, he was still a strange being to her, someone who fell into her world and into her life. He had his own goals and intentions.

And what about the reason for his fall? Cassie stared at the sun falling behind the distant mountains. *What did he do that was so bad he'd be cast out of his world, cut off from his source?* Too many questions remained unanswered. Yet, he was willing to protect her even when he could gain his redemption faster by destroying her. *Has to count for something.* She took a deep breath as night descended.

By the time they entered Vegas, Cassie's head swam. She had to get away for a while, to think on her own. But being alone in a hotel room just didn't seem like a good option. She chose not to mention that to Gabe.

Inside the city limits, Gabe drove like he'd been to Vegas numerous times, though Cassie suspected that was impossible. They never hit the strip but instead veered toward a string of small motels behind it. She could see the bright lights of the strip illuminating the evening sky, whereas these backstreets flooded the area with darkness. The occasional neon light would announce a *No Tell* motel, a grimy casino, or a seedy strip club.

Gabe drove much slower now, obviously trying to choose the right place. At last, he turned into the tiny parking lot of an ominous looking building. It sat two stories high. Most of the windows were black behind crass green curtains. A midnight blue sign, half-lit by the light from the street lamp, pronounced the motel's name as "Desert Breeze". Cassie tried to hide her distaste by covering her face with her hands and faking a sneeze, which Gabe ignored.

They entered the cramped lobby. It possessed one central desk and a couple of uninviting armchairs. A heavyset man in his mid-forties sat behind the desk. A thick hand covered his yawn as they approached. Stains spread across his shirt, appearing to be the same green hue as the motel rooms' curtains.

"Can I help you?" He sounded as bored as he looked.

"We'd like a room, please," Gabe said.

"By hour or day?"

Gabe's gaze shot to her with a hint of amusement in them. "We'll be staying for a couple of days," he said, turning back to the man.

"Cash or credit?"

"Cash." Gabe reached into the inside pocket of his coat and took out a wallet. Rifling through it, he placed four twenties on the counter.

Cassie wondered, not for the first time, where a fallen angel would get money. He never seemed to have a shortage of it. Another question she put on her mental checklist of unanswered mysteries.

"Room seven. Up the stairs and down the hall."

As soon as they entered the room with their bags, Gabe went through it, looking in all corners. He peered out the window, nodded to himself as if in approval to his own thought, and closed the curtains. Cassie watched him, crossing her arms over her chest and letting her weight sag to one foot.

"I'm going now," Gabe said, returning to the door, where she stood. "Lock the door behind me, and don't let anyone in. Do you understand?" He waited for her to nod, before he continued, "Don't open the curtains. Unpack and rest. I'll be back when I'm done with business."

"Yes, master," Cassie said and bowed in mock obedience.

"Cassie, this isn't a joke." Gabe's fists tightened at his sides.

"You just don't have a sense of humor," Cassie muttered as she moved further inside the room and put her bag on the lone bed.

Gabe looked at her for a long minute. "You can be a very irritating woman," he said. And, as if an afterthought, "Keep your cell phone near." He closed the door and disappeared.

Cassie exhaled. She didn't know if it was out of relief or something else. One thing was for certain, she did not intend to stay in this room. "If he needs me, he can call my cell." Nodding at her approval of the plan, she rummaged through her suitcase. A shiny material at the bottom caught her eye. "Danger be damned. I want a distraction. Shit. I need a distraction." Donning an outfit she would never have considered before her life turned upside down, she winked into the mirror. "And this *is* the city of ultimate distractions."

Half an hour after Gabe left, Cassie called for a cab.

FIFTEEN

A repugnant smell akin to cheap cigar smoke and raw sewage wafted through the Vegas back streets. Gabe tried to ignore it as he wandered through the night. Neon lights flickered and gleamed. Casino bells screeched a shrill chime. Hopeless bums begged for spare change. Working girls offered him a "good time". Still Gabe trudged on as the sights assailed his senses from all directions.

"What a paradise," Gabe said, shaking his head.

"Don't knock it, 'til you've tried it awhile," answered a man in a nasal voice. The stranger stepped from the darkness into the harsh orange glow of a door's overhanging light. He leaned against a building's cement wall, crossing his arms and smiling at Gabe.

"I've no desire to try it at all," Gabe said as he examined the stranger. Two muddy brown eyes stared from under a pair of stringy black bangs. The hair, slicked back in a ponytail, was thin, shoulder length, and oily. It couldn't have been washed in several days. The rust colored leather jacket covered a gangly frame. Dark blue jeans hid long thin limbs. The whole picture spoke of awkwardness and deceit. Gabe's disdain brought forth an unbidden whisper, "Who are you?"

A high-pitched squeal echoed along the street. "I'm not surprised you don't recognize me." The stranger stepped nose to nose with Gabe in one smooth motion. "But I know you."

Gabe angled his head and stood still, disoriented by the sudden movement. He recovered, however, as he stared in disbelief. *Why didn't I see it sooner?* The stranger was one of the fallen. Recognition crossed Gabe's mind. "You can't be..."

"No, of course not. That name is long gone," the stranger interrupted. "They call me Snarky now. A great name, no?" Another strangled laugh erupted. "I work for Rafe." After a pause he added, "He's tickled pink you've arrived."

"I'll bet." Gabe couldn't stifle his lips from curling over his teeth.

"More than you know." Snarky sighed. "I bet him. An actual bet, mind you, that *you* would never end up here." A wiry finger pointed in Gabe's direction. "Bah. Guess I should've known better. Don't we all end up here sooner or later?"

"No." Gabe looked toward the blackened sky. "Not all of us."

"Oh, really? Time will see which one of us is right." Snarky turned to walk down a narrow alley, but whipped his head back. "Wanna make a bet?"

"No," Gabe commanded. "Just take me to Rafe."

A gruff "humph" preceded Snarky's reply. "Fine. But, personally, I think it's a fair bet." A hideous cackle. "If there *is* such a thing as a fair bet." He turned once more and continued down the side street as he struggled to get his hysterics under control.

Gabe had no desire to pursue further conversation and trailed him a few steps behind. *What's happened to him?* The thought plagued him as he peered through the darkness. *Is this the result of a life here?* Snarky's hunched back gave him no answer. *But then, Albert. He seems...adjusted. Not the same, but not this.* He looked around to underline his thought. *No point thinking about it. I won't be here long enough to have that problem.* He turned his mind resolute to his task. He had enough to figure out without pondering his own fate just now.

As they walked further through the Vegas underground, all of the buildings took on similar design of gray one-story boxes. No tourists would ever see this part of the city unless they were looking for real trouble. Not the fun and games--let's make bets, get married in an Elvis chapel, spill drinks on a half dressed woman--kind of trouble. No, not that. This area spelt supernatural--soul stealing, universe bending, demon possessing, kill or be killed, kind of trouble. Not exactly part of a tour package.

Snarky stopped dead at the front entrance of an unmarked structure. It was undistinguishable from the rest of the buildings in the area. As he wrapped on the metal door, a series of timed knocks followed. A brief pause, then the door creaked open. Stepping inside led to another metal door, this one made of steel.

"Welcome," stated a monotone computerized voice. "State designation."

"Snarky. And this here's Gabe. We're expected."

Seconds passed before the voice responded, "Proceed."

The interior door slid into the adjoining wall. The fallen pair entered single file. Down a short narrow corridor and through yet another metal door on the left led into an ultramodern office. The walls were cold, sterile, warmed only by oddly familiar scenes from 1950s black and white photos. A row of iridescent cylindrical lights created a path to the front of a massive glass desk. A set of expensive looking Italian leather shoes lay atop the desk's center but the occupant of said shoes was bathed in shadow.

"I'll be damned," said a husky voice from the darkness. "Oh wait, I already am."

Snarky's squealing laughter preceded a quick applause. "Nice one boss," he said over his shoulder as he crept out of the room.

The swanky shoes whirled off the desk and smacked the hard ivory tiled floor with a thud. A tanned face with high cheekbones, sleek aristocratic nose, and full lips leaned into the light. Jet-black hair, mixed with deep brown highlights, flowed to frame the proud jaw line. The eyes, a cool tawny hue, spoke of assured confidence.

"Ah. To see you here," said the fallen behind the desk. "It just gives me a warm feeling of..." He snapped his fingers. "...satisfaction."

Gabe narrowed his eyes, but refused to be baited by the boss of Vegas' fallen, no matter what insights he could learn. Several decades ago, he'd known Rafe when they were both still a part of the Light. Yet, *friends* wouldn't have been the term for their complex relationship, in fact *bitter rivals* fit far more. Having to come to Rafe now for help ate at Gabe.

"Still as arrogant as ever, I see." Rafe jumped over the front of the desk in one easy motion. Soundlessly, he landed and leaned back. The mod chandelier spotlighted him. A white collar peeked from under a black designer vest. The middle button of a sleek coat hinted at a tight chest and trim waist. Long tailored slacks marked him as a half-foot above the average height. He'd star in many a woman's fantasy, and proudly made such fantasies reality. "If you've come to see me, you want something, bad." He grinned. "How much do you want it, Gabe? What's it worth to you?"

Gabe continued to peer at Rafe without as much as a blink.

"You know, I think you should beg for it." Rafe motioned to the floor. "That would really get my blood going. You, down on your knees, begging. Perfect."

"You haven't changed." Gabe took a step forward, his face riddled with disdain. "All this time here and you're the same, if not worse. A perverse mess."

"Perverse? Interesting choice of words. As I remember, Ariel called it passionate." Rafe's deliberate pause left the room silent before he continued, "This was, of course, when she, how do you put it...mounted...yes that's it, when she mounted my defense to the council."

Gabe remained motionless.

"So, Ariel means nothing now, huh? It's only when I push your pride I get a rise out of you. You haven't changed either." Rafe sneered. "All right, then, tell me what was Ariel's defense for your infinite arrogance?"

Pushing the jibe aside, Gabe said without feeling, "No

defense. She's part of the council now."

A roar of laughter echoed in the sparse office. "Conniving...ha...brilliant. Then, *she* was responsible for your fall. Oh, this just gets better and better."

"I didn't come here to play games or reminisce!" Gabe's anger had reached its threshold and spilled forth unchecked. He took another step forward.

"Ah see, it wasn't so hard. That's what I've been waiting for." Rafe beamed revealing a layer of perfect white teeth. "Face it, Gabe. You're here to stay whether you realize it yet or not."

Furious with himself for giving into Rafe's taunts so quick, Gabe took a firm step back and said nothing.

Rafe waved a dismissive hand. "No matter. On to business. So, you came here about the Key."

"How do you..." Gabe couldn't hide his surprise.

"Ha," Rafe interrupted. "Every fallen and demon in Vegas knows the Sacred Key has been born." In an almost empathetic tone he continued, "Trusting Albert was a misstep. He's a born gossip, and drama ignites his fire."

The memory of Maribel's mutilated body flashed through Gabe's mind. *Albert's big mouth may have gotten his maid killed.* The blood began to pound in his ears. *And now Cassie's life is in danger...and my chance for redemption.* His thoughts turned ugly as a lifeless Cassie replaced Maribel's face. Her eyes wide, her petite frame stiff, her features distorted, all by death. Blinding rage mixed with fear as bile crept up his throat. In a guttural voice he whispered, "Damn him."

"Yes," Rafe said nodding. "But then, damn us all." A wolfish grin rose from one corner. "Come now. Don't be sullen. I haven't seen you in so long my old...well not quite a friend are you?"

"You know why I'm here, so cut the shit!" Gabe teetered close to the edge of losing all control. "She needs more protection. Are you going to help or not?"

"She?" Intrigue and desire lit Rafe's face like a forest fire. "Albert failed to mention the Key was a female."

"Not simply 'a female.' Cassie's beyond your comprehension." Gabe's mind wandered to the previous night they'd shared in the canyons; a night he hadn't let himself think about until now. Softly he said, "Dark hair, smooth skin, penetrating eyes, and a fiery spirit. A perfect combination." The words spilled forth of their own accord. "And oh yeah..." A ferocious possessiveness clutched him. "She's mine."

Perhaps it was his anger at being here, or his worry over what was to come, or the sheer stress of the past few weeks, regardless he'd declared to his rival what he'd never said to Cassie, and he'd meant every word.

"Sounds like the ideal little package. I look forward to meeting her." Rafe crossed his ankles as he continued to lean against the desk and shrugged. The body position spoke of a nonchalant attitude, but Gabe knew better. Rafe continued, "So, what will be the terms of our arrangement then?"

"You, along with anyone under your authority, agree to help me protect Cassie until it's time for her to make the bond." Gabe closed the space between him and his rival. Holding his gaze, he added, "But, you do so from a distance. You are not to have any involvement with her."

Rafe didn't flinch. "And why would I make such an

arrangement? What do I get in return?"

"Besides the ability to be taken back by the Light when Cassie bonds with an angel?"

"Yes, besides that." Silence filled the room. "As you have no response I take it you thought it'd be enough." Rafe stood to his full height and looked down at Gabe. "You forget me. The deal is as pathetic as you."

The last string of Gabe's nerves snapped. Without hesitation, he grabbed Rafe by his designer suit and hauled him onto the solid ivory floor. A slow cracking noise rippled through the room after the initial crash. The tiles split as Rafe lay motionless. After the shock of the attack wore off, Rafe sprang to his feet dodging under Gabe's blows. With an animalistic roar, he struck Gabe's neck and threw him across the office. The pictures shook from their hinges and shattered to the ground as Gabe hit the far wall. An imprint of his body remained in the cement as he tore himself out and stood for a breath, swaying on unsteady feet.

"Enough." Rafe put up his hands in mock surrender. "We're even. Now, do you want to unleash this childish anger on me or do you want to get back to business?"

Gabe thought seriously of tearing the bastard's head off, but pushed the idea aside when he realized he needed this bastard's help. He walked forward and crossed his arms instead. "Talk. Fast. What is it you want?"

"Much better." Rafe took his former position leaning against the desk as if nothing had transpired. "It's simple. I'll get you and the girl out of Vegas first. Then, make sure she lives to see the bonding." He paused.

"Get on with it," Gabe barked. "In return for this?"

"You tell the Key all about me and my...charms. Perhaps bonding with an angel or demon isn't appealing to her. Maybe she wants things to remain as they are." A wide smile spread across his face. "I can give her this."

Gabe's eyes narrowed. "How?"

"Not your concern." He waved a hand to swat away the question. "You simply allow me to meet the Key alone before the bonding. One meeting. No tricks. And I promise I will only talk to the girl. She will be perfectly safe."

"You just want to meet and talk to her?" he said, cocking an eyebrow.

"Yes. I have an offer for her alone. If you arrange this meeting, I will agree to help protect her." He brushed his hands together, emphasizing the simplicity. "And you know how much...or more important, how many...resources I have at my disposal."

Gabe remained silent as he contemplated his next move. *And he calls me arrogant, ha.* In an atypical move, he allowed reason to dictate his decision instead of pride. "Ten minutes. No longer. I wait in the next room during your meeting. And if I feel anything amiss..."

"You'll come charging to the rescue," Rafe interrupted with a laugh. "But, really ten minutes is hardly enough time to establish a...rapport."

"Take it or leave it." Gabe growled.

"Agreed." Rafe extended a hand forward and waited before retracting it. "You're in the human world Gabe. A handshake is a sign of a deal."

The two shook hands with a mutual testing of each other's strength. It lasted a good thirty seconds or so, just a tad longer than the average handshake. A few more seconds of intense staring followed, before Gabe turned to leave.

"Not so fast," Rafe said as he pulled two items from his jacket pocket. He held them out for Gabe in an open palm. "Take these."

Gabe raised a brow at the small red devices. Each was round and no bigger than a dime.

"Consider them panic buttons. One for you. One for the girl. Place it on the roof of your mouth. If you're in a real bind, just click." He made an obnoxious clicking sound with his tongue for emphasis. "A micro global positioning system, GPS for short. It's a common device nowadays. You click, it activates and we know your location."

"Ok. But, why am I putting this thing in my mouth?"

"I'll ignore the obvious pun. You're not as good at double entendres as I am." Rafe slapped a hand to his chest. "To answer your question, even if someone frisks you, takes away your weapons and beats you senseless, chances are they still won't find this little beauty."

Glancing down at the device, Gabe had a new appreciation for technology. "Clever. What will this cost me?"

"Consider the devices part of our deal."

"Fine with me." Gabe snatched the pair of GPS from Rafe's hand and turned to leave, again.

As Gabe stepped through the office door to the exterior hallway, Rafe called, "Just don't forget to tell the sweet little Key where the present came from."

A scornful laugh echoed in the hall just before the door slammed shut. It took all of Gabe's willpower not to turn around, pound a hole through the door, and cram the ridiculous red gadgets down Rafe's throat. He contained himself, barely, and opted for getting the hell out of there instead.

Once outside the light desert wind helped to cool his anger. "You got what you needed. It's all that matters." He made his way through the snaking Vegas backstreets and to the motel without incident. As he walked through the decrepit lobby and toward the room he shared with Cassie, he mused over his next problem, getting her to "wear" the GPS device without argument.

"I could tell her it'll ensure her safety," he said aloud in the empty hallway. He turned the key in the rusty lock and opened the door. "Probably won't work. And not entirely truthful anyway." He scanned the room before entering. Cassie's clothes had been tossed on the bed. The bathroom light beamed a soft yellow glow. "Cassie?"

The sound of thick tattered curtains blowing in the open window was the lone reply. Gabe tore through the room at blinding speed. "No blood. No body," he said, reassuring himself. As he was about to crush the GPS devices in his anger, he spotted a small notepad on the broken nightstand with familiar scribbles on it.

"Dear Gabe,

Went looking for a distraction. Don't wait up.

Cassie"

Gabe crumpled the note and flung it full force out the window. He then took both GPS devices from his pocket and placed them in his mouth. They sat gnawing behind his front teeth, but it was a necessary discomfort to keep both units safe until he found Cassie. "When I find that woman, I'm going to shove this tracking thing so far up her..."

A piercing ring from his cell phone broke his rant. Gabe flipped the phone open without bothering to look at the number. "Where are you?" he bellowed into the receiver.

An ominous voice from the other side responded, "We have the girl."

SIXTEEN

"Now, *this* is really the city that never sleeps," Cassie whispered while looking out of the cab window. The Vegas Strip beckoned to her with its multitude of neon lights and party sounds. Something in her had broken free after years of self-inflicted loneliness and reservations. Her life was spiraling out of control. Tonight, her mood mimicked the downward descent. She wanted to be free and crazy, at least for a little while. "And what better place to let loose than right here in Vegas?"

"Where do you want me to drop you off, Miss?" The cabbie's voice broke through Cassie's reflection. The driver, a small Asian man with not a hint of an accent, stared at her from the rearview mirror.

"How about the biggest casino on the Strip?"

He glanced into the rearview mirror and smiled. "First time in Vegas?"

Cassie returned the grin. "Yes."

"Well, let's think. There's so much to see here. You

should check out some shows. See some old classic casinos. But if you want the hottest spot, then you should go to the Obelisk. It's the most popular place right now."

"Why not? Let's go."

Ten minutes later, they pulled up to the Vegas hotspot. "Here we are, Miss."

Cassie stared wide-eyed at the tall building shaped as an obelisk. All the windows shone with glossy black glass, like something out of a sci-fi world. On both sides of the building, thin square fountains shot colorful water streams high up in the air in a joyful celebration of life. People, dressed to let loose, entered and exited the building in a consistent flow.

"Yeah," Cassie said. "This seems like a good place to start." She thanked the cabbie, paid him and exited the car, merging with the mob of people.

Cassie stood outside for a few minutes watching the water bubble in the fountains. Being here, among these party people, among all the lights...it was surreal. Looking around, she made a mental approval of her choice of clothes, a black leather mini-skirt, silver silk blouse with an open back and black four-inch pumps. The last, a gift from Zoey last Christmas. She'd fit into the crowd.

"Okay, let's do it," she said under her breath. With a surge of confidence, Cassie walked into the Obelisk.

She scanned the throng of partiers noting most were young, an under forty crowd. The place hummed with life. To the right of the entrance, above a sharp arch, the word "Casino" sat in a semi-circle. The slick black lettering glittered in the light of the overhead fixtures. The sign might as well not have been there, the buzzing of the slot machines could not be mistaken, even to a casino virgin.

A scream erupted. Cassie jerked her head around, trying to find the source of the sound. Nobody seemed to be panicking. Her heart fluttered. Then she saw it. A huge tower, almost as tall as the building itself, stood to the far left. Below it an object looked like a wide net and spread across the floor. A young woman bounced up and down in the net, happy squealing having replaced the screams of terror. The red marble letters in front of the tower announced "The Fall". A sign under it reading, "Experience the gravity defying fall of your life".

"You've got to be kidding me," Cassie mumbled.

"You should try it," a man's voice sounded in her ear. "It's quite an experience."

Cassie spun on her heel, a feat not easily accomplished in her shoes, to find a man smiling at her. A twenty-something kid with a boyish grin, he gave her the once over. Short neat brown hair and mega-watt white teeth gave him the appearance of a prep boy out on vacation with his buddies. Dressed in a navy blue button up shirt and gray slacks, he looked ready for a date.

Cassie found herself smiling back.

"Maybe later," she said. Still smiling, she turned her back on him and started walking toward the casino doors. The guy rushed to keep up with her, not dissuaded.

"You here by yourself?" he said as they stepped inside the massive room. He had to raise his voice to be heard above the casino's clamor.

"Not exactly." She lowered her lids, enjoying the flirting, but not wanting to encourage him.

"Well, my name is Dan. Dan Miles," he said and

extended his hand to her. She eyed it, then shook. "If you need company later, search me out. I'll be here awhile with my friends."

Cassie felt a pink flush creep up her cheeks. "Thanks, Dan, I will."

"Are you going to tell me your name?"

"Maybe later," she repeated. Dan raised his hands.

"It's a deal." He waved at her. "See you later then."

At least he knows how to take a hint. Cassie sighed in relief and made her way toward the bar. Dan's attention was flattering, but lack of attention was not the problem. It was just she never put herself out there to get much male notice. "Nah-uh. Not going there. Time to let loose," she reminded herself. Besides, she wasn't naive enough to think she wasn't going to be hit on in a place like this, especially with her outfit. *It's why people come here, to have fun, to let their hair down, to meet people, to flirt.* She eyed a woman whose lack of dress pegged her job description as rhyming with snore.

"Probably much more than flirt," she murmured. But that didn't concern her. She had her hands full with one man right now, sort of.

The bartender, a slim tall redhead encased in a tight black skirt suit, nodded in Cassie's direction. "What's your poison tonight, honey?"

"Let me have a...kamikaze, please." It took her a second to remember the name of the drink she liked when she ventured out on one of the rare club outings with Zoey. She remembered the smooth sensation it made going down and the relaxed feeling she experienced afterwards. Limey drinks were her choice any day, and she intended to have a few tonight. *Maybe even more than a few.* She quirked a brow, counting the liquor bottles behind the counter.

The bartender, whose shiny silver on black nametag read "Carla", nodded and produced the drink within fifteen seconds. "Nice work." She laid out a couple of bucks on the counter and cupped the drink with both hands. A few long swallows had her turning on the stool to engage in a bit of people watching. The bar sat nearest to the table games, and she became fascinated with the excited atmosphere at one of the tables.

"Craps," she said, reading the sign above one table. "A game I just don't understand." She shrugged and watched the players. The energy within the casino was contagious.

The drink began working within minutes. Cassie started to relax, the muscles in her body becoming nice and loose. She gulped the rest of the drink, anxious to hold onto the feeling.

"Another one?" Carla asked with a knowing wink.

"Yes, definitely."

"Same dice. Same dice." She heard a deep voice grow louder over the flood of noise at the craps table. A lone dice rolled down the black and red carpet to land at her feet. She stooped to pick it up.

"Right here, honey," said the dealer at the table and waved a hand in Cassie's direction.

"This what you're looking for?" Cassie asked as she got off the bar stool and came to hand the dice to the dealer.

The man with the booming voice who demanded "the same dice" looked her over with a large lopsided grin. A heavy-set guy, his round face flushed red with the excitement of the game. The big cheeks and bright eyes made it hard to pinpoint his age with any assurance.

"You ever rolled before?" he said, nodding at the dice with an incline of his head.

"No. Never." Through the light daze of the alcohol, Cassie wondered why he asked.

"Let the lady roll." The man addressed the dealer. Then to Cassie he said, "Come here, darling."

"Oh, I don't know..."

"Go on, roll these babies. You're beginner's luck and lady luck rolled into one."

The table exploded in laughter and people started nodding their heads in approval.

Cassie grinned and took the die. "What the heck." She fiddled with the die, rolling them around her palm.

After the dealer got everyone's bets in, she nodded to Cassie to roll. Aiming for the far wall of the table, Cassie threw as hard as she could. The die hit the wood and splattered across the green tarp. The dealer tapped the dice and called the number, "Seven."

"Thatta way," the heavyset man said, patting Cassie's shoulder, then clapping his hands. "Throw again."

She rolled another seven. An approving murmur spread among the players at the table.

Cassie rolled seven, seven, and seven again before she hit a number. Six, eight, four, ten, she hit the numbers over and over. The excitement at the table flared with everyone screaming and encouraging her to keep going. A throng of people gathered around to see what all the happy commotion was about. Through the thrilled crowd, a cool hand reached out to her and landed on her arm. She turned to see Dan with a drink in his hand.

"How's it going?" He winked at her.

"Great," Cassie said. "I'm having so much fun playing."

"So I see." He put the glass down in front of her in the little cup holder under the table. "For you."

Cassie's heart skipped in alarm as she eyed the limey drink. "How did you know to get me a kamikaze?"

"I asked Carla what you were drinking," he said without a moment of hesitation.

Cassie smiled, most of the suspicion flowing out of her with the first sip of the drink.

"Hey, can I ask you for a favor?" Dan leaned in so Cassie could hear him better over the noise. "Can I borrow your cell for a sec? The battery on mine is dead, and I need to let a friend know where I am so he doesn't worry."

"Sure," Cassie said, her concentration back on the craps table. She handed Dan her old flip cell phone.

"Thanks. Be right back. It's too noisy here."

She nodded and took up the die once more. Dan walked away. Somewhere in the back of her mind a little voice told her it was a bad idea to give her cell phone to a stranger. Worse even to accept a drink. But with every sip of the drink and roll of the die, she pushed the voice down deeper.

"The number on the table is six. All bets in." The dealer called to the table and pushed the die toward Cassie.

The blood pumped hard through her veins. She grabbed the die, shook them once in her hand and blew on them for luck like she'd seen players do in movies. The die flew from her grasp and hit a stack of chips. The dealer called the throw, "Seven." People around the table sounded a collective sigh of disappointment.

"You did good, sweetie," said the guy who asked her to

roll the first time. "You'll get another chance when the turn gets back to you."

Cassie nodded at the man in appreciation. Dan appeared back at her side a breath later. He slipped the phone into her hand.

"So do I get to find out your name now, seeing as how we shared a cell phone?" he asked with a quick laugh.

"It's Cassie." She tucked a stray hair behind her ear with one hand. The drink held firm in the other.

"Well, Cassie, want to do something a little more fun?" he whispered into her ear.

By now, three quarters of the drink he brought her were gone and whatever inhibitions remained dissipated.

"Sure, why not," she heard herself saying. The words surprised her. A heavy haze settled in her head. "What do you have in mind?"

They moved away from the table, Dan leading them toward the casino exit.

"I was thinking 'The Fall'." He kept walking forward, guiding her by the hand.

"Yeah. I dunno. Not a good idea," Cassie said but didn't remove her hand from his grip.

"Why not?" He raised his brows at her, but never stopped walking.

Through the heaviness of her drunken state, she tried to think of an answer that made sense, but any good reason for "why not" refused to float into her brain. They walked through the crowd, sounds and laughter mingling in a strange array to Cassie's ear. *I'm drunk? I didn't drink that much.* She wondered to herself with faint amusement. A hiccup bout threatened to unfold.

When they reached "The Fall", there was no line but many curious onlookers stood around to see the next brave soul. Cassie looked up...and up. The top of the tower loomed too high. The net underneath it swayed as if in a light breeze. Heat rose in her cheeks, sticky sweat beading at the back of her neck.

"I can't," she whispered, pulling her hand away from his hold.

"Come on, it's such a rush. You'll love it! Besides, you look like a girl who's not afraid to try something new." He grabbed her hand again and jerked her forward.

"No, you don't understand. I can't!" Panic hooked her in its grip, even through the thick brain fog.

"What if I'm next to you? We'll do it together. Don't you want to do something out of the ordinary, something to push your boundaries?" Dan nudged her forward again.

She didn't protest this time. His words struck too close to home to argue against.

Two employees were talking to each other near the sign announcing "The Fall". One of them, a tall lanky man, locked eyes with Dan. Cassie thought she detected a quick knowing look between the two. *Alcohol never made me paranoid before.* She peered at the Obelisk employee again but his gaze turned distant, bored.

"Welcome to The Fall." His tone was flat and unpleasant. "You will remember this fall for the rest of your life."

Is he repeating a script? She narrowed her eyes, trying to lay a finger on what bothered her about the employee. When she could find nothing amiss, she turned to meet Dan's gaze. He squeezed her hand.

"Come on, let yourself go," he said. The heated look in his eyes no longer matched his prep-boy style. He struck a note within her, the wild abandon of the ride somewhat appealing. She nodded.

In a daze, they entered a small lift, the lanky man behind them. The ride up took close to a minute, but in her haze Cassie lost all sense of time. She tried to pull herself out of the stupor, but after a few tries she gave up, too out of it by now to care.

Once at the top, the man said, "All you have to do is get to the edge of the lift and take a step out whenever you're ready. The net will catch you. It's very safe. Enjoy your fall."

Dan took her hand and moved them to the edge. "Are you ready?"

Mute with terror, but also excitement she could not express, Cassie nodded again.

"Okay, we take the step on three," Dan said. "One…two…three." He didn't let her think about it for another second as he took a step out and pulled her with him.

Cassie's heart went into her throat. She was convinced so did the rest of her organs. Then something changed, she floated weightless. She didn't feel Dan's hand holding hers anymore. In fact, she didn't feel any part of her body. For a heartbeat, she wished Gabe was there with her, soothing her terror.

A rainbow of brilliant colors exploded in front of her eyes. Wind rushed past her face, cooling it. She felt like she was falling forever. Then, within a second, or was it a lifetime, the colors faded to black. She tried resisting but darkness pulled her in and swallowed her up. She stopped struggling.

#

Cassie floated out of the darkness. The first sensation struck without warning, an intense throbbing in her head. "Ugh. That's the last time I drink."

The memories of the fall flooded her mind.

"Oh my God! Oh my God!" She pried her eyes open. At first, all she saw before her was gray fog. She raised a hand to her eyes and rubbed. The fog faded away. She found herself leaning against a soft couch cushion. The room came into focus but she wished with all her soul it hadn't. The next sight was something she did not want to see, ever - a face, so terrifying and familiar; a face resembling her own in so many little ways.

"Hello, Cassie," said a deep mocking voice, sending chills over her skin. "It's time you met your daddy, don't you think?"

SEVENTEEN

The cryptic voice boomed in Gabe's ear. "We have the girl. The Obelisk. D entrance. Ten minutes. Come alone or the Key dies."

Gabe tensed, ready to bolt out the door, but a moment of clarity kept his feet on the floor. He spoke into the phone, "How do I know you're telling the truth?"

"Check the number I'm calling from," said the stranger without a pause.

Gabe turned over the phone in his hand. Cassie's cell number glowed. "Damn," he cursed, and placed it back to his ear.

"No games, fallen. The girl's running out of time." Click.

Three taunting beeps signaled the end of the call and ushered him into action. Going for the quickest exit, he reached the low ledge and hoisted himself through the open second story window. He hit the ground with a thud before rolling forward and springing to his feet. With a speed imperceptible to the naked eye, he ran through the winding streets and down the Vegas strip. He reached the Obelisk within five minutes.

The ominous building loomed over him. He stalked the perimeter of the monstrous hotel and casino. Each exit point, every security flaw, all the miniscule details that could be considered weaknesses and aid in a potential escape were committed to memory. Overhanging balconies, lazy security guards, ventilation systems and garbage shoots, nothing escaped his expert eye. Satisfied with his assessment, he headed for the designated entrance with one minute to spare.

Passing several garage gates, Gabe found two massive steel metal doors branded with an unmistakable crimson colored "D". As he approached, the right door creaked open a foot or so, and a sickly looking man slid out. He appeared to be human with gray drooping eyes, brown matted hair, and an odd yellowish complexion. The black slacks and red-collared shirt he wore made his strange skin stand out even more. A plastic nametag read, "Ted."

"Excuse me," Ted said after a coughing fit. "Welcome. Good of you not to keep the Master waiting."

Gabe stood a moment analyzing Ted. *Definitely human. No power coming from him at all. Weak even for a human. Something's off.* When the silence lingered, he said, "Can't say I'm happy to oblige your Master."

"No, don't imagine you would be," Ted said sympathetically while pushing the door wider and ushering Gabe inside. "Follow me."

The entryway opened into a cavernous loading dock. The garage gates Gabe passed earlier led into the space as well. Each was marked by a number. Parallel yellow lines signified three eighteen-wheelers could fit into the space, each one lined up next to the other. Around the outer walls innumerable sealed boxes, two story ladders, mammoth waste bins, and suspicious electrical wiring blanketed the area.

With shaking legs, Ted climbed a set of narrow stairs toward the back of the dock, leading to an unmarked door. Gabe peered at the staircase, but pushed aside his reservations for Cassie's sake. *Just do what they want until you see she's okay. There's no way to know if she's alive until then.* Decision made, he followed Ted up the stairs and through the inner door. It was two narrow hallways, another flight of steps, and an elevator ride to an undesignated floor before Ted spoke again.

"You're to go inside alone." Ted pointed to the sole door on this level. It was a simple green metal door with no handle on the outside. "I wish you luck. I don't expect I'll see you again."

"Thanks," Gabe muttered as the elevator doors closed and Ted disappeared.

A heartbeat later, there was a click as the door opened and another man said from inside, "Come in. Come in."

The voice was familiar. Gabe recognized it from the phone call. He seethed and gritted his teeth as he stepped into the room. "Where is she?" he said struggling to keep his cool.

The stranger sat in an iron chair placed in the center of the room upon a low wooden platform. A hanging overhead bulb, the lone light source, highlighted the man's short brown hair. His gray slacks and navy blue shirt crinkled in a checkered pattern like the indentations of a net. Ignoring Gabe's question, the man rose and walked to the southernmost corner. A communication system, built into the solid cement wall, blinked red.

"Tell the Boss, he's arrived," the stranger said, holding a button. A voice broke through the crackling unit from the other side, but Gabe couldn't understand it. "Yes. Tell him Dan will take care of it." Another transmission echoed its static. "Blood. No kills. Got it."

Dan let go of the button and waved a hand at the chair. "Have a seat, fallen. We're going to have some fun."

"Where is Cassie?" Gabe remained in place.

"Now, now. That's hardly the way to behave when you're someone's guest. You'll see your little puppet soon enough." Dan trailed across the room and stood mere inches in front of Gabe. Inclining his head, he whispered, "But if you don't want to behave it's fine with me. I'd enjoy torturing her much more than you."

Gabe's eyes narrowed as he thrust a hand over Dan's neck. "You're not a demon. You're not even impressive for a human. Why don't I just kill you now?"

Instead of attempting to fight, Dan flicked a switch from a device inside his pocket. The door slammed shut and a TV monitor flicked on behind the pair. Gabe swung around, lifting Dan off the ground. The monitor showed Cassie in the middle of a room with four white walls. She laid face up, eyes closed, looking as if asleep or dead. Gabe dropped Dan to the floor.

Dan coughed before saying in a scratchy voice, "That'll cost you I'm afraid. But, in fairness I did warn you. You wouldn't have gotten as much warning from a demon." He rose to his feet. "But then, no demon could make you suffer as much as I will." He smiled a wide toothy grin showing off his perfect white teeth, the picture of the all-American boy. "Now, will you have a seat or should I go see her instead?"

Gabe walked toward the iron chair without further protest. A thin metal frame with nothing but space in the middle provided no relief for a person's back, and the rough solid seat ensured maximum discomfort. As he sat, thick metal restraints bound his ankles and wrists to the chair's unyielding legs and arms. The binds fixed into the chair in such a way they could turn without giving an inch of release to the occupant. They began to circle around Gabe's limbs peeling the flesh right off with each pass.

The pain ignited every nerve in his body, but Gabe knew it was only the beginning of the brutal torment. He wasn't about to let Dan have any satisfaction even if he chewed his cheek to pieces or grinded his teeth to the gums to hide the agony. He stared ahead, using the dim light to count the cracks in the far wall as a distraction.

"Aren't you a strong one," Dan said grazing a finger along Gabe's cheek. "But, you should feel free to scream as much as you like." He walked under the light and tapped on the nearest wall. "See? Concrete, over eighteen inches thick. No one to interrupt us." Turning away, he disappeared out of Gabe's view to return with a rolled up package. He placed it on the floor in front of the chair and opened it to reveal a set of tools like surgical instruments of some medieval era. "Oh, but this will be fun. I don't often get to play with a fallen. It's a real treat." His eyes sparked with madness.

Dan stroked an object as if petting an animal's fur. The thing resembled a sickle on a 1/12th scale. He held it up to the light running the thumb and forefinger of his right hand down its length. After a few seconds, he flipped it horizontal, closed one eye and examined it. He nodded at the tool, then grabbed a pair of sharp scissors in his left hand. With a weapon in each hand, he grinned at Gabe before disappearing out of sight once more.

The sound of fabric ripping was the only indication of Dan's actions for the next few minutes. The time ticked by in aching degrees before Gabe's coat and shirt were split into two neat halves. "One. Two. Three," Dan taunted as he tore the clothes from Gabe's body. Naked from the waist up, Gabe braced himself for whatever was to come next.

"Wonderful," Dan said with a squeal of delight. "This is why I enjoy my work so much when it comes to dealing with fallen." He leaned forward speaking into Gabe's ear. "The burn marks from their lost little wings are such a perfect trail to follow." With his last word, he plunged the sickle into Gabe's right shoulder blade.

Pain erupted like wildfire sending sharp flares down Gabe's arm and back. He struggled to keep from screaming. As he shot his tongue sideways and bit on his cheek firmly, he grazed the two latent GPS devices. At the same instant, Dan began to drag the sickle with infinite slowness down Gabe's back, tearing the scar open. It took an incredible strength of will not to flick the GPS devices into alertness. *Not now. Can't.* The words spilled through Gabe's mind. *Have to...Cassie...First.*

Gabe broke out in a sweat as Dan pulled the sickle

from his lower back and plunged it into his left shoulder
blade. The same excruciating dissection continued down
his second scar. The pain rose to agonizing heights as it
erupted across his entire back. *Son of a bitch.* Gabe closed his
eyes and bit on his lip hard enough to draw blood. It
trickled into his mouth, sliding under his tongue. He
swallowed the metallic taste, focusing his gaze on the wall,
and following the cracks as if they were trails to freedom.
Don't scream, damn it. When the sickle at last ended its
torments at his lower back once more, Dan twisted it and
tore it free from Gabe's body taking a chunk of flesh with
it.

"Beautiful, no?" Dan circled into view holding the
piece of bloody flesh in his hand. He dangled it in front of
Gabe's eyes as if it were a bone to a dog. "I'd ask you to
fetch, but that'd just be cruel." He laughed, the low sadistic
sound echoing through the small room. "And do you know
why else I love playing with the fallen?" He stopped as if
waiting for an actual response, and when none followed,
continued, "No? Well, let me tell you. Because they heal so
fast. And then I can do it all over again. And again… Isn't
it wonderful?" The last words were almost a rough whisper.

Placing the flesh aside, Dan knelt and examined his
tools once more. With a feather light touch, he graced the
tip of a razor, and then skimmed the edge of a saw. As his
eyes flitted between the two instruments, a loud chirping
sound distracted his musings.

"What now?" he muttered. Dragging his gaze away
from the weapons, Dan peered at the communication
system with narrowed eyes and flaring nostrils. The
continuing barrage of chirps caused his brow to furrow. He

rose, crossed the room, and pressed the unit to speaker mode. "Why are you interrupting my work?"

"Your master wants to know if you've gotten any information from him yet," said an oddly familiar voice from the other side. Gabe struggled to keep conscious and coherent through the pain. With as much focus as he could manage, he tried to match the voice with a name.

"I was getting around to it," Dan said crossing his arms.

"You didn't even ask him anything yet, did you?" accused the voice. A moment of awkward silence followed. "I'm coming up. You're done."

"This is *my* interrogation! I'll conduct it how--" A buzzing from the other side cut off Dan's protest. "Old fallen bastard! Thinks he knows everything. Just because he had some information from a ridiculous book, all of a sudden he's the Boss' favorite." Dan kicked the wall below the communication system. "Asshole!"

A slow dawning crossed Gabe's mind and he thrashed against the restraints. In his weakened physical state, however, the bindings refused to budge. His rage increased as the metal straps tore deeper into his wrists.

"Whoa," Dan said. "What's got you all hot and bothered? Found out one of your buddies is playing you for a fool, huh?" He laughed while walking behind the iron chair once more. "If it makes you feel better, I don't like him either." He patted Gabe on the head, then walked back around to collect his tools. As he wrapped them up, a knocking reverberated throughout the room.

"Open the door, damn it. I don't have time for games," the voice demanded from outside.

"Guess we'll have to continue this later." Dan smiled bright as he placed his hand in his pocket and flicked a switch. The door swung open to allow the stranger entrance. Gabe's heart kicked into high gear as he watched the fallen, whom he'd thought was a friend, enter the room.

"Your services are no longer required, Dan. You can go," Albert said low. He stepped aside to allow him space to leave.

Dan muttered something incomprehensible before slamming the door as he left. The silence followed like a blanket of despair. As the two fallen remained alone in the room, tension permeated the space thicker than oil. Gabe stared at the old fallen with blinding fury. Albert simply looked back, pity in his eyes. Neither dared speak for several moments.

"I can't imagine what you must think," Albert said. "Nor the pain you suffer."

"No." Gabe growled. "You can't. But, I'd be happy to show you." He pulled once more against the restraints causing blood to seep through the bindings.

"Please," Albert said, alarm raising his voice an octave. "You'll only cause yourself further injury." He placed a hand on Gabe's shoulder and pushed him back with delicate care. "If you want to help your charge, you'll listen to me instead of fighting."

"Take your hand off me, now."

Albert snatched his hand away and stepped back. In a firmer tone he said, "I know you're angry, but do you want to help Cassie or not?"

"If she's suffered anything because of you…" His voice deepened, a dry desert. The rage threatened to consume him.

"If you calm down, I can explain." When Gabe made no motion to relax, Albert continued, "Will it help you to know Cassie is safe?" He clicked on the TV screen behind him and switched it to an unnumbered channel.

Gabe looked at the monitor. He watched as Cassie, alive and well, stood on a balcony observing the casino games. Her smiling face eased his anger enough to at least take the edge off. He sat back in the iron chair and relaxed. With more control, he turned his attention back to Albert.

"When Rafe told me you'd mouthed off to every fallen and demon in Vegas about the Sacred Key, I assumed it was because of your curious nature. That you couldn't help yourself." He stretched his arms to alleviate some of the pressure on his wrists. "I never dreamed it was because you were a traitorous bastard!"

Albert knelt down so he was eye level with Gabe. "I deserve your wrath." His eyes filled with unmistakable sadness, the unshed tears brimming just below the surface. "But, let me at least explain."

Gabe stared back daggers but gave no refusal.

"You may not like what I have to say, young one, but here it is. I've lived on this Earth for over two thousand years. You don't yet understand what that means as you've only been here a few weeks." He lowered his head. "But, I've come to love this place, to see it as my home. I don't want it changed."

"It's not up to you to decide," Gabe shouted. "Who the hell do you think you are?" He shifted in the chair. Pain sliced up his arms. He fought to control his ire. "Change is coming. You said it yourself. 'We all knew this day would come.' It's what you told me and what's been written."

"Yes, we all knew it would come. But, we don't all agree on the outcome." Albert rose and began to pace. "I went to the angels first, of course. I tried to talk some sense into the council. Make them see the world didn't have to change. Do you know what they said?"

Gabe had an idea as he recalled his own conversation with the Light's angelic council, but said nothing.

"They want your charge dead. Can you imagine it?" His pacing increased, his hands folding and unfolding in front of him as he walked. "I've never killed one of this Earth before and I'm not going to start now."

"So, demons are the next logical choice? You don't get the answers you want, so you seek Darkness instead?"

"No!" Albert's pacing stopped at once. He fell to his knees again, his palms flat against the hard floor. "I went to our fellow fallen, to Rafe. I told him about the Sacred Key. But, he had no better solutions than me. What was I to do?" Balling his hands into fists, he banged them on the floor like a child.

"You're supposed to be a guide, a beacon for all those who fall. Look at you now, pathetic." Gabe's anger mixed with pity as he watched the older fallen's display. "You've been here for two millennia and have learned nothing, yet you have the nerve to call me 'young one'."

"The answers are never easy." Albert looked up, a harsh light shining through his gaze. "Killing the Key wasn't an option. And if the Light comes, the Earth will be unrecognizable. I will have no place in it." His eyes turned to a softer glow. "I had limited options. The demons seemed the sole choice left. They're already here. They mix with humans every day, more and more of them. I thought they would keep things the same. Preserve the status quo if they bonded with your charge. I was a blind desperate fool." He caught Gabe's gaze once more. "All this time I always believed curiosity led to my banishment from the Light. I see the truth now in your eyes, my young friend. All of my convictions are nothing without the courage to back them up. This lack of courage has led us here." He stretched a hand forward. "I will make amends."

"You want to make up for your insane decisions, for your cowardice, then get me out of this chair and take me to Cassie."

"I'm sorry, young...Gabe. But, if I do, you'll be spotted. Since I also can't allow you to hurt yourself anymore..." Without warning, he sprung from where he knelt, and clapped Gabe on the side of the head. Gabe's chin fell onto his chest as his head rolled. His eyes widened for a split second.

In the last instance of coherency he heard Albert say, "Rest now. Regain your strength. You'll need it soon." Then he watched as Albert left, shutting the door behind him.

EIGHTEEN

"Who...? How...? What the...?" Cassie struggled to vocalize even one of the myriad of questions swimming through her mind. *How did I get here? Who is he?* Her eyes darted around the room taking in her surroundings. She lay on a white sofa in the middle of a room with four white walls. No windows, no doors could be spotted anywhere. With panic threatening to take hold, she focused back on the man in front of her. *Why does he look like me? Why is he calling himself "daddy"? It can't be.* She sat up and settled on, "What the hell's going on?"

"Easy, child," the stranger said. He stood over her, a tall and imposing figure from her seated position. A dark wool suit made his fair skin appear like polished ivory, while serving to cover his massive frame. The long roguish dark hair matched his black bottomless eyes. His size might make him the envy of any athlete, but his striking features would win him the heart of any nosferatu fanatic. He knelt, grazing a hand over Cassie's knee. In a mocking tone he added, "Daddy would never hurt you."

"You want to explain yourself or do you want to keep up the ridiculous sarcasm?" Anger won out over fear and she opted for a strong offense. She stood up, pointing her chin in the air. "You're not 'daddy' and even if you were I sure as shit wouldn't call you that. So, start talking or I start making things messy." She squeezed her hands into fists for evidence, and prayed her bluff would work.

A low laugh filled the room. "I had a feeling I'd like you." He narrowed his eyes, letting his gaze linger on her face. "Yes, we'll get along just fine."

The stare brought her chin down and she fought the urge to shuffle her feet. Fighting back the dread, she met his intense look with one of her own.

His eyes softened. "Well now, let me explain." Waving a hand at the couch, he made a motion for her to sit. She remained standing. He didn't push the issue further, and continued as if the suggestion had not been made. "I've brought you here because there are some things you need to be made aware of. You already know I'm your father. You dreamed about me, did you not?" Cassie started to speak, but a hand prohibited the action. "You're about to utter denials, but think first. A part of you has always known the truth. It would save us time if you acknowledge this. Do you want to know more or not?"

Cassie closed her eyes as the hand moved away from her mouth. She tried to let her instincts guide her, but curiosity bubbled inside. "I'll admit you're somewhat familiar, but I'm not about to accept anything at face value." She crossed her arms. "So, you want to talk, I'll listen. But, you give me a name to call you, a real name, and let me out of this room. Then, you can talk yourself red in the face."

"Brave." He grinned, a warped set to his lips. "Very brave. Your terms are fair enough and I have nothing to hide from you." He looked toward the ceiling in the right hand corner of the room. "Open," he said to the empty space. From the middle of the closest wall, a hidden door materialized and slid open. With a flourish of his hand, he said, "After you my dear."

Cassie tried to make her strides calm and even, despite having the desire to bolt through the door. Since having awoken in the white room, she'd wished like hell she'd just listened to Gabe. The thought of him caused her heart to do a small somersault even now. Yet, pangs of guilt swept through her as she imagined him returning to the motel room to find it empty, her one lined note the only clue of her fate. *If I can just get to a phone or pretend to have to use the bathroom, I'd have a chance.* Her musings of escape didn't last long because the man's next words were not what she expected.

"Your mother had similar eyes, you know." The statement was uttered in a soothing manner as he walked a step behind her. "She'd been here for some time when we met, so they'd turned from gold to hazel."

The comment caught her off guard and she stopped just outside the room. All plans to run halted as well. "My mother?" she whispered as she turned to face him once more.

"Yes, your mother. She was an amazing woman. Quite a lot like you actually. Beautiful, courageous, cunning. I fell in love with her," he said, passion breaking past the surface.

"It took some time to win her over, but eventually she fell for me too."

Cassie allowed herself a moment of absolute stillness. Logic and reason fought against a deep yearning to know more, a yearning she'd felt for years. Unresolved, she stalled. "You haven't told me your name."

"Valefar," he said smiling. "But, just call me Val." He held out his bent arm to her.

"Val," she said as she took his arm. "You're a demon. I have no reason to trust you."

"Ironically, child, your mother said the same thing."

#

Cassie sat on a plush antique chair. The detailed woodwork featured hand-carved floral leaves. The gold trim around the edgings of the arms and legs complimented the burgundy seat cushion. Val sat across from her in a chair of similar design. Stonewalls of deep reds and burnt oranges gave the room a warm feel. A paned glass window at least five feet high and equally wide allowed light to filter through the room in shades of blue and green. Upon the far wall, a high sleek desk with carvings as intricate as the chairs laid pushed aside. Val had wanted to make the space more compatible for intimate conversation, or so he'd claimed.

Time had passed without measure. It could have been hours or days; it was impossible to tell. Val had a way of entrancing a person with his voice alone. After listening to him speak about nothing more than the mundane, Cassie realized why her mother, a fallen angel, would risk all to be with this demon. He was without question, charming. But,

Cassie had been hurt enough times and endured as many hardships to be cautious, naivety having long been cast aside.

"You've told me a lot about my mother, and I don't want to seem ungrateful," she said, choosing her words. "But, you haven't said a word about why you really brought me here. I know what you want."

"Spirit. It's what makes you so unique. You have such a spirit. I wish your mother had half of it, maybe then I wouldn't have lost you for so long." He breathed deep before continuing, "When you were born, she feared those of the Light would try to take you or kill you. Keys aren't supposed to exist. To protect you, she gave you up. She wouldn't even tell me where she sent you, fearing I'd go and claim you right away. She was right. I didn't want to lose my daughter." He brushed Cassie's cheek with the back of his hand. "Then, she disappeared. She left a note saying she was going to seek redemption for all of her wrongdoings, but she'd always love me...even if it was wrong."

Cassie tried to keep her emotions in check. *This same man killed your parents. The dream was clear. Don't forget it.* She took a breath. *He's trying to use you. A good actor. That's all.* She chided herself, even though a part of her so wanted to believe him, to believe he cared for her. Because, after all, demon or not, he was her biological father. A part of him was in her.

"I spent years trying to find you. By your seventh birthday, I had finally tracked you down. I thought you'd be ascending into your powers. I didn't want you to go through it alone."

Squirming further back in the chair and struggling not to leap from it, she screamed, "Enough tricks, damn it. You want those powers for yourself. You killed my parents just to try to get them. To get me."

All of Val's sweet pretenses eroded for a heartbeat while he stared at her as if he could bore a hole into her mind. For that single second, Cassie could distinguish his true face. The sudden anger disappeared, however, replaced by his bewitching charm. As if speaking to a cornered animal, he continued, "I wanted my daughter to stand beside me. But, I didn't kill your adopted parents. By the time I arrived on that highway, you were already going through an episode, your headache. The car started to spin out of control. I had only seconds to get you out in time. I couldn't save them. I'm sorry." He paused with, what to Cassie's ears sounded as, a dramatic sigh. "When I realized you weren't going to ascend then, I left. Your mother's wishes echoed in my head. All she wanted for you was a normal childhood, free from those who could harm you. If I took you with me then, you never would have had it. Leaving you there as the sirens blared was the hardest thing I've ever had to do." He leaned in closer and placed a hand on her chair's armrest. "But, it was the right thing. Every now and again even demons can do the right thing, my child."

"Demons are pure evil." The fight began to fade from her, replaced by tears instead. A lifetime of doubts and uncertainty battled her desire for familial love. Losing her parents had been the most painful experience of her life. She couldn't ignore how his words touched a deep nerve, even if they sounded put on.

Val shook his head.

"Nothing is pure, Cassie. There is no black and white. There's always shades of grey, remember. We may be born from Darkness, but we're not evil." He raised his hand and wiped away a single fallen tear from her face. "Come with me. I'll prove it to you." He rose and stretched out his hand to her.

Cassie sat frozen in place. She stared at his open palm trying to make sense of everything, anything. A laundry list of emotions tumbled through her. She couldn't decide what was right to feel. She knew one thing for sure--she didn't trust Val. His emotional depth carried only as far as his over-acting in her estimation. She could spot a con artist. Yet, despite it all, in a few short hours, he'd managed to twist up a lifetime of beliefs. *What do I do now?*

"You've come this far, child. Your choices are your own, but let me at least show you what I am." He continued holding his hand out to her.

A strange thought came unbidden into her head, as Cassie remained seated. *If you're going to dance with the Devil, might as well have fancy shoes.* It was something Zoey told her when she'd given her the stilettos for Christmas. Looking down at her feet, where the stilettos now resided, she couldn't help but laugh. Her life had been twisted upside down and inside out, no point in stopping the ride now. With resolve she didn't feel, she managed to choke out, "Okay, Val. Let's dance."

"That's my girl." He took her hand and led her toward the door. They exited the office and headed toward a private elevator. Val pressed a ten-digit sequence into the keypad, then announced "Casino mezzanine" into the speaker. The elevator ascended, then the doors opened onto a private balcony overlooking the whole casino floor.

Cassie stepped onto the balcony on shaky legs. The erratic thump of her heart beat loud against her ribs. She could hear the uncertainty in its rhythm and gripped the ledge of the guardrail to stare at the casino floor below.

"Beautiful isn't it?" Val remarked as he leaned over the railing beside her. The sparkling orange and yellow glows of a thousand plus slot machines illuminated the room. Chimes and bells of every frequency played the gambler's lullaby. In all directions people mulled about enjoying the sights and sounds. The lone exception was a sad looking worker who swept the tiled floor below them with a decrepitated push broom.

"It's all fun for guests, but what about workers?" Cassie's heart tugged as she observed the man below. His matted brown hair stuck to the sides of his drawn face. His skin sagged in odd spots and possessed a sickly complexion. The red-collared shirt only made the yellowish hue more pronounced. His sorrowful gray eyes followed the motions of the broom without interest. Cassie pointed in his direction. "Doesn't look like he's enjoying the party."

"I'm glad you noticed him," Val said smoothly. "Most people wouldn't. That is Ted, a human employee. He's been here six months, out of the eight his doctors say he'll live."

"You mean he's dying?" Cassie bit her lip as she faced Val once more. "That's terrible. Why would he spend the time working, then?"

"To show his loyalty and plead for mercy." Val's eyes possessed a strange glint as he stared at Ted.

"Why would a dying man need mercy? And who from?"

"I wanted to show you what I truly am. So, allow me to demonstrate." With sudden swiftness, he turned toward Cassie and placed a hand on each of her shoulders.

An overwhelming sensation shot through her. She grabbed her head, squeezed her eyes shut, and crashed into the demon in front of her. She clawed at him, battling against his grip. It couldn't be described as pain, but it was far more intense than any of her previous headaches. She wandered through it trying to reach for an ending.

"Relax, child. Allow me to use your power and you will not feel pain. Don't fight me." Val cooed in her ear as he held her upright. "It will show you the truth and help a dying man."

Everything inside her screamed to fight, but the horrible feeling of being pulled apart had her giving in. "All right, just stop this."

"You can stop it. Just breathe. Open your eyes and keep them fixed on Ted."

Cassie's eyes shot open as Val spun her toward the ledge. The casino floor, the people, the sick man sweeping came back into focus. The nauseating feeling began to fade as well. When the last signs of the power slipped away, she saw it. A shadow moving across the floor toward a defenseless Ted. She wanted to warn him, but a large hand motioned for silence.

"No child, watch." As Val spoke, the shadow took shape in front of Ted. It seemed to say something, but from this height, Cassie couldn't make out the words. A radiant smile that looked out of place on Ted's sickly features brightened his face. He nodded with fervor and turned in their direction. Although the sound was blocked out from the noise below, Cassie could see him mouth the words "Thank you." As he did, the shadow passed into his body. The seconds ticked by as Ted took on a different form. His matted brown hair became rich and dark with soft curls framing his face. The once yellow skin turned a deep golden color. His eyes shaped into the same bottomless black possessed by all demons. "You see my dear, demons can give life."

The shock of what had happened turned Cassie mute even as Val released his hold. She stood transfixed, her gaze unable to move from the spot now inhabited by a demon version of Ted.

"What have you done?" She managed to mutter.

"An act of great kindness. Demons cannot possess humans without their consent." Val swept a hand at the scene below. "What you have just witnessed, and contributed to with your power, is the birth of a new demon onto the Earth. The human will exist inside this new body as a silent observer."

The sudden coldness in his voice as he uttered this last pronouncement shook Cassie from her initial astonishment. "You mean he'll sit back and watch with no control? You used him? You use people? Promising them health and eternal life in exchange for what? Slavery?"

Val raised a brow at her outburst. "Everyone has a choice, child. Free will and all," he said. "When humans suffer, when their lives have become lost to nothing but pain, they *choose* what I, and all of my kind, offer." He extended a hand in Ted's direction below. "He gets to live.

Demon possession is a merciful gift." After a pause, he added, "In time, I hope you will see."

Without another word, he returned to the elevator and punched in a different ten-digit code. The doors opened and he stepped inside. Cassie made a motion to follow but he held out a hand. "Please stay here. I have to attend to our new friend and some other business." He motioned to the balcony. "Take time to consider your options and enjoy the view. I won't be long."

Cassie watched as the doors closed, before turning around to take in the sights of the casino. Her gaze drifted back to Ted and she couldn't help the little smile that slid into place. *He seems happy and so much healthier now,* she thought as she stared at the demon below. Her smile faded. "But, then he's not himself anymore." The simple statement had her mind reeling over the events of the last few hours. *Angels and demons exist. Who knows which side is good anymore?* She sighed, shaking her head. "If there is even such a thing as *good*. What if Val is right? There's no black and white." She struggled to focus on something, anything to get her mind off it all.

As Cassie scanned the crowd below, she spotted a man dressed in black. His dark hair and fair skin reminded her of someone.

"Gabe," she said aloud. The stranger turned at the same moment and disappointment flooded her. "I wish you were here." She tried to imagine his strong hands holding her, his breath as he whispered comforting words in her ear. But, fantasy did little to help her current reality. She sat on the floor as hopelessness began to consume her. The day was fast approaching when she'd have to come to terms with all of it, the day when she'd have to make a choice that would change the future. As she leaned her head against the cool marble wall and closed her eyes, she was thankful today was not that day.

NINETEEN

The elevator cables sprang to life with sharp grinding gears. Cassie rose at the noise and dusted herself off, preparing to face Val again. As the doors opened, she jerked back in surprise. Onto the balcony stepped none other than Albert Einstein. The frizzy gray hair with brown streaks stuck out in all directions. A large bushy moustache, round nose and oval mouth assured there was no mistaking the scientist. Yet, the eyes, something about the eyes didn't seem right.

"I've lost my mind. It's the only explanation." Cassie announced to the man she was convinced to be a figment of her imagination. "A straight ride to crazy town."

"Not quite, my dear. I'm Albert, but not the one you're thinking," he said smiling and extending a hand. "I'm a fallen, like your friend Gabe, and I appreciate the physical form of interesting humans."

Cassie stared at the hand he offered before giving it a shake. "Sorry," she muttered. "It's been a long day." She paused trying to get her thoughts in order. "You said, you're a fallen?"

"Yes. And I know you've been through a great deal, but we don't have much time. Please come with me." He walked back into the elevator as he spoke.

The casino commotion below seemed to grow still as she hesitated on the balcony. She looked from the ledge to the open doors. Val had asked her to wait to think things over. Yet, it hadn't escaped her attention that placing her on this balcony, with nothing but a password operated elevator as exit, left her trapped. She tapped her foot trying to decide her next move.

"You want to trust Val because he's your biological father. You share history, blood, DNA," Albert said, casting his eyes to the floor. "He will tell you what you want to hear." After a brief pause, he raised his gaze to meet her own. "But, he is a demon and thus a liar. He is using you. He used me too."

The words penetrated her psyche one at a time, echoing the red flag in her heart. She could sense Val's deceptive nature, the phoniness in his charms, but what he'd said had seemed so real. *Maybe I just want it to be real.* Her eyes flicked back and forth between the balcony ledge and the elevator door.

"I can show you the truth, Cassie, but we must hurry." He waved a hand for her to follow. When she remained still he shouted, "If you don't come with me now, Gabe will die."

The last warning got her moving. She jumped in the elevator almost breaking her ankle in the stilettos. Her hands hitting the far wall alone saved her from falling.

"What are you talking about?"

"Val is the strongest and most influential demon in Vegas, but he wants, nay, needs your power." Albert punched in a long numerical sequence. The doors swooped together and the elevator descended. "He has Gabe tortured even as we speak for more information about you. If we don't help, Gabe will be killed."

"Why? I don't understand?" She closed her eyes trying to block out images Albert's words conjured. A cold dread crept up her spine.

"With Gabe out of the way, you'd have no further doubts. You'd come to the side of Darkness without question." He sighed, a large hand smoothing down his flyaway hairs. The strands sprang up again. "It is my fault, Cassie. I gave your father the prophecy."

"Please. I don't know what you mean." She leaned against the wall, nausea rising as the elevator increased its quick descent.

"He sent that psychopath Dan, the sick human to kill poor Maribel and ransack my home." Albert looked toward the ceiling, agony written across his face. "Didn't trust me, he said. Needed to be sure I wouldn't betray him, he said. Well screw him. I've already made a mess of things, but now I'm going to fix it."

Cassie's eyes widened as she watched Albert's hand slam into the emergency button. A high-pitched buzzing rang out as the elevator stopped between floors. His hefty fist broke through the outer wall and into the electrical wiring beneath. A slight jolt passed through his body before the noise ceased.

"What're you doing?" Cassie struggled to keep her

voice from shaking.

"I'm sorry to frighten you, but there are very few places in this horrible demon pit where we may speak in private." He patted a spot on the floor after crossing his legs and seating himself on the cool tile. "Please sit down a minute. If we're to help Gabe, you must have no doubts of the truth."

Cassie stared at the point on the floor he indicated. She glanced toward the closed doors, the broken electrical panel, and the floor once again. Taking a deep breath, she sat down.

"Okay. You have my attention. What is it you want?"

"I desire to help you see through falsehoods," Albert whispered. "When you see the past honest and free, it will help you decide the future."

"What're you talking about? If Gabe's in trouble we should find him now."

"I'm afraid Gabe will have to wait a bit longer. How long will be determined by you. The sooner we can do this, the sooner we can get to him." Albert extended his right hand toward her and placed it on her shoulder. "Don't fight me, Cassie, and the memories will come to you."

"What memories? Whose?" Her heart began to beat faster.

"Yours. His. Hers. All that has been hidden from you." Just as the first, he brought his left hand to her other shoulder. "When I agreed to side with demons, I lost much of my power and the last connection I had to the Light. However, before the connection was severed I managed to learn a great deal about Val's past with your mother and your place in all of it." He leaned in close so their foreheads almost touched. "This is my remaining power. I use it now to bring those events from darkness into light."

Without warning, a gigantic wave swept Cassie away. It crashed over her head and sucked her down into icy waters. She fought against the tide while trying to hold her breath. From somewhere far away she heard a voice whisper, "Don't fight it. Let it take you." As the last bit of air left her lungs, she ignored the message and pushed harder upward. "Sink into the past. Gabe's life depends on it." The mention of Gabe's name focused her attention, pushing aside her initial panic. Steeling her nerve, she clamped her eyes shut and tensed her muscles. Then, with a brief hesitation, she let go, relaxing and allowing herself to sink into the darkness.

When Cassie opened her eyes once more, the scenery had changed. The wave that had sucked her away was gone, replaced by a cocoon of absolute nothingness. Yet the nothingness had shape and form. It surrounded her and embraced her like a warm blanket. Inside this strange space, she could look out onto the world as a spectator. It was as if the nothingness was her small couch at home and the scene before her a movie on her TV. She watched from her safe distance as the view came into focus.

A man and woman bathed in shadow stood on a rooftop staring at the moon. The wind blew around them, a light breeze caressing their skin. The man turned to gaze at the woman and his face came into view. His fair complexion, brought a snarl from Cassie, but he didn't notice her. He spoke in a low seductive tone to the woman.

"I knew you'd like it here. No rules to be bound by. No duties to uphold. Just sweet freedom," Val said to the woman dressed in an elegant black satin gown. A cascade of tiny crystals ran down the low V shaped back elongating her petite frame. Her face was still hidden from Cassie's view, but the fiery red and gold hues of the woman's stunning hair shone through the darkness.

"Yes. I'm only sorry it's taken me this long to come to you." The woman's tone spoke of sadness and longing. "I should have trusted you from the moment I arrived. I let my bias over you being a demon cloud my emotions. But, not anymore."

The woman pulled Val into a passionate kiss that left Cassie feeling like a voyeur as she looked on. Before the embrace became too graphic however, the scene blurred and reemerged. Val and the woman appeared again, but this time they stood on the corner of some city block. A yellow glow illuminated the woman's face as the streetlight reflected off the wet pavement. Anger swirled with anxiety shone in hazel eyes flecked with gold. A wrinkle appeared across her brow. She glanced down at her midsection as arms as fair as porcelain encircled the bulge in her belly in a protective manner.

"Is this what you want for our child?" The woman shouted at Val. "Death. Always to be surrounded by death. You killed that poor human for no reason at all."

"I've had enough of your arguments. I won't tolerate this insolent behavior." Val grabbed the woman's arm and ripped her from the streetlight's glow causing the image to change again.

When the scene surfaced once more, only the woman appeared. The sun sat low in the sky indicating evening was on its way. The woman wore a midnight blue windbreaker with a hood covering her magnificent hair. Wrapped in a light yellow blanket, a baby lay cradled in her arms. The pair sat under a tree, the woman holding the little bundle close to her chest and sobbing.

"Don't be afraid, my sweet Cassiel. These people will treat you like their own daughter. You can be a normal human girl." The woman kissed the top of the baby's head. "I'll find redemption. I promise. Once I am of the Light again, I'll be able to protect you. No one will ever hurt you."

Tears clouded Cassie's vision as she watched the woman wish the baby goodbye. The pain cut her exposing a nerve long buried, but she didn't have time to wipe the water from her eyes before the scene disappeared to be replaced by another.

The sun blazed down strong and hot. It lit the pavement like glowing candles. An all too familiar highway looped around a mountainside. A rumbling car approached the bend.

"How many times do I have to see this?" Cassie cried inside the nothingness.

"The day has arrived, child. Your birthright. My power." Val trod on the road as if his feet didn't touch the ground. "So long I've waited. So long I've watched you from the shadows. You will bring me ultimate power."

The boxy blue Oldsmobile Cutlass Supreme rode into view. Val took a heavy step forward extending a hand toward the vehicle. A powerful energy broke from his palm and crashed head first into the car's front grill. It caused the car to spin out of control and land unmercifully into the mountainside. At the exact instant of impact, Val reached into the car at inhuman speed to rip the little girl from the back seat. He placed her on the ground looming over her as the girl gripped the sides of her head. A terrible coldness emanated from Val as he said, "Hello child."

A low roaring echoed through the nothingness as the scene went black. Cassie believed herself blinded. She opened her eyes wide to be hit with a strong wave. It encircled her inside the nothingness, forcing her upward. As it strained against her body, she attempted to relax into it. Yet, the unstoppable current made her fearful. She cried out and shut her eyes.

When Cassie opened them, she was staring into Albert's dark brown eyes. She watched as the last glint of light dissipated from his gaze. Her head leaned forward making the connection between them far too intimate, uncomfortable. She shot back from his grip, his hands slipping from her shoulders.

"Breathe, my dear," Albert said softly, remaining still beside her. "Just take a breath, slow in and slow out."

Cassie tried to do as he instructed. Shock had hit her so hard she hadn't realized she'd been holding her breath. It came out in a harsh wheezing sound as the air pushed between her teeth. When she trusted herself to breathe again, she turned toward Albert. The fallen before her blurred from her vision as tears filled her eyes. With a raw and heavy heart, she said, "I don't know what to say."

"Of course not. What's there to say?" Pity filled Albert's words. "I know this causes you pain, but that was not my intention." He patted her hand where it lay flat against the tile floor. "There will be time to grieve later. Now, you must use this knowledge to act. We must help

Gabe." He rose to his feet and extended his hand. "Come."

Cassie stared up at him with eyes wide like those of a frightened dear. Yet, bit-by-bit, her features changed. She raised her chin and hardened her gaze, motivated by a steely determination. She stood without his aid, her hands balled into fists at her sides. "Let's go."

"Good girl. Follow me." The doors groaned in protest as Albert forced them open. The elevator sat about three feet shy of the landing. He hoisted himself up and out with ease and then turned to offer his hand to Cassie. She ignored him and crawled out on her own.

Once free, the pair found themselves in an empty corridor. Albert moved along, checking every intersection before proceeding. No one hindered their progress. "This way," he called over and over as he ushered her through a series of hallways and staircases. When she was almost out of breath, they stopped at yet another elevator. "This is it."

"You can't be serious." Her every nerve caught on fire and she couldn't keep the edge out of her voice.

"Gabe is in a restricted part of the building. The room holding him is soundproof and almost impossible to reach without clearance." He pointed to the elevator doors. "This is the lone way in or out. And to work it you need the code." The buttons gave off a digital melody as Albert's fingers moved across the keypad. In an instant, the doors opened and he stepped inside. "Do you want to help him or not?"

Cassie muttered a string of expletives before entering. From the interior, Albert punched in another sequence and the elevator shot upward. It gained speed as it ascended causing Cassie's stomach to drop. She covered her mouth and prayed to hold onto her...*When was the last time I ate?* The thought passed through her mind in a flash as her hunger made it known with a gurgle.

Albert stared at her, his thoughts written across his face.

"Don't worry I'm not going to lose it," Cassie said, then laughed again. "My mind or my lunch."

"I hope not. Especially since the sights hereafter may cause your stomach more grief than the mere rocking of an elevator." He turned away as their journey upward ended with a rough halt. The doors opened on a screech. Albert exited into the small space beyond. A large metal door lay ahead, designating the lone room on this floor.

Cassie followed a step behind as she tried to prepare for what was to come. The door creaked open. Stale air mixed with the repugnant scent of sweat and blood assailed her. She scrunched her nose in an attempt to block the odor. With another step, she noticed a glow coming from the center of the room, but Albert's form blocked her view. Frustrated, she shoved him forward and stomped.

"Move it." The words barely left her lips when she saw him. Bound to a chair with thick metal restraints sat Gabe, beaten and bloody. His rich dark hair stuck in clumps to his head. His body sagged forward as if he'd been struggling to break free and lost the fight. Hands, blue from lack of circulation, drooped. She absorbed the horror with a single word, "Gabe."

For the briefest of moments, Gabe's eyelids fluttered. Cassie held her breath in anticipation and moved closer while Albert stepped away, hugging the far wall. "Gabe," she called louder and placed a hand on his knee. "Can you hear me?"

An eternity seemed to pass before Gabe lifted his head and whispered, "Cassie?"

"Thank God," she said with a sigh of relief. "I'm here. It's me." She looked into his eyes to reassure him while bending down to examine the bindings. She brushed the cuffs with the tips of her fingers. The metal had torn into his wrists and ankles.

He stared back at her. "Don't worry. It'll be okay. I'll get you out of here. I promise." He winked at her then and clicked his tongue. "I have help."

Her heart weighed in about a hundred pounds too heavy. *He's been tortured and he's worried about me.* She shook her head in disbelief and concentrated on getting him out of the chair. On the underside of the steel arms, she found a manual release lever. "You don't worry, Gabe." She cupped his cheek then tried the lever. "We're going to get you out of here."

"We?" he asked without taking his eyes off her.

"Yes, we." She glanced over at Albert while continuing to work on freeing Gabe. "Come over here and help me."

Albert stood fixed to the far wall. He stared at Gabe, remorse and guilt filling his eyes. He took a step forward to help, only to be stopped cold by Gabe's heated gaze.

"When I get free, I'm going to rip your head off." Anger so palpable filled the room and turned Gabe's words raspy.

"Funny," a voice echoed from the doorway. "I had the same thought." All eyes turned in unison toward the sound, but before anyone could capture the source, it moved away. An indistinguishable blur crashed through the confined space and landed beside Albert. As the form stopped dead, Val appeared. "You old fool. And here I thought you'd seen the error of your ways. Pity."

Cassie's gaze drew to Albert. His shoulders sagged low like an unbearable weight pressed down upon him. She caught the look of resignation in his eyes. Words formed in her mind as if he spoke into her ear. "Tell Gabe how sorry I am, dear child. My time here is done. I no longer deserve to be a part of this world. And I leave it now of my own free will." She stiffened as his eyelids fluttered down. He didn't even put up a struggle as Val latched monstrous hands against both of the old fallen's ears. In one agonizing motion, Albert's head tore clean from his body. The snapping of bone, the ripping of muscles and flesh, the severing of veins and arteries created a horrific clamor of death.

Albert was right. Cassie almost laughed at the bitter irony as her stomach reared and the bile rose.

TWENTY

Cassie wanted to turn her face away from the horror but found herself glued to the scene. Shock and disbelief rippled through her. She considered it a great testimony to her resolve that she managed to push the acid down without divulging the contents of her stomach. A few months ago, she could say she had never seen a dead body, save for her parents after the accident. Now she had seen enough violent deaths to have the images haunt her for several lifetimes.

With effort, she tore her eyes from the violence and stared at Gabe. Color returned to his hands as she managed to pull the manual release lever. When he leaned forward, she noticed the scars on his back seemed fresher, as if they had only recently healed. Before she could comment, Val stalked toward them.

At the same moment, as if on cue, the elevator doors opened just outside the room with a screech. Val halted in his tracks.

Within the elevator car stood a man Cassie didn't recognize. The casual grin he wore looked out of place with the heavy load slung over his shoulder. It bore down on him and crinkled his shiny gray suit. It took Cassie a second to identify the metallic black load.

"Oh shit." The thought hadn't left her before Gabe grabbed her around the waist propelling them across the room and inside the elevator with dizzying speed.

"Rafe, now!" Gabe roared at the man as he covered Cassie's body as much as possible with his own.

"Better duck." Rafe grinned at the demon still standing in the room and fired. The elevator doors closed at the same time as a blast shook the core of the building. The elevator car rocked, before Cassie felt the floor disappear under her feet. The cabin began to plummet.

Gabe pushed her to the far corner and peered at Rafe. "She's not going to survive this crash," he shouted over the screeching metal.

Rafe's gaze raked down her body and up again in half a second. "We'll have to get above it," he announced in a tone one would use to discuss what they wanted for breakfast. In one swift motion, he jumped up and ripped the roof off the elevator; the cabin speed ever increasing. "Ladies first."

Cassie bit back a scream.

"Just hold on to me," Gabe said to her. She tightened her arms around him and felt his muscles tense under her fingers as he jumped. He didn't pause until he had a firm hold of one of the thick cables on top. In a blink Rafe appeared, holding on to the wire across from them, still with the rocket launcher on his shoulder.

The elevator disappeared beneath them and another five seconds later, it crashed with a horrible roar. A cloud of dark smoke rushed toward them. Cassie shuddered. Gabe's strong arms squeezed her closer. Despite everything, she somehow felt safer in his embrace.

A cold sweat broke out on the back of her neck. Another pair of eyes watched her. Turning her head, she found Rafe looking at them with a devilish grin. *Who the hell is this guy?* Yet, the question would have to be saved for later.

"Let's get to the next elevator door below and get the hell out," Rafe said and started making his descent. Gabe nodded and followed his lead. As they came to the door, Rafe pried it open with ease. Gabe swung them onto the floor and finally let go of Cassie, setting her on her feet.

"You okay?" he asked, checking over every inch of her for signs of injury.

"I'm fine," Cassie said and swatted his hands away.

"Wonderful news, but we have to keep moving," Rafe said already heading down the hall.

"Just a second," she yelled more high pitched than intended. Glancing down at her throbbing feet, she saw the culprit of her pain. Balancing on one leg at a time, she ripped off the stilettos and stretched her bare feet on the floor. Her toes gripped the carpet with pleasure. "Now we can go."

Gabe took her hand. "I could carry you."

"Not a chance." She trotted down the hall until they caught up to Rafe.

When they were a trio once more, Gabe slapped the other fallen on the back, furrowed his brow and said in a sardonic tone, "Nice show."

"Hey, I like to make an entrance, you know," Rafe said with a grin and turned to look at Cassie. "We haven't been properly introduced, cherie." He checked her out with obvious appreciation.

Gabe growled. "Not the time or place, jackass!"

"You're right," Rafe said without taking his eyes off her. "They'll be plenty more."

Cassie shook her head to clear it, all the while trying to keep up with the two men. "Who," she gasped for a breath, "are you?"

Gabe didn't let Rafe utter a word. "Cassie, this is Rafe. He's an old...acquaintance." Gabe said the last word with distaste. "And he's helping us, for now."

"Let me guess," Cassie's voice dripped with sarcasm as their pace slowed to a more manageable walk, "another fallen?"

Rafe's grin widened. "Of course."

They continued through the maze of the Obelisk. At the second turn, Gabe asked, "How the hell did you manage to get to that elevator with a rocket launcher?"

Deep laughter echoed through the hallway. "Let's just say the human mind is easily swayed." Rafe winked at Cassie. "Or I'm that good."

Cassie rolled her eyes at the display. "Oh, save me from male showmanship."

A few more hallways and they reached the door leading out to the garage area. Rafe reloaded the rocket launcher and adjusted it on his shoulder.

He carries it as if it was a feather. She shook her head in wonder. *Unreal.*

"Prepare for company," Rafe said in a tone that left no doubt he was enjoying this a little too much.

Gabe leaned in and Cassie heard his low voice in her ear. "Try to get to the exit. If you manage it, run. Get to our hotel room." As she was about to start protesting, he added, "I'll be right behind you. It'll be easier for me to fight if I don't have to worry about you every second."

Cassie heard the steel in his voice. There would be no use arguing, so she nodded. Gabe squeezed her hand as Rafe opened the door. The three of them barely had time to drop and roll before shots fired.

"Don't hit the girl, you idiots." Someone roared through the commotion. "Aim only for the fallen!"

Gabe threw himself and Cassie toward the far wall, behind a stack of empty industrial sized bins. Rafe squeezed off the rocket launcher, causing Cassie to go temporarily deaf. She stood motionless between Gabe and the wall. He covered her with his body but she still felt the searing heat of the blast. Voices screamed in unison and the smell of burnt flesh hit her nostrils. She tried not to dry heave.

"Gabe, some help over here would be appreciated," Rafe shouted nearby.

"Stay here until you see it's safe to get to the exit," Gabe told her without waiting for her response. He sprang up to join Rafe, who was being surrounded by no less than five men. Humans from what Cassie could tell. Now that Gabe wasn't covering her, she could also see body parts littering the floor. More men poured out of a number of doors leading from the building's interior.

"Shit! Where are the rest of your men?" She heard

Gabe scream to Rafe as he knocked a gun out of one of the men's hands in a speed too fast for a mortal to follow. Rafe threw the empty rocket launcher and ducked to avoid more bullets flying his way.

An instant later, the large metal gate to the loading dock began to go up. About twenty men stood outside wearing black special-ops style outfits. They were armed to the boot. Their training was evident in the way they moved, spreading around the perimeter with military efficiency and crouching to avoid being hit. As soon as they detected their fallen boss unharmed, they swooped in, firing precise shots. Before Val's men had time to react, a number of them were taken out. The same voice Cassie heard before now told them to fall back and take cover. She couldn't identify the voice's source.

Despite her terror, Cassie smiled as the odds improved.

Then she heard Gabe. "Cassie, get to the exit now!"

"My men will cover you," Rafe shouted at the same time whirling to meet his next opponent.

Cassie looked around and noted no one in the immediate vicinity. Gabe and Rafe were engaged in hand-to-hand combat. *Ok, this is it.* She prepared herself. *Make a run for it.* She got up from her crouch and sprinted for the exit. She held to the wall as she ran. A few times, she heard shots fired near her.

To her surprise, she made it to the exit with no major problems. Her heart beat hard. She cursed at a painful stitch in her side. As she reached the gate, she gave herself a moment to stop, catch her breath and check on Gabe.

Just as Cassie turned to search for him, a large form flew into her, throwing her to the floor. The air pushed from her lungs as her head hit the concrete floor. A numbing pain filled her and her sight faded to black.

"You weren't thinking of leaving this party, sweetheart, were you?" A familiar voice sounded above her head. "Your daddy might get offended you didn't say goodbye." He bent over her, laughing. "To be honest, I'm offended."

Her vision cleared just before she saw Dan's hand come around her neck. He started pressing hard, the movement constricting her airway. A wild look of pleasure gleamed in his eyes. *Oh my God, he's enjoying this.* The thought seemed so absurd. Yet, it made terror much more palpable. The cold stone floor underneath her pressed into her back.

Dan kept his hold firm as Cassie tried to pry his fingers from her throat. Tears formed in her eyes causing his face to go hazy.

"Don't worry." His breathing became ragged. "I won't kill you now. I just need you to calm down and come along."

Cassie closed her eyes, blinking away the tears. Her thoughts shifted. Something primal overtook her, something she never felt before. A strange calm replaced the panic. She opened her eyes and managed to smile. She saw with satisfaction the look of surprise on Dan's perverse pretty boy face.

"You should...let...me go." A hoarse whisper came forth, but before Dan could do or say anything, she wriggled her body to create a small space between them. When it became just wide enough, she nestled her knee into his crotch and pushed with all her strength. It gave her enough time to twist further, bringing her knee up and into his crotch a second time with more force. He screamed and loosened his grip.

Cassie jolted up and her fist shot out to connect with Dan's jaw. The move surprised her as much as him but there was no time to think. She had seconds to get out and she prayed Gabe was not far behind.

One of Rafe's men, a tall lanky guy with long stringy black hair, ran to her side and pointed his gun at Dan. "Go!" He yelled at Cassie. Forcing her legs into action, she ran for it. A shot echoed behind her but she didn't turn around to see the result.

Once out of the building, she staggered against the wall, disoriented. A cool breeze brushed her heated face. Early morning sunlight peeked through the clouds. The air encompassed her, thick and misty. Looking around, she noted her location on the side of the building. "Main road. A cab." She broke into a run while trying to hug the wall for cover just in case.

Cassie's heart gave a painful squeeze. "Please let Gabe get out of there unharmed." She pleaded to an unseen force while picking up speed. She ran against the instinct telling her to go back and stay with Gabe. Any other time she would argue with him and do what she thought was right, but not this time. She was in over her head and she knew it. Gabe would have a better chance of getting out alive if he didn't have to think about keeping her safe.

Cassie rounded the building and slowed down. An ache crept up her soles as her bare feet made contact with the Strip's warming cement. Trying to stay off the illuminated pavement, she hoped her lack of shoes wouldn't garner her unnecessary attention. As she tried to mix into the remaining crowd out on the street, she soon realized these people were returning to their hotels after a long night of partying, and her bare feet didn't appear the worst of the eclectic scene. She sighed. The excitement of last night seemed like another lifetime ago. So much had changed since the time she walked into The Obelisk. She blinked trying to shake away the odd turn of events.

She found a cab and told the driver the address to the motel. As the car drove further away from the building, Cassie collapsed into the seat. Her whole body started shaking. By the time she got back into the motel room a second time--the first to grab a credit card to pay the cabbie--she shook so hard she had to lie down. Yet, not before losing the meager contents of her stomach. She stared at the mess without care and then crawled into bed.

The motel room's water stained popcorn ceiling gave her little distraction. Silent tears began to spill forth. Tears for the parents she lost, tears for the mother she never knew, tears for what her father was, tears for Gabe, and tears for herself. By the time the tears stopped flowing, Cassie sat up on the bed determined and resolved.

"As of today, things will change. I have to understand who and what I am. What my purpose is," she said to an empty room. Her hands curled into fists as if punctuating her words. Thinking about all she'd been through and all yet to come her way, she said, "No more tears."

TWENTY-ONE

Gabe cracked the door of the motel room and peered inside. He found Cassie standing by the window looking out and tapping her index finger against her forehead. Her long hair sat in a high ponytail and she had changed into jeans and a black tank top. A sigh of relief set free as he opened the door wider.

Cassie spun to face him. Her gaze travelled up and down his body. He knew she saw the numerous cuts and slashes covering his flesh as a look of terror crossed her face. For a few seconds, she stood still. Then, with unshed tears filling her eyes, she ran to him. He caught her at the waist and held her against his chest. Her arms glided around his neck.

"Are you okay?" Cassie moved back and stared. "You're bleeding all over!"

"The wounds are already healing," he said, caressing her cheek. He pulled his gaze from her face to search the room. "We have to leave now. Rafe's waiting for us outside. He's going to take us to a private airport and loan us his jet to get out of here."

"What happened back there?"

Gabe fought an internal battle. Half of him wanted to comfort and soothe her fears. The other rational sense told him to get out fast. Logic prevailed. "I'm sorry. We don't have time now. I'll tell you in the car. Grab your things and let's go."

Standing in the doorway, he watched as Cassie dashed about the room in frenzy. Within a minute or two, she managed to stuff everything in a suitcase. Her posture hinted at exhaustion, but her gaze remained firm, resolved. *She's holding up pretty well.* He gave her a reassuring smile as they headed outside.

Passing the front desk, Cassie pointed toward the unconscious clerk behind the counter. "Not very diligent, is he?" She stopped dead, just inches from the exit, pulling Gabe to a halt beside her. "You didn't do that…did you?"

"No witnesses. Makes it easier." As her eyes began to widen, he added, "He's just asleep. Like the doorman from before, remember? It's okay."

She sighed, but kept walking forward. Her eyes glazed over.

Once outside, Gabe nodded at Rafe who sat composed in the passenger seat of a sleek black Audi. Dark sunglasses covered his eyes. The driver, dressed in the special ops fatigues, stared out the front window. He didn't move at their approach so Gabe opened the back door for Cassie and hopped in beside her.

"Go," he said, not at all in the mood for argument or small talk. Rafe mimicked the order and the driver slammed on the gas pedal. The car weaved through the early morning traffic.

"It's good to see you again, cherie." Rafe reached for Cassie's hand and brought it to his lips. Gabe grunted and narrowed his eyes at the fallen boss. *Son of a...* He leaned forward ready to grab Rafe, but halted midway. His attention wavered as he noted the bloodstains and rips on Rafe's gray suit. Rafe's injuries would already be healing, but he'd sustained them on Cassie's behalf nonetheless. Gabe held back his fist.

"Tell me what happened now," Cassie said, pulling back her hand and placing it on Gabe's arm.

Gabe smirked at the small victory. "We took down enough of them to make our retreat. But, we don't yet know the extent of the damage. The room where they held me was destroyed, but the blast wouldn't kill a demon with Val's power." He put his hand over hers. "His infrastructure's been taken out, but contingency plans are bound to be in place. There's no way of knowing how fast he'll be able to come after us."

"And when he does come after us?" Cassie's voice shook.

"We need to find a place to hide out awhile." He thought about it for a moment, searching for a solution. Other than the points of power, he had limited knowledge of Earth's territory. "It has to be somewhere off the map where we can figure things out without worry. We'll need a few weeks at least, but preferably until the time of the prophecy."

"Yes, far from here," Rafe said. "The more remote, the better."

Cassie almost burst from the seat as she said, "I think I may know a place."

Gabe eased her back to the cushion and raised a questioning eyebrow.

"Zoey has a cabin in the mountains in Vermont," she said, her hands darting about in all directions. "Her grandfather left it to her a few years ago. She'd let me use it if I asked her."

Gabe nodded. He might not have a clue about Vermont, but a cabin in the mountains sounded secluded enough. "Might work. As long as it's away enough from hot zones to give us some time."

"How cozy," Rafe muttered under his breath. "Maybe I'll come join you."

Gabe remained silent, but bore a hole into Rafe's head with his eyes. *Complete and total...If I could only...Head on a platter.* His thoughts wove a violent tapestry, before he tore his gaze away. Turning toward Cassie, he saw the question in her stare, but he wasn't about to start spilling his guts about ancient history so he gave her a clear warning look to back off. She smiled at him innocently.

They arrived at a small private airport and turned into Rafe's hangar. Lying on the outskirts of the city, the area sat well hidden from would be trespassers. The runway stretched about a mile into the desert. No one seemed to be around, yet a twin propeller plane stood ready at the entry of the hangar.

The driver got out and held the doors open for Rafe, Gabe and Cassie. Gabe reached for Cassie's hand and led them toward the plane. Out of the corner of his eye, he saw another man approach Rafe and extend a package to him.

He watched as Rafe took it, dismissed the man and walked over to them.

"Here's all the documents you'll need for the flight and I suggest you keep using these for a while." He handed the package to Gabe.

Gabe spilled the contents into his hands. He nodded at the two passports, driver's licenses, and thick pack of cash. Then, the name on the ID caught his attention. "Jack," he asked, tapping the plastic. "My alias is Jack Coff?"

"Why? A perfect name for you. Jackcoff," Rafe said with a cruel grin.

"Asshole."

"Yeah. That would've worked too."

"Bella?" Cassie interrupted, looking over her own documents. "So my name's Bella Coff. Are we supposed to be husband and wife, then?"

"Well, I was thinking of you two more as brother and sister." Rafe winked at her.

Cassie laughed.

Gabe wasn't about to be so generous. "Husband and wife are far more inconspicuous. Don't you think so, darling?" he said, motioning to Cassie. He took her hand again and resumed walking toward the plane.

The sound of Rafe clearing his throat brought the pair to a standstill. "Are you forgetting our deal?"

Gabe turned around, a prickly feeling at the back of his neck. "Now? You want to cash in on it now?"

"Now is as good a time as any." Rafe shrugged. "The pilot needs time to go through the pre-flight procedures anyway. Twenty minutes at least. More than enough time for a little *tête-à-tête*." He cocked a brow at Cassie.

Cassie slanted her eyes at Gabe and withdrew her hand from his grip. "What's he talking about?"

He started to say something, stopped, started again. Yet, before he could say anything, Rafe interrupted. "You see, cherie, your guardian here needed some help doing his job. So he came to me."

Gabe felt the fire rising. He fought to contain the anger and settled on a low snarl.

"But here's the thing," Rafe continued. "We don't seem to agree on certain key...ideas about the prophecy."

"What kind of key ideas?" Suspicion laced every word of her question.

"Why don't we go into the office and discuss it." Rafe motioned toward a metal door on the opposite side of the hangar.

"Fine," Cassie said curtly and started walking after Rafe.

Gabe stood motionless despite having an overwhelming desire to run after her.

"Aren't you coming?" She tapped her foot, waiting for his answer.

Every fiber of his body tensed. "I had to promise him he could talk to you alone," he said, crossing his arms. "Go ahead. This shouldn't take long." The last part was pronounced as Gabe peered at Rafe with all the fury in his being.

#

The office turned out to be a small security room. It made Cassie fidget with her nails. It looked too much like an interrogation room, bare light green walls and a rectangular metal table with two chairs on either side. *Bet it's soundproof too.* She shifted her weight to each foot twice.

When Rafe reached for her hand, she jumped in surprise, but gained her composure and followed without a word as he led her to one of the chairs. If this would shed any light on her future, she would give him her full attention. As she sat down, he reached for the chair on the other side and set it next to hers. She forced herself to remain calm as Rafe's hands landed on either side of her chair to pull it even closer. The proximity of their bodies was far too intimate even in the unnerving setting.

"I know you feel confused," Rafe said with no further delay. "But, I want you to know I'm here for you. I can be your...friend." He smiled with those soft full lips. Her hardened resolve slipped a peg. "You will have to make some serious choices. You should know all of your options, however, before you decide on the right one." He paused, his striking face a little too near for comfort. A drone of power circled around him she hadn't noticed before. It was familiar yet different from the energy that surrounded Gabe. She couldn't quite put her finger on the difference.

"Okay, I'm listening," she said, trying to cover up her discomfort.

Rafe leaned back in his chair, his tone more serious. "After Albert talked to the angels and got dismissed by them, he came to me asking for help. He told me the prophecy, which I committed to memory." He paused and tapped his finger against the side of his head. "He urged me to join forces with demons together with him. I have to say, I had known Albert for a long time." He paused. "Never realized he was that ambitious, the old dirt bag.

Can't say I blame him though. Ambition is one of the greatest driving forces of humanity and I subscribe to it myself." He took a deep breath and his sensuous mouth twisted as if he was caught up in a private joke.

"So why didn't you join him?" she asked, crossing her arms over her chest in a protective posture. Rafe might be attractive, but he oozed danger from every pore.

"There was a difference in what we wanted." Steel sparked in his eyes, a predatory gaze. "He wanted to make sure he was on the side of those he thought would be most powerful. I, on the other hand, am happy standing alone. Well, as alone as a boss ever is. And..." He lowered his voice as if to share a secret, "And I may be a fallen, but I will never sink to the level of demons. I may be content with my position. I may not seek redemption for myself, but I'm not about to let demons run amok either."

Cassie shook her head. Her breath left her in one long whirl, pushing the air between her teeth. *Well, at least I know a little better where this one stands.* Her hands fell to her lap as she relaxed a bit.

"In any case," Rafe said. "Keys have too much power for their bodies to handle. Bonding is necessary for their survival. But, what if I said your choices weren't as limited as you think? What if there were other options besides choosing either an angel or a demon?" He leaned in, his lips near enough to kiss...or bite.

An unexplainable and instinctive pull beckoned her toward him. The energy inside her threatened to break out. She sat on her hands, begging it to stay put. *I don't need a purple fit!* She tilted forward, trying to shake off the feeling and concentrate on his words.

"Nothing in the prophecy says you have to bond with one or the other, Cassie. In fact, the prophecy says the Key will bring balance. And what would serve this purpose more than bonding with a fallen?"

Cassie couldn't find words to answer him. Her senses spun along with her thoughts. Tipping her chair back on its hind legs, she distanced herself from his shocking suggestion.

Rafe sighed and said in a patronizing tone, "Bonding with a fallen won't change anything in the world. Things will stay as they are. Everyone wins." He leaned back in the chair and waited for Cassie's reaction with a triumphant look in his eyes.

Cassie's heart raced and her mind reeled. *Could it be so simple? Is this what I'm supposed to do?* She looked over Rafe, considering her options. His long legs crossed gracefully, his right ankle upon left knee. His strong hands interlocked upon his lap. His jaw line was set firm and proud. The harsh light of the room accented the chocolate highlights in his rich black hair. High cheekbones and an inviting mouth completed the delectable picture. *Bonding with him would have its benefits.* Cassie licked her lips. As the suggestive idea of her and Rafe together began to swim in her head, a single word surfaced to the top as her heart contracted. *Gabe?*

Before she could say anything aloud, Rafe's narrowed eyes said he'd caught the shift in her thoughts. "If you're thinking Gabe could be that fallen, you might want to think again," he said, so matter-of-fact, one would think he was discussing his dinner selection.

"Why?" Suspicion wiped away all previous ideas.

"He wants redemption," Rafe said easily. "Bonding

with you will go against his orders from the Angelic Council. Therefore, no redemption." He waved his hand at her. "But if you don't care, then you should consider him, of course."

Cassie's lips curled in a cynical smile. *So, this was his plan all along.* She laced her words with honey, "And I'm assuming you have another fallen in mind?"

"I'm willing to sacrifice myself for the good of everyone." Rafe bowed his head in a gesture of feigned humbleness.

No wonder Gabe doesn't trust him. She stared at him. *Remember what they say about trusting pretty people.* Laughing inside, she disguised her amusement under a hardened tone, "Aha, sacrifice. What's in it for you, Rafe?"

"You are clever, aren't you?" Rafe's eyes gleamed. "Well, like I already said, I like my world as it is and my place in it. The status quo is enough of a reward."

Cassie remained stock still, her silence urging him to spill the rest.

"I'm starting to understand what Gabe sees in you." Rafe nodded his head in approval. "Perhaps, there are a few extra powers I might get. Can't say more. Nobody knows. We never had a case like you before."

Cassie said after a pause, "Fair enough. I'll give it some thought."

She rose from the chair, indicating to him she didn't want to hear anymore. Rafe remained sitting, giving her an appraising look, a suggestive grin on his handsome face. Cassie flushed, raised her chin and moved toward the door. She didn't have a chance to open it, however, because in the next breath, she was whirled around and Rafe's hands rested on either side of her, an effective trap.

"I know you find me attractive, Cassie," he murmured against her ear. "I suggest you think about my proposal. We could share the power from the bonding...as well as a bed."

Cassie bristled even as she resisted the heat from his body. "Let go of me!" She pushed against Rafe's chest hard but met with no success. The corner of his mouth rose. He lingered for a heartbeat and then stepped back, putting his hands up in submission. Cassie's hand found the cold doorknob. She rotated it and stepped outside of the tiny room. She took a deep breath, filling her lungs with much needed air. *I have to get it together before I reach Gabe.*

"Have a nice flight." She heard Rafe's voice behind her, loud enough for Gabe to hear as well. His laughter was enough to snap Cassie into determined action. She stalked over to Gabe, throwing at him a sharp glance before boarding the plane.

"Rafe's charming personality strikes again," Gabe said behind her. "No surprise there."

As soon as they were seated on a soft brown leather couch aboard the plane, the engine roared to life and the aircraft rolled onto the runway. Cassie observed the luxurious surroundings of the cabin with a detached coldness. They remained silent until the plane started climbing. She was lost deep in thought when Gabe turned to her. She felt his beautiful eyes examining her face.

"What did he talk to you about?"

The conversation with Rafe left her rattled as did her reaction, or rather her attraction, to the fallen boss. *I can't tell him. Not now.* She had to understand it herself first. She sighed, leaned her head against the cushion, and said, "He was just trying to hit on me. One day I'll have to hear his story."

Gabe gave a dark laugh, lacking any humor. "Yeah, sure. One day."

After their conversation, Cassie managed to nod off. Dreams came to her fast and strong. Faces went in front of her--Albert, Val, Gabe and Rafe all took turns. Then, another face appeared, a woman with golden red hair. The woman's face replaced them all. *Mother.* The fiery haired beauty leaned over Cassie, touching her cheek with slender fingers. "Make your choice with care, my daughter," she whispered as she placed a kiss on Cassie's forehead.

Cassie opened her eyes to find herself leaning against Gabe. His strong arms wrapped around her, giving her comfort and reassurance.

Outside the plane window, New York City loomed dark and rainy.

TWENTY-TWO

The sky pounded the city with a torrential storm as they approached Cassie's apartment. The cold swept through the streets, invading both outdoors and inside with equal measure. Cassie could feel the chill down to her bones and deeper still, as if it invaded her very soul. As she walked into her home for the first time in many days, it felt as if she'd been gone for years. Her safe little haven altered to something far more alien.

"It's a bad idea to be here," Gabe said for the tenth time. He had checked the exterior of the building three times before he'd allow her to enter the apartment. Now, he searched each room just as well. Cassie had to wait at the doorway.

"I don't want to argue about this again. We're already here. And it won't take long anyway." When he gave the all clear signal, she staggered to the kitchen counter. "Okay, can you just sit down now? You're making me nervous."

Gabe draped a leg over the same stool he'd occupied

when he'd told her she wasn't human, but a Key, a creature born of a supernatural union, a being who would decide the fate of the world. Cassie shook her head at the memory and focused on making tea instead. The tea had no time to brew when the bell rang. She knew who stood on the other side of the door.

"Cassie! Open up this minute!" Zoey cried from the hall. Sharp knocks against the front door preceded each word. "You can't just call me from the airport after days of not speaking to me, and then not even answer my questions."

Cassie glanced at Gabe. He shrugged as if to say, "What did you expect?" She took a deep breath, trying to prepare for this conversation. With heavy steps she skulked to the entry and wrapped her hand around the metal knob. With a jerk, she pulled the door wide and peeked with just one eye open.

Zoey stood in the hall like a marble statue--a gray, ashen, and worn out marble statue. The cat carrier weighed her down, causing her body to sag to the right. Her appearance took Cassie aback. She had never seen her friend look so serious and disheveled. Zoey's faded jeans and black t-shirt stuck to every part of her body from the heavy rain. Her honey blonde hair matted to her head and looked far browner from lack of care. No trace of light could be found in the usual happy friend Cassie knew and loved.

Zoey's gaze lay heavy upon Cassie before the stare moved to just beyond Cassie's shoulder. Surprise flashed in Zoey's eyes for a heartbeat, then disappeared.

"What's wrong with you?" Zoey asked, turning her

attention back to Cassie. Tears sprang to her eyes as her voice trembled. "Why didn't you answer any of my calls? Why would you make me worry?"

"Zoey, sweetie, please come in. I'll explain." Cassie took the cat carrier from her arms and let Maia free into the apartment. "I missed you, my baby," she cooed to the cat. Maia decided to show her obvious disdain by turning up her tail and walking away.

Zoey followed Maia's lead and cast a suspicious glare upon Gabe. She took two steps inside dragging water across the entryway.

"This better be good," Zoey muttered under her breath.

"Gabe. Don't just sit there. Grab her some towels." Cassie scowled. Gabe trotted to the bathroom without a word, and Cassie motioned to the couch. "Here, sit down. Do you want anything to drink?" She moved toward the kitchen as Zoey sat.

"No. I just want some answers." Zoey crossed her arms, rubbing her hands up and down her forearms. She shuddered.

Gabe returned and walked behind the couch. "Don't bite," he said as Zoey spun around. "I come in peace." He placed one towel around her shoulders and handed her another.

"Thanks," she said monotone and turned her full attention to Cassie once more. "Now. How about some answers?"

"You'll get them, but let's get you warm first," Cassie said softly. "I think this might help." She pulled out a bottle of vodka from the freezer. It was the only alcohol in the house and had sat in hibernation since their last girls' night almost a year ago. They had gone through half of it that evening, but it hadn't moved since.

She poured a shot for Zoey and one for herself into red plastic cups. After eyeballing the measurements, she shook the bottle toward Gabe, but he refused the drink. She shrugged and downed the shot in one gulp. Zoey's eyes widened, surprise written across her face.

"What has gotten into you?" she said. "What happened?"

Cassie sighed. She could stall no longer. "Zoey, promise me you'll keep an open mind."

"Okay, you're scaring me." Zoey slammed the cup on the coffee table, spilling some of the contents onto the counter. "Out with it!"

Cassie nodded and began talking. "You know the old saying boy meets girl, girl meets boy, well in my parents' case, my biological parents that is, it was more like angel meets demon, demon meets angel."

"Fallen angel." Gabe coughed the words out.

"Thanks for the correction." She eyed him. "Yes, fallen angel. So, basically, we're looking at a whole lot of supernatural shit..."

An hour, and four vodka shots later, Zoey looked like she didn't know whether to cry or laugh, hysterically in both circumstances. She sat on the couch, hands supporting her head, while Cassie kneeled in front of her on the carpet. Gabe sat in the chair by the couch, distancing himself as if to give the women some semblance of privacy. Cassie was grateful he let her do all the talking.

"So let me get this straight," Zoey said staring straight

ahead, her voice shaking. "Demons and angels are real, check. Fallen angels, check. My best friend's half demon, half fallen angel, check. Oh, and Las Vegas really is Sin City. Does that about cover it?"

"I know how crazy all this sounds, Zo." Cassie touched her friend's knee as if to substantiate the reality of what she just said. There were a number of facts she had to omit in the story, mostly so she would not put Zoey in danger. Like her father being the most powerful demon in Vegas and hunting her was one of them.

"I don't think crazy quite covers it," Zoey said after a few breaths. "Cassie, are you sure about all this? Are you sure he," she nodded towards Gabe, "didn't just brainwash you?"

Cassie heard pleading in Zoey's voice, as if she was making the last attempt not to believe, silently beseeching Cassie to say this was all just a joke and burst into laughter. *A sick joke, but a joke nonetheless. Oh how I wish it was, Zo.* She sighed and closed her eyes. When she opened them again, she took her friend's hands. A faint purple glow emanated around from Cassie's hands and encompassed their connection.

"I'm sure." Cassie smiled. "Besides this..." She motioned to the energy swirling around. "I've seen all the evidence I need in the last few days. Believe me, as insane as it is, it's all true. And I'll understand if you walk away from all this...and from me. I can't, but you can. No matter what, I needed to tell you this. I couldn't keep it from you. You're too important to me. But, now the choice is yours."

Inch by excruciating inch, Zoey picked up her head until their eyes met. Cassie could see resolve enter her friend's gaze and hoped it was in her favor.

"You're my best friend and I want to be in your life, Cassie. It's going to take some time to get used to all this, all this supernatural stuff. I mean, you know I like the whole gothic craze, but this is a bit out of my league." She grinned in a way somewhat reminiscent of the old Zoey, the happy Zoey. "But I will, and I want to, be there when you need me." Zoey squeezed Cassie's hands.

Cassie felt her eyes filling, but there was no time for tears. They had to move to the next step of the plan. Dropping her hands to her knees, she concentrated on pushing the energy inside her once more. She relaxed enough to accomplish the task, but the unshed tears stung her eyes.

"Zo, I need to ask you for a favor," Cassie said once she was able to swallow the lump in her throat. "We need to get away awhile." She glanced at Gabe. "I need to think about all this. Can we use your cabin in the mountains?"

Zoey laughed. "You're going on a romantic getaway with a fallen angel?"

If Cassie were a cat, her fur would be standing on end and the claws would be out. Sneaking a glance at Gabe, she noted him standing by the couch with his hands behind his back. His expression remained unreadable.

"No romantic getaway here. Believe me," she said, then bit her lip. "It's just a lot to deal with, as you know now, and I just need time. I met my father, who is not getting any awards for father of the year. He wants me to get to know him better. I have to figure things out, away from it all. And well, Gabe is part of the whole equation now."

Zoey shook her head as if to clear it. "I'm sorry," she

said. "Of course you can have the cabin, for as long as you need it." She paused and then added, "I'm worried about you. Really worried."

"I know. I'll be okay." Cassie's voice sounded firm as she said it, but she felt far from confident.

"What about your job?" Zoey asked as an afterthought.

"I think it's time for me to say goodbye to Mr. Turpis."

The two women looked at each other and broke out in giggles, which brought down the tension a notch.

Cassie had already considered her financial situation. She'd lived paycheck to paycheck because she didn't want to touch the money her parents' insurance had left. But, the rainy days seemed at hand. She'd have enough to last her for a while, if necessary. *Once this is all over and I can go back to some semblance of a normal life, I'll find a better job.* She almost believed it too, the part about a normal life.

Zoey left after a long emotional hug and promised to bring by the cabin key the next morning. She also agreed to pick up Cassie's last check from Mr. Turpis. Cassie decided to break the news to him over the phone. He didn't inspire enough loyalty to tell him the bad news in person. The call to the boss went just like this, "Mr. Turpis, I'm not coming back to work. I'm sorry for the inconvenience." He took it the way a man like him would--he cursed and hung up the phone on her.

The fabric of her life unraveled.

Deep in thought, Cassie spent the evening packing two suitcases for the trip. Gabe went out and came back with a few new shirts and pants, which amused Cassie. *Even a fallen angel needs new clothes.* He also brought back a box of pepperoni pizza, the greasy, typical New York City type.

They devoured it in a matter of minutes.

They didn't talk much. At around 2:00am, exhausted, Cassie collapsed on the couch. Gabe approached her for the first time in hours and sat down beside her.

"Cassie, I can't lie to you," he said as he massaged the knots in her neck with his strong hands. "I can't promise it'll be fine. I don't even know what fine would be in this case." He stopped and slid his hand down her back. "But I can promise you I'll do everything in my power to protect you and to help you fulfill whatever destiny lies ahead of you."

For the second time that night, Cassie's eyes filled with unshed tears.

"I know." It was all she could force out.

Gabe nodded and smiled at her. All the air in the room seemed sucked out. *When he smiles at me, I don't care about anything.* She tried to calm her racing pulse. As much as she wanted him, she was tired and needed some time alone. She touched her lips to his and got up. He didn't try to stop her.

She brought him a pillow and a blanket and said goodnight in a hurry. As she closed the bedroom door, she fought the urge to run to him. The feel of his strong arms enfolding her, the heat of his body near hers, it made her blood boil. Yet, weariness crept its way through every muscle, every bone. She looked from the door to the bed. Exhaustion won out and overtook her as soon as she lay on top of the soft sheets. Being safe in her own bed, no longer keeping secrets from Zoey, and Gabe resting in just the next room, gave her a sense of peace she hadn't felt in so long. No dreams would disturb her sleep this night.

Or so she hoped.

TWENTY-THREE

"I can't believe you had me lug this thing all the way here," Gabe said as he dropped the cat carrier on the front porch.

Cassie stood a few feet away admiring the quaint Vermont log cabin in the mid afternoon sun. It had clean white snow on the rooftop from a storm the weekend prior. Clean snow. Not something you see much in the city. Two large picture windows framed the antique oak door. A canopy covered the porch from the elements and gave the cabin a cozy feel.

"Perfect," she murmured as she climbed the rest of the way up the hillside and onto the front steps.

"Did you even hear me?" Gabe's irritation became apparent in his sharp tone. "We are supposed to be hiding out, not having a vacation." He emphasized his point by dropping her suitcases onto the porch next to the cat carrier.

"As I told you in New York, Guardian," she said the last word with mild distaste. "If you want to protect me, then Maia, who is a cat and my friend, not a *thing* by the way, comes with me. Not leaving her again." She sighed adding, "Gabe, is it that big a deal?"

"No," he said. "It isn't." His hand stroked her hair, his fingers working through the tangles. "I forget how much you've had to deal with." He gazed into her eyes before leaning in close and brushing his lips across hers.

Before Cassie could react, however, he pulled away. Without another word, he unlocked the door and brought all of her things inside. She remained stunned into immobility even after he'd finished the task and let Maia loose from her carrier.

"Did you plan on letting your cat roam free in the woods or are you going to come inside and shut the door?" He leaned against the doorframe, his emotions a blank void.

"Um. Yes. I mean no." She stuttered a bit as she struggled to get her bearings. "Yes, I'm coming inside. And no, Maia can't roam around. She's a house cat not a mountain lion!"

Cassie heard his low chuckle as she stormed past him and into the cabin. The sound was rich and alluring. She could feel his eyes on her back as he closed the door. Her heart began to beat faster, the blood pumping harder and filling her with an exquisite heat. The feel of his lips on hers, the hard stare at her back, and the memory of their intimate night together ignited needs she hadn't felt in some time.

"Get a grip," she whispered to herself as she tried to shake the images from her mind. Needing to buy a few minutes to settle her emotions, she took a long look around the room. The interior mixed contemporary designs with antique flair. The large open space consisted of a massive stone fireplace enclosed by oak bookcases on both sides, and floor to ceiling windows accented with thick bamboo shades on the adjacent wall. A burnt orange sofa with cherry end tables sat parallel to the fireplace. The opposite side of the room was dedicated to a dining and kitchen area, further back laid the bedroom. A set of six wooden chairs and table captured Cassie's attention. The magnificent wood seemed to be handcrafted by a skilled artisan. She couldn't imagine the strange pattern manufactured. "Maybe, Native American?"

"Cassie?" Gabe said still standing by the door behind her.

Trusting herself to be steady once more, she turned around to face him. "Sorry," she said. "Just find the place... fascinating."

"I see." The tone in his voice spoke of disbelief but he didn't elaborate. Instead, he said, "I need to leave you awhile."

"Why?" She couldn't keep the surprise out of her voice.

"It won't be for too long." He paused. "I think you need some time alone to sort through this. My presence may make that...difficult." He smiled with such pure, rich seduction it made her wonder if he knew his effect on her.

"Maybe you're right." She sighed as she bent down to pet her sweet cat. Maia had slumped by her feet after inspecting the place with her nose almost as thoroughly as Cassie had with her eyes.

Gabe took a step forward and crouched down so they were on the same level. He placed a hand on her shoulder.

"Use the time to think about what you want." He rose again and removed his hand, but added, his voice husky, "And who."

Cassie watched him head for the door. "Wait. What if something happens?"

"I won't be too far. I need to search the perimeter. See what our weaknesses are." He opened the door and gestured outward. "But, I'll always be in range to hear you. No one will hurt you, Cassie. I promise." He ran into the surrounding woods in a speed her vision couldn't catch. The door slammed behind him.

Her heart sank at the emptiness left by his departure. "I wasn't worried about me."

#

"Two days!" Cassie yelled for the fifth time to an unsympathetic Maia. "This is ridiculous! How could he just leave me not knowing anything for two days?"

Maia's initial response to Cassie's anger was to curl in a ball and purr. It had worked to calm Cassie down before, but after the emotional rollercoaster of the past two days, not to mention the past two months, nothing could soothe her.

Cassie paced the room over and over. Yesterday, she'd been close to calling out to Gabe just to be sure he was all right, but she'd stifled the urge in time. Today, it rose again. She plopped on the couch with a thud. She'd been replaying the events of the past in her head trying to decide the best course of action for the future. She had arrived at the moment Albert led her into that room of torment and she spotted Gabe broken and bloody.

"No! It won't help." She sprang up and ran to one of the bookcases. "I need something to help me figure this out." Looking through the stacks, she came across a blank writing pad with a pen tied to it by a pretty woven string. "Ah ha!" Grabbing it, she set back down on the couch and went to work.

Scribbling, she made three columns *Angel, Demon,* and *Other,* and wrote various comments under each. In the Angel column she put notes such as *Bring about peace. Creatures of Light. Loss of free will = hard price to pay. But, supposed to be good* and such. In the *Demon* column she wrote *Darkness. Evil. Not to be trusted.* And in big bold letters **VAL**. For the last *Other* column she paused. Rafe's proposal echoed in her thoughts. After a few minutes she wrote, *Rafe?* Then skipping down a few lines, *Would Gabe? Lost to the Light.* And finally *Has to be another way.*

Cassie stared at the last lines until they became nothing more than a blur. Frustrated, she rose with paper in hand and slammed it onto the dining room table. "Nothing," she cried in defeat. Sighing, she stripped off her heavy yellow sweater and black jeans. She entered the immaculate bathroom and turned on the water to the tub. The space was nearly three times the size of her bathroom back home. It had a spa-like feel with a jet tub surrounded by a privacy curtain, a separate glass enclosed a shower across from the tub, and a wooden bench heated from below. The controls on the wall allowed not only the bench to be heated, but the air in the room to be warmed, as well as the tiled floor. Off to the side laid a smaller room with a pedestal sink and toilet. Gold and white hues decorated both this space and the smaller room.

When the bath water gave off a slight steam, Cassie slipped in and allowed her body to relax. She leaned her head back against the cushioned side and closed her eyes. A heady scent of citrus and pine filled her nose. "Gabe," she murmured as the stimulating aroma brought him to mind.

"Yes?" Gabe said.

Cassie sat up, smacking her arm hard against the tub in her fright. "What the hell?"

"Sorry. Didn't mean to startle you." He laughed. "You looked so peaceful."

Her face ignited with heat as she gasped. "What is wrong with you? Haven't you ever heard of privacy?" She grabbed at the curtain almost ripping it from the hooks in an attempt to cover herself. "Get out!"

"I thought you'd be glad to see me." He laughed again. "Ah well, since I'm here." He pulled his shirt over his head giving Cassie a full view of his sculpted chest. Next, he undid the top button to his dark jeans and pushed them down his muscular thighs. As they fell to his feet he stepped out of them, shaking off his boots and socks with a grace no ordinary male could possess. When he removed his boxers, her face flushed deeper and she turned her head away. Yet, she still managed to keep his gorgeous, and now naked, body in her peripheral vision.

"Do not think for one second you can take off for two days, having me worried and then just show up and jump into bed with me." She bit down on her lip.

"But, Cassie, you're not in bed." The same seductive grin as before met her eyes as she snuck a peek at him.

She ducked her head away again. "You're still not getting in this tub!"

"I wouldn't dream of it." He turned on the shower across from her and stepped into the glass enclosure. Before shutting the door, he said, "Well maybe I would."

Cassie drew the curtain all the way closed and sank deep into the water. She tried to drown out the noise of the shower, and the images of the beautiful creature in it, but came up sputtering for air instead. Cursing, she clamped her hands against her ears and her thighs shut. The fiery heat pooling in her lower regions betrayed her. "Shoot."

A few minutes later, Gabe emerged from the shower. She heard him pat a towel against his skin before leaving. When the door closed, she sprang from the tub. *I'm going to kill him.* She thought as she dried off and donned a fluffy white bathrobe. *Or maybe something else.* Her mind echoed what her body craved most. Tensing all her muscles, she tried to stifle the urges.

When she was sure of her composure, she exited the bathroom to find Gabe sitting on the couch in nothing but a pair of black sweat pants. A vibrant fire blazed in the hearth, illuminating his body. As she drank in the sight of him, heat continued to spread through her every cell. Droplets of moisture clung to his hair, creating small rays of light in the dark mass. His eyes always changing, always hard to describe, now burned with a rich golden hue. His fair skin radiated power under the fire's glow. The muscles of his chest and arms seemed carved from marble.

She sucked in a big gulp of air.

Gabe turned, his gaze shifting down her body. A wolfish grin lit up his face. "Why are you wearing that ridiculous thing?"

Caught off guard, she looked down to see the oversized

bathrobe. She smiled, and then shrugged. "It might look funny, but it keeps me warm."

"I could keep you warm," he said as he rose from the couch.

The suggestiveness made her skin feel afire. She rubbed her arms to try to control the heat. *Oh, I know you can.* An image of their previous intimate night together in the canyons blazed through her mind.

Gabe took a step forward and pointed at her robe. "It's a well-known fact body heat is far better than fabric."

The golden hue in his eyes changed to a burning glow that matched her desires. His eyes, so beautiful and radiant they lacked all description, bore into hers with obvious lust. If she'd seen anything else in them, she might have lost her nerve. The realization he wanted her, however, gave her courage. She took a step toward him and said with boldness she'd never felt with any man, "You know what, you're right. If you think you can keep me warm, then I don't need this." She discarded the robe in a single motion.

"Beautiful," he murmured as his eyes drank in the sight of her. Then, he was in front of her before she had time to think further, crushing her to his chest in a fierce embrace. His mouth captured hers as his tongue demanded entry. Her lips parted as the hunger for more reached unbearable heights. He pulled back to growl, "Did I say warm? I meant hot." He lifted her onto the couch's high backing and guided her legs around his waist. "Burning, scorching hot."

As he dove to plunder her mouth once more, she wound her hands around his neck and drew him closer. His tongue darted in and out, coaxing her to follow his lead. Teasing, she flicked her tongue along his bottom lip. He groaned in response, the proof of his arousal pressing against her bare flesh. Yet, his cotton sweat pants soon became an unwelcome boundary. She swept her hand down his chest relishing in the feel of smooth skin against hard muscle. When her hand reached his waistline, he leaned back and placed a hand over hers.

"Not yet," he whispered with promise. "I have other ideas first."

Before Cassie could protest, he blazed a trail of kisses down her neck and collarbone. Tiny pinpricks of pleasure ignited wherever his tongue met her skin. Her mind reeled from the sensations, causing soft moans to escape her without thought. He worked his way steadily down her body. When he reached a mere fraction of an inch past her belly button, she yanked his hair.

"Problem?" he asked, masculine satisfaction coating the question.

A deep breath was needed before she could answer. Eventually, she managed to stutter, "I...need...you...NOW!"

Husky laughter filled the room. "Later," he said. Without another word, he bent yet lower and licked her with a long even stroke. Fire raced through every nerve ending as he increased the pressure. She melted more and more into the couch with every passing minute. He expertly used one hand to direct her legs about his shoulders and steady her, while the other hand sought the inner walls of her most sensitive spot. The ache became insufferable as her hands twisted in his hair.

"Please, Gabe," she cried losing her last grip on reality. "I can't."

"Don't wait, lover. Come for me," he said enticingly

between strokes. The simple request sent her spiraling out of control. As her hips arched, he thrust his fingers deep inside her and sucked gently on the small nub. Earth-shattering cries filled the room as ecstasy washed over her. Her insides throbbed and pulsated as wave after wave of pleasure hit. A few heartbeats later, the fire subsided, replaced by a deep satisfaction working its way into every pore.

As Cassie tried to find the strength to remain in her half sitting position, Gabe rose, discarding his pants in the process, and picked her up. Her head rested against his chest as her legs hung over his arms like jelly. He looked questioningly down at her just outside the bedroom door. She nodded in response to the implicit request.

Crossing into the bedroom, he placed her down on the hand-quilted blanket. The soft material caressed her skin as she burrowed into the fabric. A sigh escaped her as she stared up at Gabe. His dark hair tangled about his face. His eyes filled with passion and shone a deep amber hue. She drew her gaze lower down his body. His broad chest and trim waist rivaled Adonis. She bunched the blanket in her hands as the longing to feel his flesh ignited her desires anew. Blushing she brought her eyes still lower and gasped at her findings.

"I see now we ended that night in the Canyon too soon," Gabe said. "A mistake I attribute to the heated situation at the time, but a mistake I don't plan to make again." He kneeled on the bed, only inches away. "I'd stay like this all night with nothing but your eyes upon me, and still desire would consume me. Your gaze alone is an addictive drug."

Cassie couldn't agree more but for far different reasons. Just looking at him and hearing his seductive words was enough to bring back the ache with renewed vigor. Greedily she sat up enough to grab his biceps and drag him down to the bed with her. "No more window shopping," she said, the lust making her voice raspy. "I want you."

"Good." The one word packed more promise and pleasure into it than all of his previous talk. His mouth was on hers in an instant, tongues dancing to an ancient beat. His hand sought her breasts, rubbing and pinching in varying degrees. The motion had her back arching to his touch. When he pulled away, she cried out in frustration, only to have his tongue swish around one taut peak. When the blood rushed to the surface, he switched, carrying out the same torturous motion. His hand, meanwhile, stroked and caressed her below bringing flames of need to the surface.

As the need rose to a crescendo, she grabbed his rich black hair and pulled hard. His eyes shot up filled with a primal hunger. Heat radiated off his skin. Carefully, he shifted his weight to his forearms and stretched his lean powerful body atop her. Any remaining modesty was cast aside as she opened her thighs to allow him access. A last wordless question in his stare let her know she could change her mind. She wrapped her legs around him in response.

Her slow exhalation was the lone sound in the room as he buried himself inside her. Small spasms reverberated deep within as her muscles extended and lengthened to accommodate him. After a brief pause, he pulled out almost completely and lunged forward once more. He repeated the motion three more times before seeking a faster rhythm. She met his pace with a wild thrashing of her hips. Sinking the tips of her nails into his shoulder blades, she raked them down his back in a savage caress.

"Yes," she moaned into his chest.

Gabe's thrusts increased in intensity, filling her to the breaking point with each passing heartbeat. She relished in the sensation of feeling so full, so alive. None of her previous experiences had prepared her for the intimacy and the power of being with a fallen angel. Every nerve stretched to the point of snapping. Every muscle clenched and released in unending pulses. Her mind reeled, lost in the blissful chaos. Just as she thought she would die from the overwhelming sensations, her orgasm tore forth in an avalanche of pleasure. She screamed his name as the waves took her. Her cries of ecstasy mixed with a heady groan as he drove inside her for the last time.

When consciousness seeped back into her hazy mind, Cassie squirmed underneath him. He lifted his head and their eyes met. A warm golden light stared back at her. He kissed her on the cheek, then shifted so they lay side by side wrapped in each other's arms. He never broke the eye contact. Eventually, the urge to speak outweighed the afterglow.

"What now?" she said uncertain.

Gabe turned to stare at a clock on the nightstand. Cassie could see over his shoulder the red digital light shining 7:15pm. *So early.* She thought with a gasp. *How's that even possible?* The time since Gabe first got back to the cabin now seemed like years. She turned onto her back and made small circles with her hands and feet, wondering at how her body remained intact after their mind-blowing escapade.

"I suppose I should warn you," Gabe said leaning back toward her and observing her movements with a curious inclination of his head. "Tomorrow your training begins."

"Training?" She ceased all movements. "What're you talking about?"

"No reason to worry." His devilish grin made her insides clench in a way she thought impossible after being sated twice in one evening. "At least not tonight."

"Why? What's different about tonight?" Her breath caught as a familiar hunger returned to his eyes.

He cupped her cheek in the palm of his hand and kissed her once more. Fire rose between them again as if it had never subsided. His voice was low and sensual as he whispered into her ear, "Everything."

TWENTY-FOUR

Light peeked behind the curtain as the sun began to rise on the distant horizon. Cassie stretched her arms overhead and pointed her toes, basking in a satisfied afterglow. Rolling to her side she patted the bed lovingly only to find it empty. The sheet slipped down her torso at the movement, revealing her bare breasts. She glanced about the room to find Gabe watching her from a corner chair, a hunger in his gaze and a set firmness to his jaw. The predatory look dissolved to stoic composure as he rose from his seat.

Cassie covered herself with the blanket, eyeing his sudden change. "Good morning," she said, more question than greeting.

"Not today, I'm afraid. At least not for you." He strode toward the bed and pointed to a clock on the nightstand. "The sun will be up in fifteen minutes. I've let you sleep too long." He brushed his fingers over her cheek. "In fairness you are quite captivating when you're asleep."

She leaned on her elbow and raised an eyebrow at him.

"Not so much when I'm awake then?" In an effort to tease, she let the blanket drop once more.

"Unfortunately, for me, you're even more intriguing when you wake. However..." He turned away and rummaged through one of her suitcases. She would have shouted at him about privacy and all that, but he apparently found what he needed in a flash and zipped the luggage as if it had never been disturbed. All traces of amusement disappeared as he threw a pair of sweat pants and t-shirt onto the bed. "We have business to attend to."

"I take it I'm not going to like this...business?" She picked at the clothes with mild distaste.

"Not one bit." He strode toward the bedroom doorway. "You have fifteen minutes to shower and dress. I'll be in the kitchen." He closed the door.

With a sigh, Cassie stood up and arched her back. The grogginess wore off as she attempted a few more stretches. Donning the same robe from last night, she grabbed the sweats and shirt from the bed, and made her way to the bathroom attached to the master suite. The hot water felt like heaven as she showered, but she didn't stay long, anxious to get to the bottom of Gabe's morning behavior. As always, he puzzled her and she didn't like following his orders one bit. She shook her head at his nerve as she dried off and dressed. Her hair sat in a clump atop her head. She brushed the knots out as best she could and threw it into a bun. A peek in the mirror had her frowning, but she shrugged and tried to prepare herself for whatever "business" Gabe had in mind.

"Might as well get it over with," she said to her reflection. A sugary scent pervaded the air as she made her way toward the kitchen. On the antique table sat a small stack of what might have been pancakes. It was hard to tell from the burnt exterior and mound of syrup covering the plate.

Gabe waved a hand at the chair in front of the food. "Please, eat. You're going to need your strength."

Biting her bottom lip, she sat and forked the pancakes in the center. "Thanks for breakfast."

"A feeble attempt to make you more amiable to training."

"Tr-ay?" she tried to ask with a mouthful of burnt dough. She reached for the warm cup of tea and downed half of it.

"Perhaps, I should have skipped the pleasantries." A hint of a grin appeared.

"Maybe," she said honestly. "But, never mind. You mentioned training last night and now again. What do you mean?"

"I want to be sure you're well protected. Hence the enlisting of Rafe's help." He snarled at the mention of the other fallen's name. "As your Guardian, it's my duty." He reached across the table to stroke her arm. "But, now..." His fingers brushed her cheek. "I'd like to be sure you can defend yourself for my own peace of mind."

She pressed his palm against her cheek. The heat of his hand radiated over her skin. A heartbeat later, he pulled away. His eyes narrowed. "Cassie, what do you know about fighting?"

It took her a long minute to shake away the initial surprise. She stared at him registering the full weight of his question. *He wants me to be safe. Not because he's obligated. He wants me safe because...he feels something.* Joy washed over her in one momentous swoop. She wanted to shout her feelings from the rooftop. But, reality set in. Training meant grueling workouts, running, sparring, repetitive movements and who knew what else a fallen angel could come up with. She was never averse to physical activity and had practiced martial arts for few years when she was younger. But she was sure what a fallen could come up with would be much harder than anything she's done before. She groaned.

"Well..." She rubbed the back of her neck. "I practiced Shotokan when I was younger. Does that count?"

The lines of his forehead furrowed as his eyes widened. "What does a house of pine-waves have to do with fighting?"

"Huh? No, not the literal meaning." She smiled at the misunderstanding, impressed with his knowledge of Japanese. *Then again, he probably knows most languages.* Aloud, she explained, "Shotokan is a style of karate." When the confused look remained on his face, she tried, "Self-defense." Still nothing. "Martial Arts." Same blank stare. "You know, fighting!" she cried at last.

"Ah," Gabe said. "An old human style. Good, should make it easier."

Yeah, sure. The thought barely had time to register when Gabe launched himself off the chair, over the table, and at her head. On instinct, she threw her weight to the right and rolled on her side. The impact of hitting the hard wood floor startled her, but she recovered fast and rocked herself to a kneeling position. Her knees remained off the ground and the weight sat in the balls of her feet.

"You weren't lying about your previous training." Gabe

flipped after he dove over the table and stood above her. "Good."

"What the hell is wrong with you?" She shifted on her feet and remained kneeling. The ability to stand seemed an uncertain assumption in her current state.

Cassie didn't have time to remain indecisive too long. In one swift motion Gabe grabbed her around the waist and hoisted her up. Crushing her to his chest, he captured her in a passionate kiss. All thoughts of protest fled.

When he let her go, she staggered back. *Damn, but he can kiss.*

"When you're done eating, meet me outside and we'll continue the lesson." He swept out the door and into the cold without further comment.

Cassie braced her hands against the table for support. Her emotions rode on an ever-flowing rollercoaster when it came to Gabe. She couldn't determine from one minute to the next whether she wanted to kiss him, kill him, or...something else. Cautiously, she sat down in the chair, half-expecting Gabe to sneak attack her from behind. Instead, Maia jumped on her lap and meowed.

"How's my little one?" She stroked Maia's soft fur and attempted to choke down a few more bites of the pancake disaster. When she felt sturdy, she shooed Maia from her lap, grabbed a light jacket and rose to meet Gabe outside.

"We'll start easy with running," he announced as she approached him. "Three miles should be good for the first time."

"Are you serious?" Cassie couldn't help asking. While she hadn't trained in karate for years, she tried to keep in shape by exercising at home, keeping what she learned fresh, or making occasional trips with Zoey to the gym. However, running three miles, in the woods, in the winter, on an uneven ground sounded like torture.

"I am." Gabe planted his feet shoulder width apart and stared at her hard. His posture gave a clear display of his dead on seriousness. "I'll run in front of you. All you have to do is keep up."

Without giving her a chance to say another word, he dashed into the woods. Cassie sighed and followed him in a slow jog. She soon realized her pace wouldn't do. Gabe ran with ease, never faltering or breaking stride. Her frustrations mounted with each step. In the first five minutes of trying to match him, she stumbled a half dozen times, scraped both knees, and acquired a nasty bruise on her forearm that turned purple with merciless speed.

"What's the matter?" Gabe goaded her. "I'm not even going fast. And I thought you were in much better shape."

Anger washed over her, even as she recognized the infuriating tactic. Her former karate instructor had used taunting as a motivational tool as well. In theory, it was supposed to get students to work harder. Cassie never cared much for theory, but damn it if it didn't work every time. With dirt-ridden hands, she rubbed her bruised knees and forearm while inwardly soothing her injured pride. *Screw this!* The shout resonated inside her head. *I'm tough and I'll show him, even if it kills me.*

As she picked up speed, her lungs burned from the brisk air but her legs pushed forward. They didn't say another word to each other for the rest of the run. Before she knew it, they had circled back to the clearing in front of the cabin. She stood in the middle of it, hands on her thighs, panting and trying to slow down the rhythm of her insanely beating heart.

"Not bad," Gabe said. The cocky pull to his lips didn't match the half compliment.

Cassie glared at him. He wasn't even out of breath. She knew better than to ask him if they were done. When he motioned for her to move again, she followed him behind the cabin and saw a number of uneven tree stumps of various height.

"Your handiwork, I presume?" Her breath gave off a white mist from the cold, although her body was damp with sweat.

Gabe just grinned and motioned for her to start. Cassie stepped onto the first stump. Holding her hands out for balance, she jumped to the next one and then the next.

"Too slow." She heard his voice as she eyed the higher of the stumps. Ignoring him, she concentrated on the distance and leaped. Instead of landing on a smooth wood surface, her feet slipped and she rolled awkwardly onto the unforgiving ground. Her elbow caught the worst of it, and she shouted as it made contact. "Shit!"

"Start over." Gabe growled.

She grumbled, but gave no argument. Rubbing her elbow, she rose again and eyed the stumps with hatred. *You can do this. Just concentrate.*

Three tries later, Cassie whooped as she reached the last stump. "How was that?" she asked, pride seeping into her tone.

"Next go around you have to take less time," Gabe said as he walked away.

She could only stare at his back. *Jerk,* she thought, once

more mentally massaging her ego.

He let her take a sip of water before they moved on. Sets of crunches, pushups and lunges came next. As the sun hid behind a cloud, she collapsed in a heap on the ground.

"I can't do this anymore," she let herself whine.

Gabe sighed. "We'll take a lunch break. Then move onto sparring."

Cassie shook her head in disbelief. While she wasn't happy at the prospect of more training, she was more than happy to get into the house for a snack and hopefully a nap. She trotted into the house, not caring if Gabe followed or not, and went straight into the kitchen. She tugged on the fridge door just as Gabe intercepted her. He grabbed the door handle with one hand and laid his other hand on her shoulder.

"You did good, Cassie." He said, rubbing her tight shoulders, and eyeing her elbow. "Go sit and rest. I'll make us something to eat."

Despite his earlier failed attempt in the kitchen, Cassie didn't have the strength to argue. Dragging herself to the table, she sank into one of the chairs before her legs could give out. Gabe prepared simple sandwiches with ham and lettuce. Yet, they tasted like a five star meal to her. She drained a big bottle of Gatorade along with two sandwiches. After the meal, she curled up in a ball on the couch, and passed out as soon as her head hit the cushion.

Gabe shook her. "It's time to get up. We have more work to do."

Cassie opened her mouth to yell at him. *Two minutes is not enough time to sleep. He's insane.* Before she could get the words out, a glance at the clock above the fireplace showed an hour had passed. She sighed. "Can't we leave this for tomorrow? I'm exhausted." She hated the desperation in her voice, but she had reached a breaking point.

"We don't know what tomorrow will bring." His brows pulled together in a ferocious scowl. "I don't know how many days we'll have to get you ready, Cassie." He sounded upset but determined. "We need to use every day, every moment."

She shivered. *If that's the case, a few weeks of intense training won't be of much help anyway.* Fighting to find courage and strength, she nodded in his general direction. Pealing her aching body from the couch landed her face to face with Gabe. He leaned in to close the distance.

"If you work hard, you may earn a reward later on tonight." It was just a whisper but full of so many promises. Cassie couldn't help but smile as he lightly kissed her. Before her body had any more time to react to his touch, he took her hand and led her outside. The chill evening air had a sobering effect.

For two more hours they performed various sparring drills and exercises, with Gabe explaining both attack and defense positions. They resonated with her, recalling to her mind lessons once learned earlier in her days in a karate dojo.

"Many of these are natural reactions," he said in the little break between the drills. "You just have to trust your instincts, trust those reactions. They won't fail you."

They finished when the sunset colored the sky. Exhausted and in major pain, Cassie took a long hot bath. Afterward, Gabe delivered on his promise of a reward, easing her aches and pains with a different type of aching. When the evening ended and she lay sated in his arms, she whispered, "The day may have been rough, but if I get to spend my evenings like this, it might just be worth it."

#

Weeks passed in cycles of pain and relief. The pain came during the daylight hours with unending series of fighting drills, running, sparring, and the rest. Relief came in the evenings when Cassie could revel in Gabe's touch, and then drop into bed exhausted but satisfied. Somewhere in between food, calls to Zoey, and showering took place, but the blessed events were mere blips in the training regimen.

Around week four or so, all count of days lost, she had been given an early reprieve as Gabe went to prepare some gauntlet like test for her in the surrounding woods. She sat on the couch dreading whatever new torment he had in store for her.

"If this doesn't kill me, I'll be the strongest woman in history!" She leaned her back against the soft cushion. The TV showed the latest weather report for the area, but she hardly registered the program. Pulling her knees to her chest, she hung her head. A chill enveloped her as the temperature dropped. It took but a heartbeat to notice the change in the air. The TV clicked off and the surrounding space charged with electrical currents.

"I can feel you there," she managed to say without shaking. "What do you want?"

A soothing voice spoke in her ear, "Please bring me through Key. I need to talk to your Guardian."

While the request seemed polite enough, something inside her ushered a warning. She'd never used her powers to bring an angel to Earth before. Whenever Cassie's abilities had been harnessed, it always had a demon behind it. Those creatures forced her to experience terrible headaches and as a result pushed their way into the world. A strange foreboding filled her soul.

"I don't know how and I'm not about to bring on a headache willingly." Cassie squared her shoulders and looked around the room for signs of the angel.

"It will not be painful." The disembodied angel's voice rang high like raindrops upon tin. "Concentrate on the energy around you. Feel it becoming a physical entity and I will appear."

Curiosity warred with caution. "You want me dead," Cassie said, eyes narrowing. "Why should I help you?"

"Angels do not kill humans, Key. The fallen must accomplish that." The angel paused. "I cannot force him do anything, but I will speak with him." The tone changed from a soft cadence to something far more powerful.

Cassie considered her options. *Gabe wouldn't hurt me, so talking to him will change nothing.* She stood up and began to concentrate on the energy around her. *Probably better not to give an angel another reason to want to kill me.* The seconds ticked on as a shape started to form in the center of the room. Dancing lights zipped along the air and materialized in the space. After a minute or two the outline of a woman appeared. Her limbs stretched forward, her hair swept a long golden wave down her back, and two shining wings expanded from between her shoulder blades.

The angel flashed the wings outward in a dazzling

display of white light. Cassie's jaw dropped before she could help it. Brilliant feathers, appearing made of light, arched in a symmetrical pattern from the top of the angel's head right down to her feet. The angel retracted her wings and stared at Cassie with head held high and confident.

A flash of inadequacy swept across Cassie as she looked upon the magnificent creature before her. Yet, frustration soon replaced self-consciousness. The muscles in her neck tensed at the recognition. The angel was no stranger. Ariel stood before her in all her glory. Their last meeting in the Grand Canyon did nothing to prepare her for seeing Ariel in the flesh. When Gabe performed the communication ritual, the Angelic Council appeared on Earth in a temporary form. To gain any type of permanent physical shape, a Key needed to perform the act. Yet, Gabe had told her angels stayed only long enough to perform whatever their assigned mission, and then returned to the Light.

"Well done," Ariel said with a hint of condescension. "I will speak with Gabe now."

"He's not here." Cassie crossed her arms in an effort to shield herself.

"No matter. I will find him." Ariel said nothing further and brushed past Cassie out the door.

Cassie followed her outside and stared in awe as the angel took to the sky. Like her or not, the image of the golden-haired white-winged angel against the darkening sky was a sight she would never forget.

TWENTY-FIVE

Gabe took a step back to admire his work. Ten wood pylons stood like soldiers as they drove through the snow to the strong earth below. Each had been cut and erected at a different height to create an obstacle for anyone foolish enough to attempt walking through or upon them. He couldn't suppress a laugh as he imagined the curses Cassie would have for him at this latest challenge. This obstacle course was twice as hard as the tree stumps she'd went through on her first day of training.

All things considered, Cassie's training turned out to be quite effective. Granted she complained at just about every interval, but her surprising resolve and determined nature guaranteed she would keep going, keep trying despite any pain she felt or setbacks she encountered. For one fallen angel that type of courage and plucky spirit turned into dangerous aphrodisiacs. Even now, he shook his head of baser thoughts, looked toward the sky, and considered stripping down into the snow to cool the growing fever.

"Cassie," he growled low and began walking toward the cabin. A chilling sight stopped him in his tracks as he caught a glimmer of white against the gray evening sky. "Seems I've found the cure for lust after all. Cold shower no longer required." He grumbled as the white speck landed and came into full view.

"Gabe. It's been too long." The angel shone bright and made the pure snow around her dance in an array of colors.

"Not long enough. What do you want, Ariel?" Gabe's voice sounded harsh even to his own ears. But, he couldn't keep the anger from reaching outward. This seemingly beautiful creature had caused him nothing but grief for far too long, and now she wanted the woman he loved dead. Worse, she wanted his lover's blood on his hands. *I'd die first.* His back stiffened.

"Tsk. Tsk," Ariel said, shaking her finger at him. "So much emotion will cause you nothing but trouble."

"I'm not in the mood for games." He stormed past her, intentionally brushing against her outstretched wings. She recoiled at the contact, retracting her wings close to her body.

"Neither am I," she shouted as she outpaced him and blocked his path.

Gabe halted and his jaw muscles twitched. He struggled to keep his emotions in check. For a moment, he closed his eyes and took a deep breath. When he felt steady, he said, "Talk."

"You have been here too long." A hint of sadness emerged from the usually frosty angel, but passed just as it appeared. The light emanating from her became more subdued as she spoke. "No matter. Your responsibilities have not changed. And you put everything in danger the longer you drag your feet."

"I've given you my answer already. You have no further business here." He sidestepped Ariel in an attempt to shake her off, but she mimicked his movements, a second ahead of him at each turn. After a minute or so of this cat and mouse game, he roared, "Get out of my way."

Without warning, she faced him nose to nose, two inches of space between them. In a feral tone she whispered, "If I could do the deed myself I would."

A wild image flashed through his mind. His hands wrapped around Ariel's throat, slowly, ever so slowly, squeezing her windpipe. Bone and muscle crushed together, the sound echoing through the woods. A hideous gasp as the angel takes her last breath. The silence that follows after her body falls to the ground...deafening.

Gabe pushed the gruesome picture away. He took a pointed step back, frightened by his rage. Steadying his breaths, he let the tension drain from his body. "You push your luck, Ariel."

"I only remind you of your place." She leaned forward but made no further move toward him. "This world makes you forget yourself, who and what you are."

"I've never been more myself." The words spoken aloud took a weight from his shoulders he didn't know he bore. He rose straighter, taller somehow with the revelation. His soul exploded forth as if released from a cage. The pine-scented air filled his lungs. *What is the human expression? The truth will set you free. So be it.*

"Really? Shall I remind you?" She waved her hand from sky to ground. "You are a fallen angel. One who betrayed our laws. You are outcast, banished. If you ever hope to see the Light again, you will seek your redemption." She paused and placed her hands on her hips. Power exuded from her body, dripping from every pore. "Our word, our judgment is the Key must die."

"Then, I challenge the Angelic Council."

"You dare question us?" A melodious laugh like the ringing of church bells cut through the air.

"Yes. I question the Council's hypocrisy. One day setting me on a road to protect this Key, the next demanding I kill her. I question the sanity of believing even one life is expendable." He fixed his gaze on her, eyes burning. "But, most of all I question your motives."

"Those are not questions, Gabe. No. They smell much more like accusations." Ariel thrust her wings forward in a fierce display that shook the very earth around them.

"Call it what you will." Gabe ran a hand through his hair weary of this conversation. The angel's power began to creep upon him like pinpricks on his skin.

"You think me heartless, but I am not." Her tone changed again, now dripping with sweetness. "She is dangerous, Gabe." Her lashes fluttered like flower petals in a breeze. The energy pinpricks turned to teasing strokes. Stepping closer, she draped a hand on his chest.

It was an old act of hers and one he knew all too well. He grabbed her wrist, clenching his fist over the delicate bones, and threw it off as if it were a snake that bit him. Putting more distance between them he said, "Not this time." His hands came up. "Just go home, Ariel. There's nothing for you here."

She gazed at the ground, pouted lips and tear-filled

eyes. In a breath the moment was gone, her face masked once more. She met his eyes with absolute impassiveness. "We'll see." Her last words uttered as she took to the sky.

A blaze could be viewed from below as the angel returned to her world. The sight would appear as a shooting star to any human who might be watching. Gabe knew better. An explosion of heat and fire emanated from an angel's body when it shook earthly form to pass through to the world of Light beyond. Ariel would emerge into that existence, a place he once called home, with perfect ease and grace. A pang of envy hit him as he watched her disappear.

"The Light," he said. "Peace. Peace of mind. Peace in my heart." He laughed. "Even a creature as cold as Ariel can feel the pull of human emotions, earthly emotions, in this world. Even she can't fight it." He sighed, trailing his eyes across the sky to watch the last flicker of light. "What hope do I have then?"

A voice flew on the wind. A name reverberated. "Gabe." Cassie called to him. Even at this distance he could hear it, feel it, the connection with her.

"Cassie." Going back to the Light would mean leaving her behind. Leaving all he'd learned, the pleasures and pain, the emotions, the joys and sorrows, the love; none of it could return with him. *Cassie.* If she would only bond with an angel, all would be different. Worlds would merge. Life would be forever altered. If the Light descended upon the Earth, could they be together?

Gabe walked toward the cabin with heavy steps and a heavier heart. All the days of his long existence he had been sure of his decisions, certain of his way. Since the day he had fallen, everything changed. With absolute tunnel vision, he'd sought redemption. Now, when it seemed closer than ever before, he pushed it away for a woman he never knew he wanted, never imagined he needed.

By the time he trotted through the woods and reached the front door, his head pounded in his ears. He rubbed his temples, then opened the door. Cassie sat on the couch with hands folded to her chest and an unreadable look on her face. Bypassing any greeting, she said, "Well?"

A hint of fear ran through her question. Her doubt was more than he could handle. In two strides, he stood before her. She unfolded her hands and rose atop the couch, matching his height. Her gaze felt hot on his cool skin as if her searching eyes could see straight to his soul. He wrapped his arms around her and kissed her neck, her cheeks, her nose, her mouth. He wished to answer her question, to ease her fears without words.

When she pulled away, he let her go. Her expression altered. A blush appeared on her cheeks, but doubt lingered in her eyes. "Tell me what happened, Gabe." She traced his jaw line with a delicate brush of her fingertips.

"Ariel came to remind me of the Angelic Council's decision." He paused, hesitant to recall the details of that decision. He took Cassie's hand and gave it a squeeze.

"You mean she came to tell you *she* wants me dead and you're supposed to kill me." Cassie pulled her hand away.

"*They* want you dead. Though I'm quite sure it's by Ariel's persuasions. She's very good at getting her own way." He growled low. The image of the angel's taunts a constant vision in his mind. He shook it away. "None of which matters anymore."

"Why?" She barely spoke it aloud. Gabe strained to hear her.

"Because..." It would be so easy, so simple to tell her how he felt. But, he couldn't. He wouldn't be so selfish. Too much was at stake now. The day of the bonding drew near. She needed to decide for herself the right thing to do, not be influenced by his feelings. "Because I won't be connived into committing murder. I've killed before, but never an innocent woman."

"I'm not innocent. I'm guilty of a lot." She looked down and tried to wipe her eyes discreetly.

"Cassie, I..." He turned away to stop himself from taking her in his arms and showing her how much he cared. "You're not guilty of anything." He walked to the dining room table and took a seat. Struggling to make his voice more neutral he added, "And you have more important things to consider now. Don't worry about Ariel or the Council." He swallowed hard. *Or us.* His fist landed on the wood table. "I'll deal with them."

He watched her brow furrow and eyes narrow. She didn't say a word. As if coming to some decision, her face went blank. She hopped off the couch and joined him at the table.

"Speaking of things to consider, I've been thinking about the bonding." Her tone sounded too clinical, too matter of fact. "What do I have to do?"

He ignored the change in her demeanor, and tried to match it instead. "Every bonding is different. Sometimes it's a simple blood exchange, sometimes it requires oaths, or it can be a complex ritual." He shrugged. "It all depends on the participants. Both sides, angel and demon, must be present to assure the Key's free will. But, the bonding will change depending on the Key's choice."

"So, whoever I choose to bond with will determine what I have to do?"

"Yes. But, it will come. You'll know what to do when the time is right." He sighed and wished they were talking about something else. He didn't want to picture her bonding with anyone, in any fashion.

"I don't understand. *How* will I know what I'm supposed to do?"

Gabe thought about the last time he'd heard of an Angel-Key bonding. "I knew several angels who were sent to Earth to bond with new Keys. One of them described the act as being as natural as breathing."

"Doesn't really help." She leaned back in the chair making it tilt at an awkward angle.

"I'm afraid it's all I can tell you." He placed a hand on her shoulder. "Just trust yourself. You have keen instincts. Use them."

"What if I choose wrong? What if I do something wrong?"

A lump formed at the base of his windpipe and he swallowed it down. He trusted her, but her concerns mirrored his own. If their roles were reversed, he couldn't be sure he'd be confident in his decisions either, not anymore. He said what he'd want to hear. "You'll be fine. I have faith in you."

Her eyes welled up but the tears didn't fall. "Thank you," she whispered.

The chair screeched across the floor as Cassie jumped up. She reached for him as if caught on fire. Wrapping her arms around his neck, she fell into his lap, and pressed her lips to his. He met her fervor after only a moment's hesitation. So much had passed between them, and so much more lay on the horizon. He felt dazed by the force of it all, but refused to fight it.

Pulling back a fraction of an inch, he said, "Don't think this will get you out of training."

She laughed. "Wouldn't dream of it."

They made love that night as if the chance would never come again. Unspoken emotions surfaced in every kiss, every look, and every touch. The days ahead would lead them to a future neither of them could foresee, but the nights until then were theirs alone.

TWENTY-SIX

Cassie came out of the shower with a fluffy yellow towel piled high on top of her head and a flimsy white t-shirt hugging her still moist body. Tiny beads of water fell from her lean legs onto the carpet. She caught Gabe's heated gaze on her and batted her lashes with a *come hither* stare.

"I'm not taking another shower today," she huffed at him, suppressing laughter. "I'm too exhausted." Her body betrayed her as it came alive and tingled in all the right places.

Gabe got up from the couch, where he'd sat watching the news on TV. *How human,* she thought with a sigh as he made his way toward her. *How normal.* The months they'd spent in relative peace created a surreal atmosphere. She could almost believe they were just another average couple on a private retreat, almost forget the decision that lay ahead. *Almost.*

"Well, if you're too exhausted, maybe I can find a way to relax you," he said, stalking toward her. His muscles rippled in an enticing display as he closed the distance. He reached for her and jerked her forward so that she stumbled into his arms, finding herself pressed against his hard chest. The cotton fabric of her t-shirt tickled her breasts.

"And how are you planning on relaxing me?" she said, warmth filling her cheeks.

"Do you want me to describe it," he whispered into her ear, sending a shiver up and down her back. "Or do you want me to just show you?"

"I don't know." She feigned seriousness, trying to push away from him. "I don't want to take another shower."

"What if I promise to wash you? All you'll have to do is stand there and let me do the work?"

Cassie wiggled her brows. She put her arms around his neck in surrender, not that she ever considered giving him a fight, when her phone's musical ring sounded nearby. Sighing, she let him go.

"Just as it was getting interesting. Ah well. Must be Zoey," she said, grabbing the phone from the side table by the couch. Over the past seven weeks, no one had called except Zoey. In fact, no one else knew how to reach Cassie and Gabe at all. Cassie didn't like the hiding but if she were going to live to see her birthday, then it was a necessary inconvenience. For good or bad the day would arrive very soon.

"Wonder why she's calling so late," she said to Gabe as she flipped the phone open.

Gabe just shrugged.

"What's up, Zo? You're not at a party or a club?" Cassie laughed, waiting to hear her friend's bubbly comeback.

Instead, a frosty voice came through the line. Her blood ran cold, recognition causing her head to swim. She knew that voice though she would far prefer to forget it.

"You didn't want to play with us so we had to settle for your friend," the caller said into her ear with no preamble. She glanced at Gabe, horror written on her face. In one smooth movement, he was at her side, his ear pressed to the side of the phone. His arm went around her waist and pulled her close. A protective growl escaped his throat.

"What have you done, Dan?" Cassie didn't let an inch of fear slip into her question. She surprised even herself at the amount of control and coldness she could muster into her tone. The terror mounting inside didn't equal her stoicism.

"Oh, nothing yet. We'll make your friend's stay with us as pleasant as possible. Well, as pleasant as one can be in restraints and with a gag in one's mouth. But I'll try to at least keep my boys away from her." He paused allowing the commotion in the background to break through the line. A muffled feminine cry along with several male threats echoed in Cassie's ear. "Although she looks too damn tempting all tied up."

Cassie bristled. *Hold it together.* Mounting courage against this bastard felt like an impossible task. He was taunting her, yet his sadistic tendencies meant Zoey could already be hurt or worse. Her heart dropped. She turned eyes full of dread to Gabe. He squeezed her waist.

"What do you want?" The words came out through gritted teeth, but her tone remained even. *Don't let him shake you.* Why didn't the bastard do the world a favor and die back in Vegas?

"Daddy wants to see you again." Dan's tone became smooth, velvety, as if he was trying to seduce her through the phone.

Motherless... Cassie shook enraged, and Gabe tensed beside her. "When?"

"He wants to spend your birthday with you. You know, catch up."

A manic, hysterical laugh threatened to bubble up, but she didn't let it reach the surface. "I'll bet he does."

"You should give him a chance. He has so much to offer you," Dan said, a hint of sincerity breaking through the cold exterior.

Psycho! He believes this shit. Her thoughts became bitter before she could respond. The urge to hurl became so strong, Cassie had to pull the phone away and take a deep breath. It didn't help.

"You are the last person I would take advice from, you stupid son of a bitch!" She screamed into the phone with all the vehemence she could summon.

"Hey, just trying to make it a little easier for you, darling."

"I doubt that very much. Your only concern is making things easier for yourself." Despite her rage, logic kept her thoughts on track. She was getting sucked into pointless banter. Holding hand over the receiver, she counted to three, then said, "Just tell me what you want me to do to get Zoey back."

She locked eyes with Gabe. Sympathy and support etched in his gaze. It was enough to keep her steady, an anchor to grab on to as the water closed over her head.

"Well, we'll pay you a little visit, you know, to talk things out."

She could practically hear his sick grin through the phone. *No more games for this asshole.* In as low a voice as she could manage, she said, "Let's cut through the B-S, shall we? Your 'little visit' is to force me to bond with him, correct?"

"Hey, that's your daddy's business. I'm just the messenger."

"And you know what they say about messengers, don't you? They tend to get shot." The image of Dan with a bullet through his brain and the gun in her hand was seriously appealing at this moment.

"I knew I liked you." He laughed high and wild. "But I'm just your father's humble servant."

"Please, like you don't stand to profit from your work."

"More than you could ever imagine, darling." He cooed the term of endearment at her like a lover might.

She tapped her foot against the hardwood floor. The rage and agitation built to its breaking point. She tried to get her nerves under control and form a plan. After an awkward silence, she decided to keep the home field advantage. "Well, I'm not going anywhere. I'm assuming you don't need directions to us."

"Oh, I like you more and more," he whispered, the sound reverberating through the line. "Now, tell your guardian." The last word elongated in an obvious manner of distaste. "Tell him not to try any heroics."

"You better make sure Zoey is unharmed." Cassie's words escaped as a hiss through clenched teeth. "Or 'daddy' dear will lose me for good. Wouldn't want that now, would you?"

Dan's cackle preceded a harsh beeping as the line disconnected.

Every muscle in her body pulled tight. She gasped trying to suck in some air.

"Shhh, stop shaking, love." She let Gabe's voice penetrate the fear that overtook her. Her whole body shook. Her breath hitched and tears spilled. She let Gabe comfort her within his strong embrace, wiping the tears away with his fingertips.

She took a long shuddering breath and pushed away from him. "We have to figure out what to do. We need a plan."

Gabe smiled down at her, an unspoken pride radiating through his eyes. His faith in her gave Cassie the ability to think through the pain. She was discovering all kinds of power within herself and she couldn't help but wonder the source of that strength, her angel or her demon side.

They sat on the rug in front of the fireplace and gazed at the crackling heat inside.

"We've been avoiding talking about it all this time, Gabe," Cassie said. "We can't avoid it anymore. My birthday is coming and whatever needs to happen will happen."

"We haven't spoken about it because we needed to concentrate on getting you ready. And I needed your head clear. I needed you focused." Cassie felt his eyes on her face but didn't turn toward him.

"Yeah, well, I'm as prepared as I'm ever going to get but my head is not clear anymore." She bit her bottom lip as thoughts of Zoey filled her head. "Any suggestions?"

"First priority is your friend now. Am I right?" He turned her face to stare into her eyes. "You don't have to say anything. I didn't expect it to be otherwise."

She nodded unable to find the words. He spoke for her. "If we can figure out a way to get Zoey out safe, then you'll be able to think without distractions, without impediments to your decision."

When she found her voice again, she muttered, "Sounds so simple." The floor suddenly held her interest. Well, anything would do as long as she could look away from his knowing gaze.

Gabe took one of her hands in his strong grip, and tried to meet her eyes once more. "If we can't get to her..." He paused and started again adapting a more even tone, "Cassie, as your guardian, I need to remind you..." He stopped again to sigh, and then bent down further so Cassie could not avoid his gaze. "I appreciate this is your friend. I get it. I do. But you need to understand she can't be your number one concern. There are much bigger things at stake here." He touched his finger to her mouth when she made a move to speak. "I know this sounds heartless to you. But please believe me, it's not. The lives of many people rely on this decision. I wish it wasn't so. I wish I could take away that burden from you. But I can't and nothing can change it."

"You're wrong, Gabe." She stood up, pulling her hands away and crossing them over her chest. "Zoey's life is my number one priority. The second that changes, I lose a piece of my humanity, a piece of myself. I give into whatever demon blood flows inside me." She started to pace, lost in her emotions. Memories of their friendship bounded through her mind like an old filmstrip. "I have to think of Zoey above all else right now because she's what makes me human. Her friendship, what we share, it's something no demon or angel could understand."

She regretted the last words the second she uttered them. A fleeting look of pain passed on Gabe's face, but it was enough for her to catch. She shook her head.

"I didn't say that to hurt you, Gabe. But the way you're being honest with me, I need to be honest with you. My humanity is what I have to hold on to, it's what will balance me. It's who I am."

Gabe didn't speak. His breathing slowed. At last he nodded, his face a mask of resolve. "I understand," he said. "We'll do it your way. Your humanity is what I love most about you and I'll do what needs to be done to preserve it."

A floodgate of emotions opened in Cassie's heart at his words. She knew no matter what might lay in their future, she could never, would never love any man more. Yet, plans had to be laid out. Declarations of love would have to remain on the back burner.

Over the next two days, Cassie tried not to let herself think of Zoey, to little avail. Horrible images of her friend being tortured, eyes swollen, bruised skin, lips blue, kept plaguing Cassie. She thought of the way Gabe had looked just after Vegas. The nightmare of his experience kept her worrying about Zoey all during her waking hours and late into the night. Gabe had a chance to heal and recover, but he was a fallen angel. Zoey was only human. *How could she survive?*

The seconds, minutes and hours dragged on as Cassie practically drove herself mad with worry. During the day, training, which she demanded be more intense than ever, kept her exhausted and helped block out the vile thoughts. The rest of the time, planning their moves against Val's "visit," helped as a distraction.

But the nights provided no escape. Twisted dreams filled her restless sleep. When she'd wake up panting in the middle of the night, she'd stare at the ceiling for the remaining hours until the sun rose. It was the most haunting two days of her life. When the day she'd been waiting for in agony arrived, the morning of her birthday, Cassie would be ready to meet whatever came her way head on, even if only to escape the nightmares.

TWENTY-SEVEN

The woods cast eerie shadows along the floor of the clearing as the full moon shone bright from above. Cassie paced amongst the shadows as the midnight hour approached ever nearer, ushering in her twenty-eighth birthday. Yet, as her steps increased with each passing moment, all she could think about was Zoey.

"You don't think he hurt her, right? He's not that stupid." Cassie's voice cracked as she fought back tears.

Gabe placed two strong hands on her shoulders, kneading the tension at her neck. "You have to hold it together. Whatever you decide is about to change everything." He took a deep breath before continuing, "I know you're worried about your friend, but there are bigger things at stake."

She bit down on her lower lip to fight the pain. "I know, but I can't... I won't..."

"You're not alone in this," he said wrapping his arms around her in a tight hold. "I'm here with you." He pulled back just enough to look into her eyes. "I also made a few calls to invite some other guests to this little party." He half smiled, before his face fell serious. "You should be able to choose freely. I won't let anyone force your decision."

"If he tries to kill Zoey, I may not have a choice." Her arms dropped to her sides. Her head hanging low.

He placed a hand under her chin, raising her head to meet his eyes. "There's always a choice, Cassie. We have a plan. Just trust me."

Gabe drew his tongue across her lips, and she shivered at the contact. *I don't want this to be goodbye.* Her muscles tensed and her heart seemed to stop for a moment at the thought of losing him.

"Go," she whispered.

"I won't be far. If anything goes wrong..."

"Just get Zoey."

He nodded and disappeared from her sight. In an instant, the air around her began to change, crackling with unknown energy. She jerked her head from one direction to the next, scanning the woods.

"Zoey?" she called out afraid of what might answer from the darkness.

Heavy silence filled the night. From the tree line, shapes emerged. Narrowing her eyes, Cassie began to distinguish the figures. Val appeared first, wearing a blank expression. Behind him trailed Dan with an unconscious Zoey in his grip. Cassie made a move toward them, but snatched back her step, forcing herself to remain still.

"Hello, child. I'm sorry we're not meeting under better circumstances," Val said, extending his hand toward her. "Your disappearing act left me with few options."

"What did you do to Zoey?" She managed through gritted teeth.

"The girl? Oh, yes..." Val glanced over his shoulder at the pair. "She'll be fine...eventually." He smirked. "As long as we can come to a suitable arrangement."

"Okay then, what the hell do you want?" She stole a quick glance to the right trying to spot Gabe.

"Clever child. You're too smart for such tactics." With a fluid motion, he ripped Zoey from Dan's arms and held her by the neck. She hung like a rag doll in his grip. "Let's not play games."

"You're right. Let's not." She inched closer. The adrenaline and months of training put her body on instant alert. "You're pathetic. Some all-powerful demon hiding behind a human. If you want me, here I am. But, I want you to spell it out. What *exactly* do you want?"

"Hold this." Val laughed a cold sinister sound in the night. He flung Zoey behind him as if discarding a piece of trash.

A harsh cry rang out as Zoey regained consciousness and hit the frozen ground. Dan stalked her like a hungry predator. His lips curled in a sadistic sneer. Without warning, a jolt of energy hit him square in the chest knocking him backward. Gabe stood over him, anger radiating from every pore.

"Tell me, you sick bastard, how do you want to die?"

Dan cackled. "Maybe I should ask you that question." A sharp whistle pierced the air. "So fallen, how many demons can you handle?"

Gabe looked up to find a ring of demons closing in on him. "We'll finish this later," he spat and threw Dan aside.

Cassie watched in horror as Gabe braced himself to meet the onslaught of demons. Struggling with indecision, she tore her eyes away and focused on Zoey. Her friend's broken body lay a few feet from where Val stood. As fast as she could, she sprinted forward.

As she closed the distance, a blur of movement caught her eye. It passed in front of her too fast, powerful hands encircling her waist. She spun around to stare into Val's bottomless black eyes.

"Now, back to business." He let go of her waist to grab her by the wrists. "You can see you're outnumbered and out of options." He cast his free hand around as proof. "Be smart. Do the right thing. You have my word your loved ones will be safe."

"The word of a demon? What's that worth?" A familiar husky voice sounded over Val's shoulder.

Cassie never thought the sight of Rafe would ever be so welcome. He winked at her as he circled around into full view. Black jeans, combat boots, and a burgundy-collared shirt replaced his usual suit. His casual posture might have fooled the novice onlooker, but the steel in his eyes revealed his true purpose. He wasn't here for small talk.

"You're not welcome here, fallen," Val said as he tightened his grip on Cassie. His large palm cut into both of her wrists as the bones pushed together. "This is a private party."

"But, I've been invited." Rafe shot them a wolfish grin. "And I brought some friends."

All around them fallen and demons clashed. On the outskirts of the melee, Gabe fought with abandon as he made his way back to Cassie. A demon tore at his arm only to be thrown off with a powerful hook punch to the jaw. A second demon flew to his side and was greeted with an elbow to the nose. These moves by themselves would do nothing to take down the demons but the pulsing energy around Gabe grew stronger.

Cassie screamed as a third demon, his large body all muscle, slammed into Gabe. The impact took both of them to the ground. The demon wound his arms around Gabe's neck, trying to put him into a blood choke. Sparks of electricity, given off by their combined energy, flew all around them as they struggled on the cold ground. The demon's energy threw off black flickers. Cassie had never seen anything like it before. But the all too familiar stench of standing water reached her nostrils. The black demonic energy had its own distinct smell. Gabe's energy had a blue tint to it but never gave off any aroma.

"No!" She screamed as Gabe gasped for air.

"He's one of my strongest," Val whispered into her ear.

Fear tingled through her, but Gabe gained the upper hand. He stood on top of the large demon, his own energy rippling with blue fire under his fist. The battle raged on as Gabe smashed his hand through the demon's stomach. When he pulled it back out, a black oily substance coated the limb. The demon's body stopped moving and Cassie turned her head away. She had imagined Gabe had done many violent things in his life as a warrior angel. After seeing the manner of the Angelic Council, she could have no doubts as to their nature, but to see it firsthand left her shaken. Yet, the fight marched onward and she could not take a backseat.

Cassie struggled to break free as she watched the

surrounding chaos. Val's hold proved ironclad. She waited for any opportunity to catch him off guard. Rafe kept Val's attention, but it wasn't enough to get him to loosen his grip. Her patience served her well as a voice rang in her ears like church bells.

"It is time Key. Let us through."

No arguments here. She laughed inwardly, grateful for once to hear Ariel's voice. The Angelic Council's presence surged forward, pressing on her mind. The angels might not be on her side, but they sure weren't on the demons' side either. Their company might help even the odds.

"Okay," Cassie said in a hushed tone. The pulls of celestial energy permeated her psyche. They begged for release, trapped behind an unforeseeable barrier. Concentrating on each of the angels distinct energy patterns, she imagined a wall falling away. The angels took shape, molding and forming in the physical forest clearing. As if by her will alone, a flash of light signaled their arrival and provided the perfect distraction.

Cassie didn't dare look to her handiwork. The angels could do whatever they liked. She had bigger problems, getting away from Val her number one at the moment. As Val focused on the angels, the tension on her wrists eased. She pulled back with impressive stealth and broke free of his grasp. Booking it, she dove for the cover of the tree line. Hidden behind a thick elm, she only then dared a look at the angels.

From the clearing, Ariel glided to the forefront, her face a mask of neutrality. Her dazzling white wings arched over her head, vibrating as she spoke. "We will not intervene, but the balance must be preserved."

The angel Remiel floated next to her, his feet never touching the ground. "Yes. We will stand watch." His tone ushered no argument. The bright golden hue of his wings stood in stark contrast to his dark hair. It made him look like one of the Egyptian gods etched in gold.

The remaining angels, the soldiers of the Angelic Council, stood behind their leaders. The darker, almost copper color of their wings radiated a light through the clearing. The ground shone as if ignited by liquid fire.

A snort broke the lull that had descended on the battle. "Wallflowers," Rafe murmured with a shrug, then engaged Val with a fist to the jaw. As if on cue, the fighting resumed in full force.

Ariel and Remiel folded their wings. The four angels beside them followed their lead. The display snuffed out the celestial light and punctuated their words. They had no intention of helping the fallen or Cassie.

The sight made Cassie bristle. *Look on the bright side, at least they're not trying to kill you.* The screams and cries of battle filled her ears. "No time to rest. Focus".

Glancing around, a familiar face caught her eye from the edge of the clearing. The fallen who had saved her from Dan in Vegas smashed a demon's head into the ground. His long lanky frame and oily hair could have pegged him as a rocker instead of a fallen angel, but the energy surrounding him could leave no doubt.

"Hey Snarky, could you get your ass in motion?" Rafe called to the same fallen as he continued to engage Val.

Cassie tore her eyes away as Gabe reached her at the same moment and pulled her further into the cover of the trees. "Are you all right?" He asked looking her over.

"I'm fine," she said. "I feel a little strange, though."

"It's your power starting to come through. You have to make your choice." He brushed her cheek with the tips of his fingers. "And I want you to choose me."

"What are you talking about?" Surprise made her hesitate, before she realized the weight of his words. "I can't do that! What about your redemption?"

"The Light will always be a part of me, but my future is with you." He stared into her eyes, and she found herself lost in his gaze. "I love you. I've made my choice."

Cassie remained speechless. Unshed tears of joy sprang to her eyes. More than anything she wanted to tell him how she felt, but as she began to respond, a bloodcurdling scream shattered the moment. A shared look of understanding had them both running toward the sound.

The scene playing out in the clearing shook Cassie to the core. Dan crouched over Zoey's body, a bloody knife in his hand and a grin of satisfaction across his face. Cassie's heart twisted and a shout of denial escaped her as she raced toward her friend. Only her connection to Zoey and the shock of the situation made her reach them a second before Gabe, just enough time to put her training into good use. Dan's head snapped back as her fist, encased in purple light, cracked against his temple. She'd never let loose such force before. The bastard fell to the ground in a heap.

Demons descended upon them as Cassie knelt at Zoey's side, her friend's head cradled in her lap. She fought to stop the blood that ran from the knife wound in Zoey's stomach. "Please, don't die."

"We're running out of time," Gabe said as he fought off the approaching demons.

"I don't know what to do." She sobbed.

Zoey's eyes flickered open. "Cassie," she whispered.

Warm lavender colored light glowed from Cassie's hands as they pressed into the fatal wound. Energy radiated up her arms into her chest and flooded her body. The feeling of strength and power overwhelmed her with its intensity. The choice became clear.

"Zoey." She wiped away the blood and dried tears from her friend's cheek. "I'm going to save you." Lifting her hands from Zoey's body, she grabbed for the discarded knife. With expert precision, she sliced a thin line on each of her palms. As the blood flowed down her fingers, she pressed them back to the wound, and chanted words in an unknown language. They spilled forth from her as if she'd known them her whole life.

Shudders racked Zoey as the energy poured into her. Flesh and muscle forged together as if the wound had never been there. Purple light now encased her entire body in an otherworldly glow. She stared ahead as if looking through Cassie, not at her. A glow of health and life began to form in her eyes and the waves of energy dissipated.

"Cassie?" Zoey said, a hand touching the spot where her wound had been. "What happened?"

Cassie couldn't find the words. Instead, she drew Zoey close to her chest, and sobs of relief rocked her. For some time, they lay on the ground just crying and hugging one another. When the tears had passed, Cassie picked up her head and realized for the first time that the fighting around them had stopped. Fallen, demons, and angels surrounded them in silence.

Ariel emerged amongst them all and leaned down to

whisper in Cassie's ear. "You're quite a surprise." She beamed, a golden light in her eyes, then turned to the rest of the observers. "The bond has been made. The Key has chosen. So, let it be." At her words, the angels disappeared within a hazy light.

"Well, that was unexpected." Rafe laughed. "But then I had a feeling you'd be entertaining." He grinned at Cassie. "Offer still stands." He inclined his head toward Zoey. "When you change your mind."

"Thanks," she said. "But, I'm good."

Val strode toward them. A heavy hand landed on Rafe's shoulder and hauled him back. "This isn't over between us, fallen. You've overstepped this time."

"You know where to find me, demon," Rafe said steadying himself and brushing Val's hand off. He walked away without a backward glance. Snarky followed behind his boss, a strange wild glint in his eye.

"As for you," Val said turning his attention to Cassie.

"Back off." Gabe's energy flared a dark blue blaze. "You have no power over her anymore."

"We'll see." Val sneered before surveying the scene and calling to his lackeys. "You there," he said to a surviving demon. "Pick that up." He pointed at Dan. As he walked away, he turned back with one final look at Cassie, a strange expression crossing his features. "Just like your mother." In the next breath, he was gone.

Cassie couldn't even begin to define the torrent of energy and emotions raging through her. But, as she stood to meet Gabe, the strength of her love for him rose to the forefront. Nothing else mattered. She placed a hand on his chest, not sure if the gesture would be met with acceptance or disappointment.

Gabe extinguished all of her doubts by placing his hand atop hers and pulling her in for a kiss. After a heartbeat, he pulled back and smiled. "You surprised everyone. Me most of all."

"I'm sorry I didn't choose you," she said lowering her eyes. "But, I couldn't let Zoey die. If circumstances had been different..."

He raised her chin. "I understand," he said. Then laughing added, "Just tell me one thing. Is life with you always going to be this crazy?"

"Well, I can promise you it'll never be boring," she said smiling.

"I hate to ruin the moment," Zoey said, her voice still hoarse. "But, can someone please tell me what the hell just happened?"

EPILOGUE

In the month since the bonding, Cassie still hadn't adjusted to her new abilities. Purple energy flowed through her in tangible waves as naturally as her blood and breath, yet it felt foreign. Strangeness aside, being a Key had its perks. Her new strength and speed had her giddy during the training sessions with Gabe. And her increased appetites, emphasis on the S, drove her crazy with lust every time he entered the room. If he were mortal, she probably would have killed him by now.

As it stood, Gabe seemed to be enjoying her ramped up libido. The first few days after her change had been one glorious marathon that brought a blush to her cheeks at the memory. She glanced over at where Gabe stretched out on her--scratch that--*their* new sofa. One arm draped over the back of the couch as he rested his head on his bare chest. His long legs covered in black sweats took up the rest of the cushions. She licked her lips at the same instant he opened his eyes.

"Now, why would you be all the way over there?" Gabe grinned as he moved to make enough room for them both to fit.

"Good question," she said and hopped off the high stool. As she ran from the kitchen and across the living room, she knocked over several half opened boxes, spilling the contents across the floor. Their shared apartment in Manhattan was a recent purchase from Gabe's inheritance of Albert's former estate. Cassie tried not to think about the old fallen angel's death as she tripped over the knickknacks now littering the floor. A stinging on the sole of her foot brought her attention back to the present.

"You all right, sweetheart?" Gabe knelt beside her, examining her foot.

"I might be a Key, but I'm still a klutz," she said with a halfhearted laugh.

"Sit down. Let me get a bandage for that cut." He helped her to the couch and kissed her once before heading to the bathroom. "Be back in a minute."

Cassie bent over the mess below and picked a small piece of glass from her heel. She'd managed to break one of her favorite frames into tiny shards. Wiping the broken pieces aside, she plucked the photo from the wreck. In it, she stood shoulder to shoulder with Zoey, arms wrapped around each other in a hug, in front of the Empire State Building. Zoey had planned the outing as a gift for Cassie's twenty-fifth birthday three years ago. They'd spent the day shopping in Soho, eating lunch in Little Italy, catching a play, and then taking the elevator all the way up to the top of New York's famous landmark. The memory came through as if it were yesterday.

"You wanted stars," Zoey said. "Well, we have to get above the smog. So, up we go."

Cassie had complained she missed the night sky; the city lights always blocked out most of the stars. So, Zoey surprised her with the solitary place in the city you might catch a glimpse of the true sky above Manhattan. It was one of the happiest birthdays she ever had.

"Gabe?" The unanswered questions swirled in her mind and sent her nerves racing. "Do you think I should try Zoey again? I mean I know she said she needed time and all. But, it has been a couple of weeks. And..."

Gabe dropped the bandage on the floor and placed a kiss on her cheek, erasing the worry lines on her forehead for a heartbeat. Her insides tightened. She arched her back and wound her hands through his hair pulling him closer. When she began to wrap her legs around his waist, he pulled back.

"Whoa, wait a sec. Let's take care of that foot first." He disentangled her limbs, caressing her calf muscle in the process and working his way down to her ankle. He set her foot on his thigh and retrieved the bandage. As he went to clean the cut, he said, "Already healing, my Key." His smile lit up the room. "Now, back to your rant about Zoey."

"I wasn't ranting," she cried but then caught herself.

He cleared his throat. "As I was saying. You need to give her time to adjust. She'll come to you when she's ready. She's also going through changes right now. Being bonded to someone brings change."

"I know. But she shouldn't be alone. What if..." The quiver in her tone gave away her fears.

"When she's ready, Cassie." He climbed next to her on

the couch and put a consoling arm around her. "You kept the world in balance. No demons, no angels, not even fallen angels can use your abilities unless you will it." When she tried to interrupt, he placed a long index finger to her lips. "You saved your best friend from dying and in the process shared a great gift with her."

"She didn't ask for it." Cassie blurted out against his finger.

He sighed. "No, but sometimes we get things we didn't ask for and don't necessarily want. She will learn how to handle it."

"I don't even know how it affected her. She won't return my calls."

"If I remember correctly, you weren't embracing the truth at first either." He laughed heartily. "In fact, I believe you threatened me with a knife when I told you what you were."

"That was different." She took a deep breath and tried to find the words to explain. "This bonding, somehow...I can feel her." She shook her head. "Well, at least some of the time. I know she's confused and there's something else. Like's she's afraid of something, something she thinks is coming." Her sigh came from deep within. "I don't know. I just want to help her. I want her to know I'm here. She's not alone."

"No, she's not. And neither are you." Gabe pulled her onto his lap. "You have me now, and whatever happens, whatever comes, we'll face it together."

Cassie's heart beat a little faster as she stared into his eyes. A rich golden hue shone out from them, his gaze revealing his beautifully human emotions.

"I love you." She pressed her lips to the center of his chest, just above his heart.

"I know." He ran his hands down her back in a soothing caress. "And I love you with all that I am. I won't leave you. This is my home, our home."

"Home," she echoed. As she rested her head against the solid wall of his chest, she found true contentment for the first time in many years.

THE END

Thank you for reading! Find the sequel short story to A TOUCH OF DARKNESS featuring Zoey and Rafe available now free at all digital outlets: EMBRACING DARKNESS!

Book Two in the Key Series, A KISS OF SHADOWS, arrives on shelves Spring 2016!

Please sign up for the Ninja Newsletter or join our street team, Team Ninja, for chances to win special subscriber-only contests and giveaways as well as receiving information on upcoming releases and special excerpts.

www.tinamoss.com

www.yelenacasale.com

All reviews are welcome and appreciated. Please consider leaving one on your favorite social media and book buying sites.

For books in the world of romance and speculative fiction that embody Innovation, Creativity, and Affordability, check out City Owl Press at www.cityowlpress.com.

ACKNOWLEDGEMENTS

Two people may have written this novel, but a community of supporters created it. We have so many to thank and apologize for anyone left off this list. Please consider this our thank you to you too.

A partner in life makes everything easier. To our wonderful husbands for their unwavering love and support in all we do. None of it would be possible without you.

To our amazing family and friends, you are the glue that keeps us together and the inspiration for our creative endeavors.

Melissa Cordone, our first beta reader, friend and fellow martial artist. You helped us find our title, brainstorm ideas, and make this novel shine. You're a true friend and are always there whenever we need you.

Everyone at WritersRoad for the support and community, especially Heather McCorkle, L.M. Preston, Tee Tate, Krissi Dallas, Brenda Dunne, Kristie Cook, and Melinda S. Collins. You are our sanity and inspiration in the writing world.

To all of the amazing individuals involved in RomCon and the Readers Crown Award for making us the 2014 winner in Urban Fantasy.

The members of CFRWA for believing in the book before publication and giving us the 2011 Touch of Magic Award in the Paranormal category.

To you, the reader. Without you, we're writing into the void. We've dreamed about having our book in another person's hands for a long time. You are our dream made real. We cannot thank you enough and hope you enjoy!

Special addition from Tina:

Jamie, you are my best friend and confidant. I would be nothing without you. Granny Bird, you are simply everything. You taught me a lifelong love of books. No words could thank you enough. Norine, my aunt and my friend. You keep me laughing and believing in myself. My brother and cousins, each of you brought a new joy into my life.

The writing community is the most wonderful group in the world. I could write an entire novel on the people in it, but here are a few I need to thank. To Pitizens who always speak the truth even when it's hard to hear. Norma, Tracey, Jenna, Rick, Steve, Bob, Katherine, Vanessa, Traci, Carla, Theresa, Mario, Tiffany, Melissa, Teri and all of you, thanks for making the gloom a little brighter. To Purgies for the sunshine and rainy days. To Kris Mehigan from Team Ninja for never giving up. To Lydia Aswolf and Nicole Camp, for their easy smiles and kind words. And finally, to my Fearless Blogger, Danielle DeVor for all of the shared experiences and unflinching generosity. For any writer I missed, I'm sorry and I thank you!

Special addition from Yelena:

To my brother Oleg, sister-in-law Irina, and absolutely awesome nieces Rebecca and Emily, for all of the support, help and love. And most of all to my incredible parents for raising me to be the person I am today, and for always encouraging my writing and any creative endeavors I ever undertook.

ABOUT THE AUTHORS

Yelena Casale is an award-winning author of urban fantasy and paranormal romance. Born in Kiev, Ukraine, she moved to New York at thirteen. Being very curious, she has been a devoted reader and writer since childhood. As a 2nd degree black belt and instructor in Shotokan karate, an avid traveler, and history and art enthusiast, she weaves universal themes with martial arts philosophies into her stories. She lives with her amazing, supportive husband and the best Siamese cats. In her spare time, she reads, paints, watches cool shows on TV and tries to get more sleep.

Tina Moss is an award-winning author of urban fantasy, paranormal romance, romantic suspense, and New Adult novels. She lives in NYC with a supportive husband and two alpha corgis, though all the males hog the bed and refuse to share the covers. When not writing, she enjoys reading, watching cheesy horror flicks, traveling, and karate. As a 5'1" Shotokan black belt, she firmly believes that fierce things come in small packages.